# A CATERED COSTUME PARTY

Books by Isis Crawford

A CATERED MURDER
A CATERED WEDDING
A CATERED CHRISTMAS
A CATERED VALENTINE'S DAY
A CATERED HALLOWEEN
A CATERED BIRTHDAY PARTY
A CATERED THANKSGIVING
A CATERED ST. PATRICK'S DAY
A CATERED CHRISTMAS COOKIE EXCHANGE
A CATERED FOURTH OF JULY
A CATERED MOTHER'S DAY
A CATERED TEA PARTY
A CATERED COSTUME PARTY

Published by Kensington Publishing Corporation

A Mystery with Recipes

# A CATERED COSTUME PARTY

## ISIS CRAWFORD

KENSINGTON BOOKS
www.kensingtonbooks.com

Longely is an imaginary community, as are all its inhabitants. Any resemblance to people either living or dead is pure coincidence.

Library of Congress Control Number: 2017940665

ISBN-13: 978-1-61773-337-6
ISBN-10: 1-61773-337-7
First Kensington Hardcover Edition: September 2017

eISBN-13: 978-1-61773-338-3
eISBN-10: 1-61773-338-5
First Kensington Electronic Edition: September 2017

10 9 8 7 6 5 4 3 2 1

Printed in the United States of America

*To Anna, The George, Mila, Cora, Anya, and Aiden.*
*You brighten my life.*

# Chapter 1

*Third time's the charm*, Darius Witherspoon told himself. He'd tried killing his wife twice before—once in Taos and once in Stowe—and all he'd gotten for his efforts was having to take his wife back and forth to her physical therapist when the cast on her ankle came off. But this time would be different. This time he was taking a more direct route.

He studied his hands. The long fingers. The carefully shaped nails. The signet ring. The activity he was about to embark on was not what his hands were meant for, but there came a time when you had to step things up a notch and do what you had to do. Heaven only knows, he'd tried everything else. He shook his head ruefully. He had never thought—not in his wildest dreams—that he'd be doing something like this. *Funny the places life takes you.*

After all, he had a BA from Penn and an MFA from Yale, he co-owned an art gallery on Madison Avenue and a one bedroom co-op on Park Avenue, yet here he was, getting ready to bash his wife's brains in. On top of everything else, the action was so . . . so primal. So déclassé. So lacking in subtlety. In truth, he thought he'd be horrified by what he was about to do, by the up-close-and-personal nature of the operation. But he wasn't, not even a little bit. Okay, maybe he felt a tinge of remorse, the same tinge he'd felt that time in the jungle, but that was all it was—a tinge. Did that make him a bad person?

He knew he should feel something—anger, regret, horror—at what he was about to do, but he didn't, and that disturbed him more than the deed he was about to commit. Was he really a psychopath? He'd never thought of himself that way. After all, he gave money to the ASPCA and the Red Cross, he was kind to children and dogs, and he was understanding of rush hour subway delays.

No. This was Penelope's fault, Darius decided, trying to convince himself of that fact. If she'd kept her nose out of his business, if she'd left things alone, if she'd let him handle things the way he'd asked her to, if she hadn't talked to his partner behind his back, this wouldn't be happening.

He remembered how happy she'd been when he told her he'd bought a condo at the Berkshire Arms. Then that pain-in-the-ass friend of hers, Dorothy Evans, had gone and told her about what had happened at the Berkshire Arms before they did a full-scale renovation, and she'd flipped out. Said she wouldn't stay there, not even for a night. Said it was a bad luck place.

Darius smiled as he remembered how he'd convinced her that she was being ridiculous. That Dorothy was ridiculous. After all, this was a woman who wouldn't make an appointment before she'd consulted her astrologer. The place had been completely remodeled. It was a wonderful space, with a new kitchen and French windows that led onto a balcony that overlooked the Hudson.

Darius had reminded her that she'd been saying she wanted to get of out the city for years now. Well, this was her chance to have a second home, to explore Westchester. If they liked it, maybe he'd establish another gallery here in Longely or in Rhinecliff, or in one of the other communities that dotted the area, and they'd buy a house. Then he'd told her he'd let her furnish the condo the way she wanted—even with modern furniture—and that had sealed the deal.

If only Penelope hadn't been so damned nosy, Darius thought regretfully. If only she'd minded her own business. If only she hadn't kept reminding him how much he owed her. If only she hadn't threatened him, but she had. So here they were, in a situation he would rather have avoided—if possible.

Heaven only knows, he had given her plenty of hints, had even told her directly that he was working on a special project, and when the time came, he would tell her what it was. But she wouldn't take the hints, wouldn't go away. She always had to be right on top of him, always asking him whom he was talking to, where he was going, what he was doing.

It made him wonder if she wanted to know for a different reason, instead of out of sheer bloody-mindedness, as his father used to say. A couple of times he'd even caught her hanging up when he walked into the room. She'd had that guilty look she got on her face, which had made him start to wonder, and then he had started thinking about his partner. What a scum that man was. It wouldn't surprise him if he and his wife were scheming together to take the credit from him.

Darius was thinking about that when his thoughts were interrupted by his wife's oohing and aahing over the fall colors on the banks of the Hudson. God. That was the other thing about Penelope: why did she always have to be so damned effusive? Why couldn't she ever just say something was nice and get on with it?

Everything was such a big deal, and everything was spelled out in capital letters, Darius thought as he stood there contemplating the best angle to connect the pipe with her head. It required some thought since it was not as though he'd done this kind of thing before. It would have been so much better if she'd broken her neck falling off the ski trail instead of her ankle. But it was what it was, Darius thought as he got back to solving his current dilemma.

So should he aim for the top of Penelope's head? No. That wouldn't work. She was too tall, which would limit the pipe's impact. The side? No. She'd see him coming out of the corner of her eye, and he didn't want that. That would be horrible. The back of her skull? Yes. That was it. There'd be no sorrowful looks then, because she wouldn't know what hit her—literally.

It would be over before she could ask him, "Why? Why are you doing this to me?" in that irritatingly pitiful little girl voice of hers. His wife had no idea of what was to come. None. For which he was profoundly grateful. He rubbed his hands together, realized what he was doing, and stopped. This was better. More humane. He didn't want Penelope to suffer. After all, he wasn't a monster.

Darius took a deep breath and let it out. Then he took two more breaths. *Be calm,* he told himself. *If you show any anxiety, she'll want to know what the problem is, how she can help.* Not a discussion he was going to have. Actually, there wasn't a problem. Or, he thought, correcting himself, there wouldn't be soon. Darius took a fourth deep breath and looked around. It was indeed a gorgeous fall day, he thought. Penelope was right about that.

Most years the leaves on the trees along the Hudson River were down by October, but it had been an unusually long, warm fall, so they were still there glowing red and gold in the sun. It was, he decided, a good day to die—if you had to. His wife thought they were going on a romantic getaway. A thought that thrilled her. As far as she was concerned, all their differences had been reconciled. In her favor, of course.

Romantic? Now, that was funny coming from her. He

looked at this woman, this woman with whom he had shared his bed for over thirty years, and he couldn't imagine why he'd ever found her attractive. If he ever had. Even back in the day she was big. She had big hands, big feet, a big nose, a big mouth, and a loud voice that trumpeted the rightness of her opinions.

She was one of those WASP women who rode horses and played tennis. There was nothing dainty about Penelope, nothing feminine. Not then and not now. Maybe he had married her because she was there when he decided he should get married, or maybe it was because she had led the kind of life he thought he wanted to live. That was probably the reason, he decided as Penelope turned toward the water and studied the scene in front of her.

"We should get a boat and sail down the Hudson," she said, smiling.

Darius agreed.

"A thirty-six-footer. Maybe we'll do it this summer," Penelope continued as she clasped her hands in front of her breasts. "Just the two of us. It'll be like the honeymoon we never had."

"That would be lovely, dear," Darius said, thinking that he'd rather be chained to a rock and have the birds peck out his eyes than spend a week on a boat with her.

Penelope turned toward her husband. Her eyes were brimming with tears of happiness, which just showed you how clueless his wife was, Darius thought as he patted her shoulder.

She took his hand in hers. "I'm so glad we could put all this nastiness behind us," she told him.

"Me too," Darius replied.

"For a while I was afraid that . . . you know . . ."

"No reason to be," Darius said, loosening his hand from his wife's grip. "We'll be together till death do us part." Then he pointed to a dirt path a couple of feet away that wove in and out of a copse of trees, and suggested they walk down that way so they could get closer to the river.

Penelope was only too glad to oblige. A mild wind blew off the river, bringing the slight briny scent of the water to her. Even though it was warm and sunny, no one was out on the river. It was, she reflected, too late in the season. All the boats were safely stowed away in dry dock. She watched the waves sparkling in the sunlight and listened to the ducks quacking as they paddled around in circles, while the sea-gulls squabbled overhead.

"Wait," Darius told his wife when they were almost at the river's edge. "I have a surprise for you."

Penelope let out a squeal of delight. "Oh, you shouldn't have!"

"I want to," Darius told her, his voice conveying nothing but sincerity. "Now, cover your eyes and don't peek."

"I won't," Penelope said, thinking about how sweet Darius was. How cute he was to insist they sneak out of their Park Avenue building by the side door so no one could see them early that morning. In case anyone was following them, he had said, and she had giggled. Not that there would be. It was just a game she and Darius had played when they began dating. She hugged herself, adjusted her bag, then put her hands over her eyes. This was so exciting!

Maybe her husband was giving her one of the coins he insisted he hadn't found. He'd probably had it made into a necklace for her. She let out a sigh of happy anticipation. This was what it had been like when she and Darius had first gone out together, when they'd spent every moment they could together, when all they'd needed was each other. Everything was going to be all right, after all. She'd had her doubts, but now she was glad that for once she'd listened to her heart instead of her head.

And that was the last thought that Penelope had, because a moment later Darius Witherspoon picked up the length of lead pipe he had leaned up against the trunk of an oak tree and brought it down with as much force as he could manage on the back of his wife's head. There was a wet sound, a kind of a thunk. Penelope wobbled but remained upright. Darius brought the lead pipe down again. This time Penelope crumbled and fell to the ground.

Darius put the lead pipe down and stood over his wife. Then he leaned closer and studied her back. She didn't seem to be breathing. He walked around to the front and squatted down.

Her eyes stared back at him, conveying what? Surprise? Dismay? Darius wasn't sure.

He put his hand close to her mouth. He didn't feel her breath. He stayed like that for a minute just to make sure. Then he got up and brushed the leaves off of the knees of his corduroy pants.

The leaves crunched under his feet as he walked back to the tree he'd leaned the lead pipe up against to grab the dive weights he'd stashed there earlier in the day. He heard something. He froze as his heart began to knock inside his chest. Then he realized it was just a squirrel running through the fallen dried leaves on the ground.

He laughed at himself, picked up the square, flat pieces of iron, and walked back to his wife's body. He carefully placed the weights in the pocket of the skirt she was wearing. For a moment, he stood there questioning whether he should do that or not and then dismissed his doubt. The material the skirt was made out of would rot, and the dive weights would fall to the bottom of the river, and even if they didn't, it didn't matter. Given the situation, no one would question their presence, anyway.

They were just one more indication of Penelope's determination to kill herself à la Virginia Woolf. Hadn't she referred to Virginia Woolf's death at the dinner party they'd hosted last week in the city? Hadn't Penelope said she admired Virginia Woolf for weighting herself down with stones? That she admired the finality of her act?

Yes, indeed she had, Darius thought as he grabbed both of Penelope's arms and began dragging her toward the water. She was heavy, she weighed as much as he did, and it took him a while to get her down to the water's edge. Well, it seemed that way to Darius, but in reality it was less than two minutes. When he got to the edge of the riverbank, he rolled Penelope into the Hudson. The ducks squawked indignantly and flew away.

"Good-bye," Darius said to Penelope as he watched her floating in the water, her body bobbing up and down with the rhythm of the waves. He waved. "Adieu. Adios. It hasn't been fun."

For a moment, Darius was afraid that the current would tangle Penelope up in the tree branch that was arching out into the water, but then she began to sink. Little by little, she became less visible.

From what Darius had learned in his research, it would be springtime before the river threw her back up from the bottom. At the minimum. Plenty of time to be eaten by the fish. Or, even better, she might stay down there forever. As he walked back up the riverbank, he rehearsed his call to the New York City police about his missing, suicidal wife. No, he'd just gotten back from Longely and found his wife gone. No, he was absolutely sure she hadn't gone out shopping. No, she wasn't with any of her friends. Yes, he was very concerned, because she had been very depressed lately. Very depressed. Could he please file a report?

And then he thought about the masked costume party he was throwing in the common room of the Berkshire Arms on Halloween Eve, the one that was being catered by Libby and Bernie Simmons. Given the circumstances, they'd probably offer to refund his money, but he would look away, with tears in his eyes, and say, "No, but thank you, anyway. This was my wife's favorite holiday. . . ." *Sniff.* "And I want to carry on with it in her honor."

Then Halloween Eve would arrive. He'd smile and be charming—with just the right tinge of sadness, of course—and everyone at the party would pat him on the shoulder and murmur to their partners about how brave Darius was being, given his wife's disappearance. How well he was holding up under the stress. How unfortunate the situation was.

Darius grinned. Everything was going perfectly. He believed in advanced planning, he believed in thinking before acting, and in this case, it had definitely paid off. Now that he'd solved his most pressing problem, he really did have something to celebrate.

At least, that was what he told himself as he locked away the small screaming voice inside his head, the voice telling him to leave. Because he couldn't leave. Not now. Not when he'd made the discovery of a lifetime, a discovery that was going to make him rich and famous. Everyone had laughed at him. Told him he was crazy. Well, they wouldn't be laughing soon.

# Chapter 2

*Three weeks later . . .*

Darius Witherspoon walked through the door of A Little Taste of Heaven for the last time six hours before the start of his Halloween Eve party. He didn't have too much longer to live, but of course, he didn't know that then. If he had, perhaps he would have conducted himself differently.

It was a little after four in the afternoon, the sun was setting, and the crows were flying home to roost. A cold wind had sprung up out of the north. The dried leaves on the sidewalk skittered and crunched under his feet like small bones, but Darius didn't notice. Nor did he notice the plastic bats lurking in the dwarf evergreens in the planters outside the shop, or the zombie mannequins in the shop window, or the moms and kids in front of the counter, clamoring for ghost-shaped sugar cookies and devil's food cupcakes, as he elbowed his way through the crowd.

He hadn't been sleeping well. Even his sleeping pills hadn't helped. He kept thinking he saw something out of the corner of his eye whenever he was in his living room or bedroom, but when he looked around, nothing was there. And then there was the other stuff. The stuff he was busy attaching explanations to. Explanations he desperately wanted to believe. The fact that the Berkshire Arms had gone all out with their Halloween decorations didn't help. They were reminders. Avatars. The skeletons, the skulls were supposed to be fun, but they weren't for him. Not at all. They called up the old and the dark, the tales told at night.

Darius shook his head. No. He had to get a grip. He had to stop acting like some hysterical schoolgirl. The dead stayed dead. They didn't come back and hover. They didn't move things around. They stayed where they were put. His wife was at the bottom of the Hudson. But what if she wasn't? He should have stayed to make sure. No. If she wasn't, if someone had found her body, he would have been notified by now.

He took a deep breath. Three more days and everything would be over. Three days and he would be famous. Three days and he would finally get the respect he deserved. He smiled, thinking of the expression on his partner's face when he found out. The superstitious old goat. Always tut-tutting. Calling him a treasure hunter. Calling him unscrupulous. A grave robber. Telling him he would come to a bad end. As if he wouldn't take advantage of the opportunity to rewrite history if it came along.

Darius put his hand on the small of his back and grimaced. His back was bothering him. All that digging and dragging, and let's face it, Penelope was no lightweight. He needed to find a chiropractor up here.

Maybe he'd ask the old lady across the hall. She'd probably know. She was an interesting lady, with her stories about the crows. She'd even gotten him feeding them. He had to admit, he enjoyed doing it. It took his mind off other things, things it did no good to dwell on. He shook his head. He just needed a vacation. A change of scene. Maybe he'd go to the Canary Islands or Malta. Or Spain. Yes, Spain would be nice. He'd go right after the costume party.

# Chapter 3

Bernie Simmons was sliding two more trays of ghost-shaped shortbread cookies into the display case and hoping that she and Libby had made enough of them when Darius came through the door. As she watched him weave his way through the crowd, she thought about how tired he looked.

Exhausted really. And anxious. And sad. And stressed. He looked worse every time she saw him, Bernie reflected. He was no longer the "natty suit and tie" Darius Wither-spoon she'd first met. He seemed to be becoming less substantial. She guessed he wasn't eating very much, because he'd certainly lost weight, his skin had acquired a grayish cast, and the bags under his eyes were taking over his face. Instead of a jacket and tie, he was wearing an old shirt, a pair of baggy jeans, and a beige barn jacket. There were smudges on his clothes. He looked as if he'd been digging in the dirt.

Bernie couldn't imagine the stress he was under, not knowing whether his wife was alive or dead. The NYPD hadn't turned up anything, and neither had the private detective Darius had hired and dismissed when it became obvious the man wasn't doing anything except taking Darius's money.

*It must be awful living with the uncertainty*, Bernie thought. *That is probably the worst thing of all. At least if his wife had killed herself in their apartment, he would have known. Which is an awful thing to think, but true.*

Given what had happened, she'd expected Darius to stay in the city and cancel the party. Instead, he'd done the opposite. Two days after his wife had disappeared, he'd moved into the Berkshire Arms and told her he intended to stay there for a while—or at least until after the party.

"I admit I'm tempted to go home," Darius had continued, rubbing his hand over a two-day growth of beard. "But sleeping in the bed I used to share with my wife . . ." He'd stopped talking, and Bernie had waited. He'd sighed. "There are just too many memories there. Anyway, Penelope would have wanted me to stay here," he'd added, squaring his shoulders. "This was her dream come true," he'd confided to Bernie. "She'd been begging me to get out of the city for years, and I'd finally agreed. We were going to make a new start. I was going to open a little shop up here. Just a branch of our store in the city. Nothing spectacular. At least that was the plan. I should have done more to help. I should have insisted she go see someone. I should have pushed harder. Then . . . maybe . . . she'd still be here."

Bernie remembered he'd shaken his head again. "Funny how things work out. I should have done this years ago. Stupid. Just stupid." He'd hit his forehead with the palm of his hand. "It's the not knowing that's driving me crazy."

"It must be awful," Libby had said to him.

Darius smiled weakly. "It is. It's so unreal. I keep thinking that Penelope's going to call or show up any minute. That she's lying in a hospital bed, in a coma, somewhere and that she's going to wake up. I know that's ridiculous, because the police have checked for Jane Does, but I still can't help thinking that's what happened. I'd just like to know, you know?"

Bernie nodded sympathetically as Darius spread his hands in front of him and stared off into space, as if he was hoping his wife would find a way to communicate with him. Bernie and Libby exchanged glances.

"We'd be happy to give you your money back," Bernie said, even though on the one hand, she wouldn't be happy at all, but on the other hand, she would be ecstatic.

Darius shook his head. "Thanks, but Penelope would have wanted the party to go on," he asserted, his voice growing stronger. "Halloween was her favorite holiday," he added.

"So that must make this doubly hard," Bernie said, taking Darius's hand in hers and patting it.

Darius teared up then, and Libby and Bernie looked away, giving him a moment to compose himself.

"Anyway," he said when he could speak again, "the invitations are already out."

"I'm sure people would understand," Libby began, but Darius held up his hand, indicating the matter was not open for discussion.

So that had been that. Bernie shut her eyes, thinking about the fit Libby had pitched when she first told her she'd taken the catering job for Darius's party at the Berkshire Arms. Not that she blamed her. Not one single bit. Considering.

"I don't care if they've gutted the place and done a major reno," Libby had said when her sister had relayed Darius's request to her. "The answer is no. I don't care what they've done. That place will always be the Peabody School to me. I still have nightmares about that head rolling down the steps." She had shuddered. "The farther away I am from there, the better I like it. And on top of everything else, this is going to be on Halloween Eve. A masked costume ball on Halloween Eve. What are you? Nuts? Have you lost your mind?"

"Possibly," Bernie remembered saying as she'd avoided her sister's glance.

"And you didn't think to consult me first?" Libby had demanded, puffing up like an angry cat. "Why would you do that?"

Bernie held up two fingers. "Two words, Libby. Sales tax."

"Oh," Libby said, deflating. "I forgot."

"Well, I didn't," Bernie replied, although she would have liked to. She watched Libby groan.

"I guess we're really not in a position to throw business away, are we? Not even this business."

"No, we are not," Bernie replied grimly. "Unfortunately. Although I wish we were."

"Me too," her sister said. "If Michelle—" Libby began, but Bernie cut her off before she could continue.

"I know," Bernie said, not really wanting to hear yet another rant about how their father's fiancée's coffee and bake shop was cutting into their business.

"I was just sayin' . . . ," Libby said.

"I know what you were going to say," Bernie replied.

"No, you don't," Libby challenged.

"Yes, I do." Bernie remembered she'd crossed her arms over her chest. "You were going to complain about Michelle's shop again."

"So what if I was?" Libby said, sulking. She sighed. "But I guess we don't have a choice, do we?"

"Not with our current bank balance," Bernie answered.

If they didn't pay their sales tax on time, they'd owe the state even more because late payment penalties went up really, really fast. Postponing Peter to pay Paul was how small businesses got themselves into bankruptcy court, and Bernie was damned if that was going to happen to them. Her mom had started A Little Taste of Heaven, and it wasn't going to go down on her and her sister's watch. She'd been thinking about that as she watched Darius weaving his way through the crowd.

"We need to talk," he said.

# Chapter 4

Bernie looked at the crowd in front of the counter and looked back at Darius. "Can it wait for a few minutes?" she asked him. "Like ten?" She'd sent Googie, her second employee, out to the store for an emergency napkin run, so at the moment they were short staffed, but he'd be back very soon.

"No, it can't," Darius snapped. "I have things I have to do."

"Don't we all," Bernie muttered.

"What was that?" Darius demanded.

"Nothing." Silently, she repeated, *The customer is always right*, three times. "What can I do for you?"

"I want to give you something," he told Bernie.

"Okay," she said, wondering what the something was. "Like a present?"

Darius gave her a wintry smile. "I guess that depends on your point of view."

"I guess I'll find out, then, won't I?" Bernie replied, then nodded to Amber, her other employee, and mouthed, "I need five minutes."

When Amber nodded back, Bernie, ignoring the baleful looks of her customers, poured some freshly brewed

Guatemalan coffee into two mugs and added cream and sugar, then got a couple of scones out of the display case. She was carrying it all over to one of the small café tables she and her sister had recently installed in A Little Taste of Heaven when Darius shook his head.

"In your office," he said, taking a mug of coffee and a scone from Bernie's hands.

"Fine," Bernie replied, then led the way. "Are you ready for tonight?" she asked, making small talk.

"Got my costume all set," Darius said. He laughed. "All I have to do is shave and clean the dirt out of my finger-nails."

"What are you going as?" Bernie asked.

"You'll see," Darius replied. "And you and your sister? Are you ready?"

"We're ready. Libby is loading up the van as we speak," Bernie said. They had already made one trip up to the Berkshire Arms this morning and were planning on doing their second and last trip in a half hour. "So," she said when she and Darius had stepped inside the office. "What's up?"

Darius put his coffee mug and scone down on the desk, reached into his jacket pocket, pulled out a white envelope sealed with Scotch tape, and held it out to Bernie. "I want you to take this and put it in your safe until the party is over," he said.

"And then?" Bernie asked.

"And then I'll come and get it," Darius told her. "But if by chance I don't, I want you to open it up."

"Why won't you come and get it?" Bernie asked as she noticed a slight tremor in Darius's hand. She was fairly certain it hadn't been there before, or maybe she just hadn't noticed it.

"I will," Darius replied. "I just like to cover all my bases. I'm a great believer in insurance. If you have it, you won't need it."

"I guess that makes sense," Bernie said. It sounded like something her dad would say. "So what's in the envelope?" she asked. To her eyes, it looked as if it contained a document of some kind.

"Papers," Darius told her.

"They must be pretty important papers," Bernie observed after she'd taken a sip of her coffee. Not bad, if she did say so herself. Certainly better than Michelle's or the new coffee place that had opened last month. Maybe they needed to run a special on coffee, she reflected. A dollar for a small cup, a dollar and a half for a large one. Or start a reward program. Something like that.

Darius smiled. "They are. Would you believe these papers contain the secrets of the universe? I don't want the dark forces to get them."

Bernie laughed. "Naturally, you don't. I know I wouldn't want to be responsible for the end of the world. Seriously. What's in the envelope, and why do you need me to take it? For that matter, why do you think you won't be coming back to get it?"

Darius took a bite of his scone. "Nice," he commented as he brushed a few crumbs off his shirt. Then he answered Bernie's last question. "I guess I've just gotten paranoid, what with my wife disappearing and all. . . . Do me a favor. I know I'm probably being crazy, but could you just humor me?"

"Are you sure you're okay?" Bernie asked Darius. "Do you need me to call a doctor?"

He realized his hand was on his chest. He could feel his heart hammering away. He dropped his hand to his side and faked a laugh. "I'm fine."

"Because you have a funny look on your face," Bernie told him.

Darius forced out another laugh. "A back spasm. I must have pulled a muscle," he lied. He wasn't going to tell Bernie or Libby, or anyone else, for that matter, what was going on. To do that would make it real. He lifted up the envelope. "Please take it. I know I'm being silly, but it'll make me feel better."

"Fair enough," Bernie said. Really, how could she say no to a grieving husband? She took the envelope and put it in the safe.

She and Darius chitchatted for a few more minutes, agreeing to meet up at the Berkshire Arms to firm up some last-minute details later in the day. Then Darius took off, and Bernie went outside to help Libby finish loading up. They were almost done when their dad's fiancée, Michelle, pulled into A Little Taste of Heaven's parking lot in her brand-new Infiniti. Bernie wondered how she could afford a car like that, while she and her sister were driving around in an eleven-year-old van, as Michelle parked next to them and rolled down her window.

"I'm collecting your dad," she chirped in her annoying Barbie doll voice. "He agreed to help me give out cookies at my shop tonight."

Bernie felt a stab of jealousy as she forced a smile. She'd asked her dad whether he wanted to stand in for them this evening and give out cookies at their place, but he'd said, "Thanks, but no thanks," which was why her two employees, Amber and Googie, were holding down the fort instead.

"I knew you wouldn't mind," Michelle said. "Especially since you two will be off working. Have fun."

"We intend to," Bernie lied.

"Good. I wouldn't have it any other way," Michelle said, flashing Bernie a smile, a smile that made Bernie wonder for a brief moment if Michelle was responsible for their getting the gig at the Berkshire Arms. *Now I'm the one being paranoid*, Bernie thought as she watched Michelle get out of her vehicle and saunter over to the side door, the door that led up to the Simmons' flat.

"I don't think those jeans could be any tighter," Libby sniped once the door had closed behind Michelle. She could hear the tapping of Michelle's heels on the wooden steps as she made her way up to the second floor.

"Well, she does have a nice ass," Bernie remarked. "I'll give her that. Do you think that's why Dad likes her?"

"That and the fact that she's younger and she laughs at his jokes."

Libby bit her lip. "The fact that she could be our step-mother is too depressing to contemplate."

"I know," Bernie said. "Which is why I'm not thinking about it," she lied.

"I wish I could say the same," Libby said. "We have to do something."

"Like what?"

Libby shook her head. She didn't have a clue.

"Exactly," Bernie told her. "I'm just afraid that the more bad things we say about her, the more defensive Dad is going to get, and that will make things even worse."

Libby clicked her tongue against her teeth. She knew her sister was right, but there had to be something they could do, a sentiment she repeated out loud.

"I'm working on it," Bernie told her.

"Well, work faster," Libby said.

Bernie sighed. "I'm doing the best I can." Then she looked at her watch. It was time to get going. Even though all the food was prepared, they had a lot of setup work to do before the party got started.

# Chapter 5

The sun had set and the moon was a sliver hiding behind the clouds by the time Bernie and Libby pulled out of A Little Taste of Heaven's parking lot. It was dark out, and it got even darker once they turned onto the roadway that led up to the Berkshire Arms.

The narrow two-lane road was full of hairpin twists and turns and lined on both sides with overgrown stands of oak, sycamore, and birch. The tree branches swayed in the wind, knocking against the streetlights and throwing dancing shadows across the road. Tonight, in honor of Halloween, the oaks and the sycamores were hung with plastic skeletons and leering severed heads, which twitched and jerked in the wind.

"Lovely," Libby said sarcastically when the van's high beams picked up a skeleton decked out in a top hat and an orange muffler, holding up a sign that read WELCOME TO HELL.

That was the first word either sister had uttered since they'd left the shop's parking lot. Both women had been remembering the last Halloween Eve they were at the Berkshire Arms. When they'd catered a fund-raiser there, it had been called the Peabody School. The school, once an expensive boarding school, had closed suddenly due to the unexplained death of one of its students and had stood vacant for years, falling further and further into ruin, until someone had decided to stage a haunted house there. That hadn't worked out too well, though.

"You were right. I shouldn't have taken the job," Bernie suddenly blurted out when she spied a head with an ax stuck in its skull grinning at her.

"No. I was wrong. You were right. You should have. We need the money," Libby replied.

"Yes, we do," Bernie agreed.

There was no arguing about that. Still, she should have tried harder to drum up more business. No. *You're being ridiculous*, she told herself. She was giving in to hysteria. She and Libby had been up at the Berkshire Arms before to check out the facilities, and everything had been copacetic.

Bernie held on to that thought as their van rounded the last curve in the road and the turrets of the Berkshire Arms sprang into view. The developer who'd bought the place was based in New York City. He'd gutted the inside of the building, but he'd left the outside, which had been modeled on an old French chateau, intact. As Bernie looked up at the last turret on the left side of the building, she had an uncomfortable feeling that someone was watching her—a feeling she instantly dismissed. *Get a grip*, she told herself.

"Do you think she's still here?" Libby asked, having gotten the same feeling. Libby didn't have to explain whom *she* referred to. She knew that Bernie knew.

"No," Bernie lied. "I don't think she ever was here." She corrected herself. "I mean, she was here when she was alive, but that's it."

Libby turned toward her sister. "I notice you're not mentioning her name."

"So?"

"So naming something . . ."

"Does not summon it," Bernie said, having had this conversation before.

"Because ghosts—"

"Can we just drop the subject?" Bernie asked, raising her voice a little. "Seriously, can we do something a little more fruitful and concentrate on what we have left to do?"

"There's no need to get huffy," Libby replied.

"I'm not getting huffy," Bernie told her. Bernie didn't believe in ghosts, she really didn't, but she couldn't explain what had happened to them at the Peabody School any other way, and that made her uncomfortable, which, in turn, made her angry.

"Because I'm just saying," Libby continued, undeterred, "that Halloween is when the membrane—"

"Between the living and the dead is thinnest," Bernie said, finishing Libby's sentence for her. "And all I have to say to that is blah, blah, blah."

"Now you're just being rude."

"But accurate."

"Then why are the crows here?" Libby demanded. The noise had become overwhelming.

"Plenty of trees, lots of bugs, not too many people," Bernie said, raising her voice above the racket. "This is probably crow heaven."

Libby humphed. "You know a flock of them is called a murder. A murder of crows."

"What's your point, Libby?"

"I read somewhere that the Greeks thought they were messengers of the dead."

"I think you have your mythology mixed up. I think they're Odin's eyes and ears in Norse mythology. Or is that ravens? At any rate, there were two of them. Heckle and Jeckle. No. Those are a cartoon. Huginn and Muninn. I think. Actually, I don't remember too well," Bernie confessed. "It was a nine o'clock class, and I usually over-slept."

"Why don't you believe in ghosts?" Libby asked, changing the subject.

"Because I believe that the dead stay dead," Bernie replied. "I don't believe that they get up and go traipsing around, bothering people."

"So then how do you explain what happened?" Libby demanded, pointing at the Berkshire Arms.

"I can't," Bernie admitted.

"And there you have it," Libby crowed. "An admission."

"However, that doesn't mean there isn't a rational reason for what occurred," Bernie countered. "Maybe ghosts are like electricity. Five hundred years ago, people would have thought electric lights were magic. Maybe ghosts are like that. Maybe they're a natural phenomenon. Maybe some scientist will discover why they exist—if they exist—one hundred years from now."

Bernie tapped the face of her watch with a maroon fingernail. "We have an hour and a half before the guests start arriving. I think if we're smart, we'll stop talking about ghosts and goblins and start concentrating on our prep. I think the only thing we should be thinking about now is figuring out when Darius wants the dessert served and where we should put the spiced nuts."

Libby nodded. She hated to admit it, but Bernie was correct. At least about this. She needed to focus on the job. She took another look at the turret as she stopped the van. That person whom she couldn't bear to name, the person who she thought was watching them from the turret—well, she wasn't there now. Probably never had been. Her mind was playing tricks on her, that was all. At least, that was what she was going to keep telling herself. It was the wind and the dark and the jangling skeletons that were freaking her out.

Halloween was just doing a number on her head this year, and that was due to a confluence of unfortunate incidents, the major one being having to be at the Peabody—no, she corrected herself, the Berkshire Arms—tonight. It was just bringing back too many bad memories. She was PSTDing. Or was it PTSDing? She could never get the order straight. In either case, there was the explanation. Problem solved. Libby took a deep breath and let it out, counted, and repeated the process. After a few times she felt calmer, at which point she turned her attention to her to-do list—which was fairly extensive. If she wanted to get hysterical about anything, she told herself, she could get hysterical about that.

# Chapter 6

Darius Witherspoon's costume party was taking place in the common room of the Berkshire Arms. It was the new thing, Bernie had informed Libby. Residential spaces were being built with individual units upstairs and shared spaces below. In past times, Libby reflected, the area they were giving the party in would have been known as the ballroom, with its chandeliers, gleaming hardwood floors, and French windows opening onto a garden.

Whoever had designed the space had done a good job. It was warm and welcoming, fulfilling its multipurpose-use mandate. It worked for upscale birthday parties or more informal shindigs. For openers, the space was sited right next to the kitchen, which meant it was easy getting food in and out. In addition, the room was large but not large enough to feel lost in, and to make sure that wasn't the case, the interior designer had visually divided the room into two parts. The first half had scattered area rugs, cozy leather club chairs, and a fireplace; while the second half, the half closest to the garden, the half Darius Witherspoon had reserved, was all shiny wood floors, which made the space perfect for dancing.

Darius had arranged for the maintenance man to set up

the buffet tables near the French windows and the ten six-tops around the room's perimeter, which left the center of the floor clear for dancing. Dinner, according to Darius's desires, was on the simpler side, more fall than Halloween themed, and was self-serve style.

Which was fine with Libby and Bernie, because it meant they didn't have to hire extra staff. This way they could manage with just the two of them, and with Brandon, Bernie's boyfriend, as the bartender, even though a masked party conjured up images of formal dining. At least it did in the minds of Bernie and Libby.

The menu the sisters had worked out with Darius was equally informal and featured cider-braised beef short ribs with leeks and parsnips, scalloped potatoes, a green salad with sliced pears, walnuts, and blue cheese, plus fresh baked corn bread, challah, and warm cracked-wheat rolls served with salted butter made at a local dairy. Dessert consisted of a devil's food cake, a salted caramel apple cake, French macaroons, coffee, and a variety of liqueurs.

Bernie and Libby had kept the appetizers simple, because neither one of them believed in a long cocktail hour when serving a full-course meal. The appetizers consisted of two different kinds of spiced nuts, mini crab cakes topped with micro greens, mini Vietnamese spring rolls, and freshly made butternut squash chips, which were always a big hit, because they looked pretty with their bright orangey color, tasted good, and were more or less healthy. The beauty of the menu, as far as Bernie and Libby were concerned, was that everything in it had been prepared ahead of time and could be reheated and replated with a minimum amount of fuss or loss of flavor.

It took Libby and Bernie half an hour to unload the van and put everything away. Then they got to work setting the tables, which the maintenance man had already set up. Bernie went over and lit a fire in the fireplace and put bowls of spiced nuts on the side tables, while Libby placed the three flower arrangements they'd purchased earlier in the day along the center of the buffet tables. She'd just put the last one down when she realized Darius was still upstairs.

She wondered where he was as she studied the arrangements. The new vendor they'd picked had done a good job. Lisette had combined sprigs of rosemary and Russian sage with dusty pink gerbera daisies, and the combination worked. It was unexpected, festive, emitted a pleasing odor, and set off the burnt orange table linens—burnt orange being a nod toward Halloween and as far as Darius was willing to go.

"I'd prefer to celebrate the holiday with a traditional bonfire," he'd told her, "instead of with all this ridiculous folderol." A reference, Libby was sure, to the decorations hanging from the trees surrounding the Berkshire Arms.

"Where is our client, anyway?" Libby asked Bernie. "I thought he was going to meet us downstairs."

"I thought so, too," Bernie said, stepping back to look at the buffet table.

It was all good. She liked the tablecloth with the oxblood-red plates she'd chosen. She'd debated about the color before showing her selection to Darius, but she needn't have worried, as he'd been complimentary about the combination.

Libby moved one of the flower arrangements fractionally to the right so it would line up with one of the two French doors. "We need to talk to him."

"I'll text him," Bernie said. Which she did.

Ten minutes later, Darius hadn't answered, and Bernie tried again. Five minutes after that, when Darius still hadn't responded, Libby volunteered to go upstairs and knock on his door. There were eight apartments on the second floor, and Darius's was the last one.

A wide staircase, replete with an oak bannister and

spindles, led up to it. The floor in the hallway was covered in wide-planked oak, but as she rang the doorbell, Libby couldn't help remembering that it had been originally made of concrete and covered with a ratty green rug. When Darius opened the door, she stepped inside.

She'd been in the apartment once before. The developer had done a good job, Libby reflected again. He'd taken a dingy, claustrophobic space and turned it into something bright and cheerful. Darius's apartment was spacious and well proportioned, its open floor plan making it seem even larger than it was.

The apartment had oak flooring, high ceilings, and floor-to-ceiling windows that afforded a distant view of the Hudson. The open floor plan allowed for maximum flow. The living room, dining room, and kitchen were all interconnected, while the single bedroom was off to the left-hand side. It was a space made for entertaining, and Penelope had furnished the place with that in mind. The plump sofa and club chairs, the Navaho rugs and wall hangings were inviting, calling one to come in and sit for a while.

Darius frowned. "To what do I owe the honor?" he asked Libby.

"You didn't answer my sister's text," Libby explained.

"Oh, dear." Darius put a hand up to his mouth. "Sorry. I didn't hear the phone ding. I probably turned it off and forgot to turn it back on." He scratched his head. "I seem to be doing that a lot lately." He glanced down at his watch. "You're right. I did lose track of time. That's another thing I seem to be doing a lot lately. Before Penelope went missing, I was the poster child for prompt." He ran a hand over his cheeks and made a face. "Of course, before Penelope went missing, I never would have not shaved—or uttered a sentence like that, for that matter. I guess I should stop what I'm doing and clean up."

He pointed to the stains on his pants. "After all, I certainly wouldn't want my guests to see me like this." He brightened. "Of course, I could always come as a gardener. Unfortunately, I don't think gardeners usually wear masks. Not usually. Unless, of course, they're spraying their plants with insecticide."

"The dessert," prompted Libby, who had no opinion about that question one way or another. "Remember, you said you wanted to talk about the timing for dessert."

Darius waved his hands in the air. "Actually, I don't remember what I had in mind, so whatever you want to do is fine with me."

"Are you sure?" Libby asked.

"Positive," Darius said. "Because, you know what? I really don't care." He checked the time again. "Now, if you'll pardon me, I have a call I have to make. Then I'll jump in the shower, shave, put on my jester costume—what could be more fitting?—and be downstairs in fifteen minutes. Hopefully. I might be a little longer, so don't panic if I'm not down when everyone starts arriving. Just tell everyone I'll be down as soon as I can."

Libby nodded and turned to go. She heard the door lock behind her as she started down the stairs.

# Chapter 7

"Darius said to do whatever we want about the desserts," Libby informed Bernie when she ran into her in the hallway.

"Okay by me," Bernie replied. She started calculating when she had to begin warming up the apple cake and caramel sauce while she placed a chunk of dry ice in a container near the entranceway. It was the only really Halloweeny thing at the party, and Darius hadn't been sure about it. "What do you think?" she asked Libby as clouds of vapor began rolling out and creeping along the floor. "Too much?"

"Nope," Libby said. "I think it sets the proper tone."

"Me too," Bernie said, and then she went off to consult with Brandon, who was busy setting up the bar, which was located off to the right side of the buffet. According to Darius's request, Brandon was serving hard cider, sidecars, a good vintage French champagne, and old-fashioneds before dinner, and red wine during the meal.

"I like to curate everything," Darius had explained when he'd told Bernie and Libby what he wanted to serve in terms of drinks. "I guess Penelope was right. I am a control freak." Bernie remembered she hadn't said anything at the time, even though she'd agreed with Penelope.

Twenty minutes later everything was good to go. The appetizers were plated, the salads were in their bowls, and the meal was warming in the oven. All that was left for the sisters to do was light the Sterno, bring out the food, and put it in the chafing dishes.

Ten minutes after that, the guests started trickling in, and Bernie and Libby got busy hanging up coats, passing appetizers, checking to make sure the food in the kitchen was warming up properly, as well as apologizing for their host and assuring the guests he'd be down shortly.

Everyone had come as requested. The room sparkled with masked figures holding drinks and nibbling on appetizers. It reminded Bernie of pictures she'd seen of Venetian balls, even though no one was dancing. Everyone looked elegant, but there was a sinister undercurrent inhabiting the room, which she couldn't explain.

Maybe it was the masks, she thought. They ranged from the kind you bought at a place like Michaels for two dollars and fifty cents to elaborate, expensive confections crafted out of silk, gold, and black lace. Some of the masks followed the contours of the human face, while others were designed to look like birds of prey, animals, or satyrs. But all of them turned the people who were wearing them into something else. As did the clothes they were wearing.

Most of the men were decked out in tuxedos, but there was a small percentage who had come in costume. The costumes were elegant, ranging from musketeers to Zorro. Half the women were wearing ball dresses, while the other half were wearing costumes that ranged from gypsy to leopard. Bernie thought that the ball dresses were particularly elegant. Some were backless, others had plunging necklines, while others were columns of lace, chiffon, and taffeta that whispered and sighed when the women walked.

A few of the men and the women arrived wearing billowing hooded black cloaks that further hid their faces.

At one point, after most of the guests had arrived, Bernie thought she saw a tall, cloaked figure—she couldn't tell if it was a man or a woman—floating down the hallway toward the stairs, but when she looked again, no one was there. She shook her head to clear it. *It's probably a trick of the light*, she told herself as she focused on Libby, who was unobtrusively counting heads.

"I think we have forty-eight," she told Bernie when she was done. "More or less." It was hard to count with everyone moving around the way they were.

"And we're supposed to have between fifty and fifty-three."

Libby nodded. "So almost everyone is here."

Bernie made the obvious comment. "Except for our host."

She glanced down at her watch. It was time to serve dinner. Bernie stepped over to the side, away from the groups of chattering, laughing people, got out her phone, and called Darius. He didn't answer. An uneasy feeling began to settle into the pit of Bernie's stomach as she walked over to Libby.

"He isn't answering his phone," she told her sister.

"I hope everything's all right," Libby said in an aside as she smiled at a tall blond woman sweeping by her in a jaguar mask and a strapless red velvet gown and offered her a tray filled with mini crab cakes.

"You and me both," Bernie told her sister as the woman took a crab cake and a napkin and moved on. "My message went straight to voice mail."

"How about texting?" Libby suggested as she watched the woman in red velvet sip her champagne and wondered what it would be like to be on the other side of the equation. "Maybe he's on the phone," she said, remembering what Darius had told her about making an important call.

"Maybe," Bernie said, sticking her cell back in her bag. "You know what? I think I'll just nip up there and make sure everything's okay."

Libby nodded as she offered her tray to a tall man in a silver mask with a long pointed nose. After this tray was gone, there was only one more tray left. She'd underestimated the crab cakes' popularity.

"Good," she told her sister. "Because the potatoes have to come out soon, otherwise they're going to be too dry."

"I know," Bernie said as she made for the staircase. She hurried up the steps. "Darius," she cried as she rapped on his door. "Is everything all right?"

"Fine," Darius replied. "Absolutely fine." Later Bernie would think she'd heard a catch in his voice, but she wasn't sure. Given what happened next, she might have been reimagining how he sounded.

"Because we're about to serve dinner," Bernie continued.

"Go ahead," Darius told her.

"Everyone is asking for you."

"I'll be right down," Darius assured her. "Five minutes. No more."

"Okay," Bernie said. Then she turned and hurried back down the stairs, not thinking about the fact that Darius hadn't opened the door.

Ten minutes later the food was out on the buffet and everyone was lined up in front of the table, serving themselves, as Libby and Bernie made sure that everything was proceeding smoothly. The room was filled with the pleasant hum of people having a good time. Libby was refilling a chafing dish with scalloped potatoes and congratulating herself on how smoothly things were going when she heard the sound of something heavy hitting one of the French windows.

# Chapter 8

Bernie heard the noise, too. There was a thud, then a pause, then another thud, another pause, and then another thud.

A woman wearing a black lace mask and a silver lamé ball gown screamed and dropped her plate. It crashed to the ground, spewing its contents on the wood floor.

There was a fourth thud.

Another woman, her eyes wide with terror, screamed and pointed.

Bernie and Libby whirled around.

Darius was dangling in front of the French windows, swaying in the breeze.

Libby put her hand to her mouth. "Oh, my God," she said. For a moment, she and Bernie were rooted to the spot.

"Talk about entrances," Libby heard a woman behind her say, while a man said, "It's not funny. He could give someone a heart attack."

"He's dead!" someone else cried.

"Don't be ridiculous, Edmund," snapped a woman in a cat's mask and an electric-blue taffeta gown. "He's wearing one of those harnesses, you know, like the ones they wear in circuses, although I have to say this is in very poor taste."

"He always had a sick sense of humor," a man wearing a satyr's mask said. He pushed the mask up on the top of his head. "Look at the crows," he said, indicating the two birds that had just landed on each of Darius's shoulders. "That's odd. Don't birds sleep at night?"

"They're messengers come to take his soul down to hell," a woman said as the crows opened their beaks and cawed.

Libby half expected to see fire coming out of their mouths.

"Don't be a moron, Betty," someone snapped at her. "I don't know where you get this kind of stuff from."

"It's true, Allison. Everyone knows that."

"I don't know that," Allison replied. "Neither does anyone else. You're spending too much time watching those trashy horror movies you like."

"Can't you see it's a joke?" said a woman in a pale chiffon evening dress and matching half mask.

"Well, the joke's gone on for long enough," the man standing next to her observed, looking thoroughly put out. "Someone should go out and tell him to stop it. It's really not funny. Not funny at all."

"Look at the way he's hanging," the man next to Libby cried. "Can't any of you see? His neck is broken."

The woman called Betty put her hand to her mouth. "Oh my God. Jack is right," she said as the two crows cawed again.

Another one lit on the top of Darius's head. Libby could have sworn the crow was holding something shiny in his beak, which it dropped on the ground. She heard someone else say something, but she couldn't make out what it was, because suddenly she realized she was moving. She looked up to see that Bernie was in front of her. They elbowed their way through the people crowding around the French windows, exited the common room, and ran into the hallway and up the stairs.

Bernie got to Darius's door first. She tried it, but it was locked. "We need the key," she yelled down to Libby.

Libby turned and ran back down the stairs. As she was heading for the management office, she saw the maintenance man. "We need the key to two-G," she cried. "Hurry!" she added. "It's an emergency."

He nodded, turned, and ducked into the office. A moment later he was out, with a key in his hand.

"Hurry!" Libby cried again as he came toward her.

They both ran up the stairs. Bernie stepped aside as the maintenance man put the key in the lock and turned it. The door swung open, and the three of them rushed inside and headed toward the open window. Darius was hanging from a rope that had been looped around a hook sticking out of the upper window sash. As Bernie looked out, she could see four men lifting Darius's body up to take the weight off his neck.

"We need a knife," she yelled to Libby.

"Got one," the maintenance man said. Bernie watched him take out a pocketknife from his front pocket and open it up. She moved aside, and he went over to the window and began to saw on the rope with the blade. She watched the strands untwist themselves. A minute later, he'd cut the rope, and the men below laid Darius's body on the ground.

# Chapter 9

Bernie took out her cell, punched in 911, and told the operator what had happened. After she got off, she said, "We should get them back inside," referring to the guests converging on the spot where Darius lay. "They shouldn't be out there. Our police chief will have a fit."

"I don't think they'll listen to us," Libby replied as she watched the crows gather. The two birches in the garden were black with them. She shivered. "Those birds give me the creeps."

"Maybe they're saying adios," the maintenance man reflected. "After all, they did like him."

Bernie looked at him. It was an odd thing to say.

The maintenance man explained. "He fed them. I told him not to, but he and Mrs. Randall, the old lady who lives across from him, kept doing it. Every day. Regular as clockwork." He shrugged. "Go figure. Me, I don't like birds. Especially crows. They're bad luck. I put baited food out for them, but after a couple died, they never came back."

"They're supposed to be smart," Bernie replied. She snapped her fingers. She remembered the envelope. "The envelope," she said. "I need to get the envelope."

Libby gave her a blank look.

"The envelope that Darius had me put in the safe," Bernie explained. "The one I wasn't supposed to open unless something happened to him."

"Oh yes," Libby said. "How could I forget?"

"Well, I think it's safe to say something's happened to him," Bernie observed.

"You should wait for the police," Libby advised.

"No," Bernie answered. "I want to see what's in that thing first."

"Why?" Libby asked.

Bernie gave her a look. "Obviously, in case there's anything in there we don't want the cops to see."

"Like what, Bernie?"

"I don't know, Libby. That's why I want to look. I'll be back with it as soon as I can."

Then she was gone before Libby could say anything else.

"What envelope?" the maintenance man asked.

Libby shook her head. She was too tired to explain. One thing she did know, though. The chief of police was not going to be pleased when he got here and Bernie was gone. And Libby was right. He wasn't.

Bernie returned to the Berkshire Arms three-quarters of an hour after she left. She parked the van in the lot, now crowded with police cars, an ambulance, and the CID vehicle, and trotted over to where her sister and Lucas Broadbent, the chief of police, were standing, waiting for her. She knew this because her sister had sent her three texts that read: **Where are you? When will you get here? Lucy's really pissed.**

A fog was rolling in, and wisps of mist floated above the ground. It made the air smell of dried leaves, haloed the lights inside the common room, made the grass slippery, and outlined the CID vehicle and the ambulance that was waiting to take Darius Witherspoon's body away.

Bernie paused for a moment and watched the four members of the CID unit working as the two ambulance drivers talked to each other and Darius Witherspoon's guests watched the proceeding from the common room windows, having been corralled back in by the police, while they waited to give their statements to two patrolmen.

"It's about time," Lucy, aka Lucas Broadbent, said to Bernie as she approached him. "I should have you arrested for leaving the scene of a crime."

"Do you want to see the envelope or not?" Bernie asked, ignoring his threat.

Lucy stuck out his hand. "Show me."

Bernie handed him the envelope Darius had asked her to put in the safe, having already read the contents.

"You opened it," Lucy said.

"Very perceptive," Bernie said as she watched Lucy take out the note, read it, put the note back, and take out one of the bills. "A hundred-dollar bill," he said, raising an eyebrow.

"Five thousand altogether," Bernie told him. "I counted it."

Lucy grunted. "For you and your sister."

Bernie nodded. "So it would seem."

"Waste of good money, hiring you, if you ask me," Lucy observed as he put the bill back in the envelope and returned it to Bernie.

"That's all you have to say?" Bernie asked him as she passed the envelope to her sister, who proceeded to study its contents.

"What else do you want me to say?" Lucy asked her.

"Something along the lines of . . . 'Gee. I guess we're looking at a homicide investigation instead of a—' "

"Suicide," Lucy said, interrupting. "Or a practical joke gone wrong."

Libby read the note Darius had written out loud. " 'Please take this money and find the people responsible for what happened.' " Then she said, "Sounds to me as if he knew someone wanted to kill him."

"Not to me," Lucy snapped. "Maybe he was talking about something else entirely."

Bernie snorted. "Like what?"

Lucy glared at her. "How the hell should I know? Maybe he's asking you to make a year's worth of meals for a friend of his. Did you see someone kill him?"

"No," Bernie admitted, "but something wasn't kosher." And she told Lucy about Darius's behavior.

"That doesn't mean anything," Lucy retorted.

"How can you say that?" Bernie demanded.

Lucy stuck out his belly, which only made it look bigger and his bald head smaller. "Hey, missy, for all I know, you or your sister could have written the note. I only have your word that Darius left this for you." He pointed to the envelope. "The note is printed out. It's unsigned."

Bernie felt her face flush. "Why would Libby or I do something like that?" she demanded, taking a step forward.

Lucy shrugged. "For publicity. Bring people into your store. After all, whenever you have a case, you get more customers. . . . And your business has been going down."

"You're nuts," Bernie said.

Lucy looked her up and down. "Am I?"

"What about the five thousand dollars?" Libby demanded. "What about that?"

"Maybe it's yours," Lucy said.

"You really are . . . ," Bernie began.

Lucy smirked. "I'm what?"

*Don't do it*, Bernie warned herself. *Don't lose it. Don't give him the pleasure.* "Nothing," Bernie told him. "Nothing at all."

Lucy pointed to himself. "Did you call me nothing?"

"No. *You* called you nothing," Bernie told him. "I didn't say anything."

Lucy was searching around for a sufficiently cutting comment as Bernie watched a middle-aged man approaching. He was wearing a trench coat with its collar turned up and moved with the ease of someone accustomed to commanding.

"How's it going, Chief?" he asked Lucas.

Lucas nodded. "As well as can be expected, given the circumstances."

"You think you'll have this cleaned up soon?" the man asked, his tone indicating that sooner would be much better than later.

"We're moving as fast as we can, Mr. Moran," Lucy told him, looking at him, then looking away.

The man who was Mr. Moran turned to Libby and Bernie and extended his hand. "William Moran." He nodded toward the Berkshire Arms. "Developer of the property. And you are?"

"Libby and Bernie Simmons," Lucy answered for them. "They own a catering business called A Little Taste of Heaven."

"Ah," Moran said, "the ones who are catering this unfortunate event."

Lucy nodded. "But they fancy themselves private detectives."

"And are they?" William Moran asked Lucy.

"No," Lucy growled. "What they are is a real thorn in my side."

William Moran turned and smiled at Libby and Bernie. It was a smile without warmth, Libby reflected. A professional smile deployed to buy time. "And what's your take on this matter?" he asked the sisters.

"We think Darius Witherspoon was murdered," Libby said.

Moran's smile got colder. "That's quite a statement."

Libby handed him Witherspoon's note.

"That could refer to anything," Moran said, echoing Lucy's statement after he'd read the note and handed it back.

"We don't think so," Libby countered. "He left us five thousand dollars to investigate."

Moran buttoned his trench coat. "I don't like to speak ill of the dead," he said, "but I've had some reports of . . . let's say . . . some odd behavior on Mr. Witherspoon's part, which suggests he was—I'm being polite here—having issues."

"What kind of issues?" Libby asked.

"I believe he was becoming quite paranoid."

"Perhaps he was correct in his assumptions," Bernie observed. "Given what happened, I don't think you can dismiss his note so easily."

Moran looked as if he could. "Well," he said, "I'm certainly not the person to make that call, but I'm sure that our chief of police will conduct an investigation that takes in all the relevant factors."

Lucy nodded. "You can be certain of that."

"Right," Bernie muttered.

It began to drizzle.

"I think it would be better if we concluded our business inside," Moran suggested. "Perhaps in the media room?"

Bernie nodded, and she and Libby followed Moran into the Berkshire Arms. She could hear people talking, but that stopped when Moran led her and her sister into the common room. Darius's guests looked at the three of them as they went by, waiting for answers.

Then, when they realized none were forthcoming, they went back to doing what they had been doing before. Everyone had removed their masks. They all looked ill at ease. They'd come for a party and ended up at a wake. As Bernie studied their faces, she wondered if Darius's killer was among the group, if he or she was pretending to be shocked but was secretly rejoicing.

Once they entered the media room, Moran closed the door, unbuttoned his coat, took it off, and carefully hung it on a coat tree in the far corner of the room. Then he said, "I have enough to deal with. I don't need to entertain some ridiculous fantasy on your part. The man hanged himself. Take the money and go on a vacation. Or buy yourself new clothes. Or something. I don't care what you do as long as you stay away from this property. Are we clear?"

"Perfectly," Libby said.

"Excellent," Moran said.

"As soon as we go up on the roof," Bernie said.

"And you want to do this why?" Moran asked, his voice crackling with exasperation.

"Because the killer might have escaped that way."

"There is no killer."

Bernie persisted. "If there was."

"He couldn't have. If he'd opened the door to the roof, he would have set off the alarm. Which you would have heard, because it's very, very loud."

Bernie raised an eyebrow.

"It has to be. For insurance purposes," Moran explained. "Now, I think we're done here."

"We're going," Bernie said. "But before we do, would you mind telling me where you were when Darius was killed?"

"Yes, I do mind telling you, because it's none of your damned business." Moran glared at them and pointed to the door. "So are you going, or am I calling Chief Broadbent?"

"Leaving," Libby said, and she grabbed Bernie's arm and pulled her out the door.

# Chapter 10

It was ten thirty at night by the time Sean came home from Michelle's place. He was surprised to find his daughters sitting on the sofa, sipping tea, eating the few leftover cookies that remained from the day's sales, and watching a rerun of *Project Runway*. He'd expected them back somewhere after twelve.

"Anything happen?" he asked as Cindy the cat leaped off the sofa and began to weave herself around Sean's legs.

"You could say that," Bernie answered.

Sean grabbed a ghost cookie off the platter and sat down, at which point Cindy jumped in his lap, circled around three times, and plopped herself down.

"Are you going to tell me?" he asked after a minute had gone by and neither Bernie nor Libby had spoken.

After another minute of silence, Bernie told him about the evening's events. Then, when she was done speaking, she handed him the envelope Darius Witherspoon had asked her to put in their safe.

Sean raised his eyebrows as he read the note and examined the contents of the envelope. "Interesting," he said. Cindy meowed, and he scratched behind her ears and watched her tail flick back and forth as he tried to reconcile what Darius Witherspoon had done and the note he'd left.

"Isn't it, though?" Bernie commented before she took a sip of her ginger tea. Her stomach was acting up. Probably due to the stress of the evening, she reckoned.

"I wish I could have seen the crime scene," Sean said, thinking out loud. "It would give me a better sense of things." But the moment the words were out of his mouth, he regretted them. Anything having to do with Michelle and her shop was a minefield in which Sean had no desire to step.

"So how *was* Michelle's shop?" Libby inquired in a steely tone. "Busy?"

"It was okay," Sean said, which was the most innocuous comment he could think of to make. Then Sean read Darius Witherspoon's note again and carefully put it on the table. "And you're telling me the property developer was there?" he inquired, changing the subject.

Bernie nodded. "He definitely wants this to be a suicide."

"I bet he does," Sean said. "Given the reputation of that place, the amount of money he's supposed to have invested, and the fact that it's still half empty, I'm sure a suicide would be preferable to a murder."

"A view Lucy seems to share," Libby said.

Sean bit the head off his cookie. "He always was politically astute."

"Which is why he's the chief of police and you're not anymore," Libby observed.

"Exactly," Sean said, remembering the case that had made him resign, a course of action he still didn't regret.

"So what do you think, Dad?" Bernie asked when Sean had finished speaking. "Do you think Darius killed himself, or was he murdered?"

Sean considered his answer as he watched the light in

the jack-o'-lantern in the window across the street flicker on and off. Finally, he said, "Although I don't usually side with Lucy, I can see his point this time. From what you tell me, everyone saw Darius hang himself. That's fifty eyewitnesses."

Libby corrected him. "Fifty-three."

"That makes it hard to call it a murder."

"He could have had help going out the window," Libby suggested.

"Maybe," Sean agreed. "But that's a long shot."

"He could have, though," Libby insisted.

"Yes, he could have," Sean agreed. "But let's not forget that Witherspoon was under a great deal of stress. One could posit that Darius couldn't deal with his wife's disappearance, that he figured her for dead, which, in my experience, is how most of these cases play out. And unable to face a future without her, he killed himself in a fit of grief."

Bernie leaned forward and pointed to the note. "How can you ignore this letter? Someone who is going to kill themselves doesn't leave you five thousand dollars and a letter asking you to investigate their death. Obviously, he thought someone was after him."

"You'd be surprised. People do strange things in times of stress," Sean observed. "And I should know. They change their minds all the time, and Darius was nothing if not stressed. Maybe Moran was right. Maybe Darius was going around the bend. Maybe he thought someone was after him. After all, his wife had disappeared out of the blue. That has to be unsettling. Maybe he left you the note in some paranoid fit, then had a change of heart."

"I find that difficult to believe," Bernie said. But was it? she wondered, thinking back to Darius's demeanor the last time she'd seen him. She thought he'd seemed nervous, scared even.

Sean brushed the crumbs off his plaid shirt, a shirt that Michelle detested but he loved, leaned over, and picked up another cookie. He bit into it and sighed with pleasure. God, he was glad that his daughters hadn't jumped on the "sugar is evil" bandwagon or gone into making kale-quinoa muffins, the way Michelle had. He'd managed to choke one down out of politeness, but that was as far as he was willing to go.

"I get what you're saying," he said after he'd swallowed. "But then tell me this. Why didn't Darius name someone in his note? He must have had an idea of who was after him."

"Obviously, he didn't, or he would have," Bernie answered.

"Okay. Fair enough. Let's assume you're right about that. But here's the other thing," Sean continued. "Where did the murderer hide? How did he get away? Precisely," he said when neither Libby nor Bernie replied. "From what you're telling me, the door to Witherspoon's apartment was locked, the door to the roof was alarmed, and since there is only one staircase, you would have seen anyone going down the stairs as you ran up. So tell me where your unsub was? You can't. At best, I think Darius Witherspoon's death was the result of a practical joke gone catastrophically wrong, and at worst, it was suicide."

Bernie took another sip of her tea and watched the rain hitting the windowpane. Then she looked at the note again and remembered Darius's insistence on her taking the envelope and his relief when she did. Even though she hadn't explicitly promised, she couldn't not do something. "I don't know about Libby, but I'm going to do a bit of poking around."

"Why?" Sean asked.

"Because something's not right about the whole setup," his younger daughter answered.

Sean turned to Libby. "How about you?"

"I'm in, too. After all, he left us the money to do it. We should follow through."

Sean shrugged. "Suit yourself, but I'd be surprised if you found anything."

"We have to go back to the Berkshire Arms tomorrow, anyway," Libby said. "We have to collect our stuff, since Lucy wouldn't let us take it when we left tonight."

Bernie finished her tea. "We might as well ask some questions as long as we're there." She looked at the clock on the wall. It was almost midnight. Time to go to bed, since they had to be up tomorrow at five to bake. Halloween was one of their busier days.

# Chapter 11

But Bernie didn't go to sleep. She couldn't. She tried, but after tossing and turning, she got up, went downstairs to the shop, and got herself a big bowl of the pumpkin ice cream she'd made the day before, went back upstairs, fetched her laptop, sat down on the sofa, went online, and began to research Darius Witherspoon. Maybe something she found out online would nudge her in the right direction investigation-wise. A moment later Cindy joined her, and after some plaintive mewing, Bernie conceded defeat and got up, went downstairs, got a tiny bowl, and came back up.

"Here," she said to Cindy as she put three tablespoons of her ice cream in the blue-and-white bowl with a picture of a fish on it and put the bowl on the coffee table. "Satisfied?"

Cindy leaped on the table and began to eat. Her purring filled the room.

"I'll take that as a yes," Bernie said, getting back to her digging.

She didn't find as much as she hoped for, but after an hour she knew more about Darius Witherspoon than she had when she started. She was just about to go back to bed when Libby stumbled out of her bedroom on the way to the bathroom.

"What are you doing?" she asked when she saw Bernie sitting on the sofa.

"Research."

"Researching what?"

"Researching Darius Witherspoon."

"Ah." It was true they didn't know much about him, Libby reflected as she sat down next to Bernie. It wasn't as if they'd asked him for his bona fides when he'd hired them. Cindy crawled up on her lap and began to purr. "I don't suppose there's any more ice cream left?"

"Nope. Sorry."

"I didn't need it, anyway," Libby said. Although she would have liked some.

She briefly thought about going downstairs and eating the last slice of the pumpkin cheesecake with the gingersnap crust left in the cooler, but then she thought about how tight the waistband on her jeans felt the last time she'd put them on, and decided against it. She knew she'd gained some weight. She just didn't want to get on the scale and find out how much. It was too depressing. Why was it so easy to gain and so hard to lose? That was what she wanted to know.

"So what did you find out about our client?" she asked Bernie instead.

Bernie told her. "Darius Witherspoon is . . . was . . . fifty-seven years old. He was born in Norwich, Connecticut, went to the public schools there, and then went on to Buffalo State for college, where he got a degree in art conservation. He got married to his wife, Penelope, in nineteen eighty-six. She's a Monroe."

Libby looked at Bernie. "Meaning?"

"The Monroes are a very wealthy family. They're on the list of the top one hundred richest families in America."

"Nice," Libby remarked. "But just because her family has money doesn't mean that she does."

"Oh no, she does." Bernie rubbed her eyes. "I found an article on Page Six of the *New York Post* that talks about the inheritance she received from her aunt Polly."

"We could use one of those," Libby remarked.

"It would be nice," Bernie agreed.

Libby waved her hand in the air. "Never mind. I wonder where Darius and Penelope met," she said as she looked longingly at Bernie's ice cream.

"Here," Bernie said, pushing the bowl over to her sister. "Take it."

"You're sure?" Libby asked.

"I'm positive," Bernie said. "I don't want the rest, anyway."

Libby sighed with pleasure as she took a spoonful. There really wasn't that much left. A half a cup at most. Which wasn't enough to make her gain weight. At least that was what she was telling herself.

"I think Darius and Penelope met at the Metropolitan Museum of Art," Bernie continued while Libby polished off the rest of the ice cream. "He was working there at the same time she had an internship. At that point he was living on the Lower East Side, while she was living on Sutton Place. Then, after the wedding, they moved into a co-op on Park Avenue."

"Not bad," Libby allowed.

"Not at all," Bernie agreed. "I'm guessing they didn't buy the co-op with his money. Then, nine months later, Darius opened up the Caldwell Gallery on Madison Avenue. That was probably with Penelope's money, too."

Libby licked the spoon. Maybe, she thought, they could make pumpkin ice cream cakes for Thanksgiving, along with the usual pies. "That must have set her back a fair chunk of change," she observed.

"That's what I'm thinking. However, there was a partner involved." Bernie looked up from her laptop. "But I'm willing to bet that even with that, Penelope did part with a lot of cash, but I suppose if you're swimming in money, it wouldn't matter. But get this." Bernie elbowed Libby in the ribs. "You know who Darius's partner is?"

"The Loch Ness monster?"

"Septimus Peabody."

"Who would name their kid that? It sounds like a disease. 'He's got a bad case of Septimus. We have to operate.'"

"I'm talking about the last name, Libby."

Libby sat up straighter. "What are the chances?"

"Agreed. But wouldn't it be something if this Peabody is related to the person who founded the Peabody School?"

"It certainly would be," Libby said, leaning back and putting her feet up on the coffee table.

Both she and her sister paused to think about what a strange place the world could be. A moment later, Bernie picked up her narrative.

"Anyway," she went on, "the gallery deals in antiquities." She stifled a yawn. She was beginning to crash.

"All this is great," Libby said. "But it would be nice if we had the guest list for the party," she observed.

"It would be very nice," Bernie agreed. "But we don't."

"What do you think our chances are of getting it?"

"Slim to none. Lucy isn't going to give it to us. . . ."

"I'd say that's a good bet."

"And Clyde is off visiting his new grandson in L.A. and then is attending some conference about community policing in Hawaii with the wife."

"Too bad," Libby remarked. She yawned, too. "Because the person who killed Darius was probably at his party."

"It gives lie to the saying 'Hold your friends close and your enemies closer,' doesn't it?" Bernie asked as she closed her laptop. It was time to go to bed. "Even if we did get the guest list," she went on, "we couldn't vet all the guests. We don't have that kind of time."

"True," Libby said. "Which is why we have to be smarter than the average bear."

# Chapter 12

Libby yawned again, took another sip of her coffee, and wished she were back in bed instead of in the van. It was only eleven in the morning, but it felt like ten at night. God, she needed a nap. She hadn't slept well once she'd gone back to bed. Every time she'd drifted off, she'd seen a crow with something in its beak, sitting on the chair next to her. She'd screamed as it spread its wings and flew straight at her, and she'd woken up with her heart pounding.

She could still see the crow. Shiny black coat. Sharp curved beak. Beady eyes. Hopping around. As if it was looking for something. She thought it was the crow that had been perched on Darius Witherspoon's head.

"Are you all right?" Bernie asked her sister as she stopped for a red light.

"Just tired," Libby said, closing her eyes for a moment. She didn't want to talk about her dream. She could hear the honking of geese flying overhead. They'd been leaving for the past week. A harbinger of winter. Why couldn't the crows go south, as well? she wondered as she opened her eyes and took another sip of her coffee. It wasn't helping.

A minute later, Libby and Bernie entered the road that led

up to the Berkshire Arms. A ground-level fog had descended overnight, shrouding the trees' low-hanging branches in a mist and making it difficult to see the road. The skeletons dangling from the trees seemed to be welcoming them, their eyeless sockets following them as they went by.

"I wish they'd take those things down," Libby said, re-pressing a shiver.

Bernie didn't reply. She was hunched over the wheel, eyes squinting as she tried to make out the road.

As they got farther up the hill, Libby could hear the crows. Their din filled the air. *There must be hundreds in the trees around the Berkshire Arms,* she thought. She shivered again. She knew they shouldn't bother her, but she couldn't get last night's dream out of her head.

Three minutes later, Bernie was relieved to be off the road and in the parking lot of the Berkshire Arms. She parked as close to the common room as she could get, grabbed her coffee, and got out of the van. The mist on the ground curled around her legs, shrouded the grass, and ca-ressed the yellow crime-scene tape as if the tape were an old friend come calling.

Bernie studied the crime-scene tape, then turned her eyes to the window Darius had gone out of. She still found what had happened hard to believe. After a minute, she stepped over the tape and walked to where Darius had lain. Libby followed behind her. The grass was trampled down in all directions. Bernie squatted down to get a bet-ter look.

"What do you think you're going to find?" Libby asked, standing right behind her.

Bernie shrugged. "I don't know," she confessed as she kept looking.

A moment later Libby joined her. The grass was damp, and some leaves were strewn across it. Libby was just thinking about how she used to collect leaves in the fall and make designs with them when she noticed something glinting in the grass.

"Look," Libby said, picking it up. "I think this is what the crow dropped next to Darius."

Bernie took the silver disk and rubbed it with her finger. "It looks like a coin to me. Or maybe it's some sort of game piece," she said, handing it back to Libby, who put it in her pants pocket, thinking she'd look at it later.

"What do you think it means?" Libby asked.

"I have no idea," Bernie told her, getting up. She picked a piece of grass off the bottom of her black silk parachute pants and went inside.

She and her sister went directly into the common room. Everything was exactly as they had left it last night. The food was still in the chafing dishes, plates and glasses were piled up on every available surface, while the food that had been dropped when people saw what was happening was congealed on the floor.

"What a mess," Libby said, thinking about how much time it was going to take to clean and pack up. She sighed.

Bernie was about to say that she figured it was going to take them at least two hours, probably more like three, when the maintenance man who had been working last night came into the common room.

"Would you like some help?" he asked.

"Love it," Bernie said, looking at the middle-aged man with the receding hairline, brown eyes, and a bit of a potbelly standing before her.

"Thanks," Libby said.

"My pleasure. Manuel," he said, extending his hand. "Manuel Rico. But you can call me Manny for short. Everyone does."

Libby and Bernie shook hands with him and introduced

themselves. Somehow introducing themselves had seemed superfluous last night.

"I wouldn't want to go through that again," Manny said, referring to having to open the door to Darius Witherspoon's apartment. He shook his head. "No, no, señor. And I took this job because it was quiet. Everyone thinks that Paraguay is bad, but I never saw anything like that there." He shook his head again and laughed. "You never know, right?"

"Right," Libby agreed, liking him instantly. "Have you been here long? Because you don't have an accent."

Manny laughed again. "I first came here when I was a kid, and I've been going back and forth ever since," he told her. Then he pointed to the scalloped potatoes on the floor. "I would have cleaned this up for you last night, but the cops wouldn't let me near the place. Mrs. Randall told me they left around three." Manny sighed and bit his lip. "I should have known something bad was going to happen," he told them.

"Why do you say that?" Libby asked.

"My *abuelita* used to say that a bat in the house means someone is going to die," Manny replied. "And when Mr. Witherspoon moved in, one flew in his window, and I had to come up and chase it out."

"My mother used to say that about birds," Libby told Manny as she went to get the garbage cans from the kitchen. She figured she'd put liners in them and then dump in everything.

Manny shook his head. "Poor Mr. Witherspoon. First, his wife, and now this. I guess he didn't have much luck."

"Apparently not," Bernie agreed.

Then, by common consent, the three of them turned to look at the place in the garden where Darius Witherspoon had lain.

"Rest in peace, Darius," Bernie murmured, after which she turned on her iPod and the three of them started cleaning. They worked at full speed, and it took a little over an hour and a half to restore the area to what it had looked like before.

They threw away all the garbage and the food that had been left in the chafing dishes; emptied out the refrigerator; packed up the dishes, glasses, serving pieces, and silverware, all of which needed to be washed when they got back to the shop; threw the tablecloths and napkins into the laundry bag Libby had brought; closed up the tables and the folding chairs; and put the furniture back where it belonged.

"You know," Manny said as he and Bernie began mopping the floor, "I can't help feeling that Mr. Witherspoon's death is on me."

Bernie stopped mopping. "How so?"

Manny wrung out the mop before answering. "Because I was the one who bought him the rope and the hook. Even worse, I installed the hook for him. He said it was for a plant he was planning on bringing up from the city. A heavy plant. I shouldn't have installed the hook so well. Then it would have come loose, and Mr. Witherspoon would have fallen to the ground."

"Did he say what he wanted the rope for?" Bernie asked.

Manny shook his head. "I figured it was for something to do with his move."

"It wasn't your fault," Libby said. She'd been wiping down the side tables and straightening the chairs on the rugs by the fireplace. "You couldn't have known."

Manny pointed at himself. "Then why do I feel so bad?"

Bernie clarified. "My sister means Darius might have had help going out the window. He might have been murdered," she explained when she saw the blank look on Manny's face.

"Really?" he said.

"Yes, really," Bernie said, and then she told him about the note Darius had left for them.

"No," Manny said when Bernie was done. "No way. Not unless the ghost that's supposed to haunt this place did it, and I don't believe in ghosts." Then he backtracked. "Well, maybe I do a little."

"Then how do you explain the note?" Bernie demanded.

"I can't," Manny replied as he moved the bucket over to the stretch of floor near one of the French windows. "But I also can't explain how anyone could get out of his apartment, either. Mr. Witherspoon's door was locked, and his windows were closed."

"Except for the one he went out of," Libby noted.

"We were up there in a minute. We looked out the window. Did you see anyone?"

"No," Bernie admitted.

"Neither did I," Manny said, and he began mopping.

"Do you mind if we take another look in Darius's apartment?" Libby asked.

"The police tape is up, but be my guest," Manny said, then told them where the key to it was. "I don't care. It's none of my business. Just don't tell the police I let you have the key if they come by."

"We'll say we took it without telling you," Bernie said.

Manny nodded. "Call me if you need me."

Bernie nodded back and turned her iPod up to drown out the sound of the crows. Then she and Libby went back to doing what they had been doing before.

# Chapter 13

Two hours later, Libby and Bernie were standing in front of Darius Witherspoon's apartment, contemplating the yellow police tape crisscrossing the door, when the door across the way opened and an elderly lady stepped out into the hallway. She looked at Bernie and Libby with bright eyes full of curiosity.

"Are you relatives of poor Mr. Witherspoon?" she asked, a slight tremor in her voice.

"No. We used to work for him," Bernie explained. Which was true. "We're just here to collect something we couldn't get last night." Which wasn't true.

"But what about the police tape?" the lady asked.

"Well," Bernie began, trying to decide on a story, but the lady cut her off.

"Don't mind me. I'm an anarchist from way back."

Bernie laughed, and the old lady extended her hand. "I'm Mrs. Randall. Who are you?" she asked.

Libby explained.

"Yes," Mrs. Randall said. "You have that lovely catering place my daughter-in-law uses sometimes."

"Who's your daughter-in-law?" Libby asked.

"Erin Croft. The one with huge boobs, thanks to the magic of cosmetic surgery."

Bernie laughed again as she watched Mrs. Randall smooth down her plaid wool skirt, make a minute adjustment to her black turtleneck sweater, and zip up her black leather jacket.

"Love the sneakers," Bernie said, changing the subject and pointing to the yellow Converse high tops Mrs. Randall was wearing. She'd learned from experience that talking about a client usually did not end well.

Mrs. Randall beamed. "My daughter-in-law doesn't."

"Then she has no sense of style," Bernie said in spite of herself.

"Strictly suburban soccer mom," Mrs. Randall informed her.

"Well, I think you look great. In fact, I think you're my new 'This is what I want to look like when I grow old' model."

Mrs. Randall's smile grew bigger, making her face look like a shar-pei's. "I figure if you can't dress the way you want at eighty, when can you?"

"You're eighty?" Libby asked.

"Eighty-two, to be precise," Mrs. Randall declared. "Which is a lot older than poor Mr. Witherspoon will get to be." She tsk-tsked as she studied the door to his apartment. "Poor man. I told him I'd pray for his wife, and now I'll have to pray for him, as well. Hanging. That's an awful way to go."

"Yes, it is," Bernie quietly agreed.

"And so inconsiderate. Those poor guests. What a dreadful thing to see. Why he couldn't have hung himself somewhere else, I really don't know. He seemed so nice, too. Not the sort to make a spectacle of himself."

"So you think this was suicide?" Libby asked.

"Definitely. What else could it be? Although, I have to say, he seemed perfectly fine when I last spoke to him."

"When was that?" Bernie asked.

"Early morning the day he died. We had such a nice chat, too. He was standing right where you're standing now. He was returning my late husband's metal detector. He'd borrowed it because his had gone on the fritz. I guess he found what he was looking for."

"Did he say what he was looking for?" Bernie asked.

Mrs. Randall nodded her head emphatically. "Yes. Mr. Witherspoon said he was looking for pieces of old ships, told me it was a hobby of his, after I told him about my husband. Then we talked about ghosts. I told him I wasn't afraid of them at my age, and he said—"

A horn sounded outside.

"He said what?" Libby asked as someone honked again.

"He said he was. I think that fact embarrassed him," Mrs. Randall confided.

The car honked again.

Mrs. Randall put her hand to her mouth. "Oh, dear. That's my daughter-in-law. I should have been downstairs already. She gets cranky when I keep her waiting. Sorry, but I really have to go."

"Anything else you two talked about?" Bernie asked. "Please. It might be important."

"Well, I suppose my daughter-in-law can wait for another minute. We talked about crows. Most people don't realize how smart they are. They can remember people's faces, people who have been nice to them and people who haven't. He started feeding them when I told him that. He said he needed all the friends he could get."

The horn sounded again.

"Now I really have to go," Mrs. Randall said, and then she turned and headed toward the stairs.

"She should be in a building with an elevator," Bernie told Libby as she went to help her.

When Bernie came back, Libby ducked under the police tape, slipped the key to Darius Witherspoon's apartment into the dead bolt, and turned it. The door swung open, and Libby and Bernie stepped inside.

# Chapter 14

"It's cold in here," Bernie complained before she realized the window Darius had gone out of, voluntarily or otherwise, was still open and the fog had crept in the room, leaving a thin layer of damp behind.

Bernie crossed the room. She was going to close the window but then thought better of it—someone from the CID might notice—and settled for turning on the lights instead. The plastic wall plate felt greasy beneath her fingers. As she looked around, she shivered, wishing she were wearing her black cashmere sweater over her shirtdress, instead of her denim jacket. The modern furniture, which had looked cheerful the last time she'd been up here, now seemed garish and mismatched. Like something out of a carnival.

"Look at the walls and the windowsills," Libby said, rubbing her arms with her hands to warm herself up. Once white, they were now full of black smudges, which the crime-scene techs had left behind when they dusted the surfaces for fingerprints.

"Repainting will not be fun," Bernie noted as she went over and began to go through the small pile of mail on the modern Danish teak dining room table.

"I don't think a coat of paint is going to do it," Libby said, looking around. "I don't think I'd want to live here, considering what happened."

"Maybe the Realtor won't tell the new tenants about Darius."

"Isn't that illegal?"

"Probably. Or maybe they won't care," Bernie said, preoccupied with what she was doing.

"I'd care," Libby said. "Wouldn't you?"

"Probably," Bernie admitted, looking up at Libby before she looked back down at the mail. She found the usual assortment of junk mail. Requests for donations. Credit card offers. Invitations for free hearing loss screenings. Garden and furniture catalogs. Some of the mail was addressed to Darius's wife, some to Darius; most was addressed to Occupant. None of it was of consequence. But what had she expected? Darius hadn't been here for very long.

Bernie sighed and studied the area some more. A couple of crumbled-up take-out bags from Harry's, a local deli/food market, and a half-empty bottle of Johnnie Walker on the coffee table caught her eye. No glasses. Maybe Darius had drunk straight from the bottle, Bernie decided as she went over and, for want of anything better to do, opened the bags. There was a half-eaten cup of coleslaw in one and a couple of crusts of rye bread in the other, along with the remains of two pears.

"Now, this could be something," she said, showing her sister what was left of the pears.

"Like what?" Libby asked as she looked around.

"Remember, Darius had some weird allergy to pears? That's why we made the caramel apple cake instead of the almond custard pear tarts."

"That's right." Libby opened the hall closet. The only thing in it was a raincoat. "He did, didn't he? Something about his tongue swelling. So maybe someone else ate here."

"That's what I'm thinking," Bernie said. She thought about Harry's. It was a popular upscale food market with seven checkout lines. The odds of someone remembering someone who bought a couple of pears and some sort of sandwich in the past couple of days were fairly slim.

On the other hand, maybe someone would remember Darius, and maybe Darius was with someone. It wouldn't hurt to have her dad ask. He knew the general manager there. In the old days, he would have leaped at the opportunity, but now, with Michelle around, she wasn't so sure.

"Found Darius's metal detector in the bedroom," Libby said while Bernie was thinking about whether going to Harry's would be worth it or not, if she and her sister had to do it.

Bernie looked up as Libby plonked it down in front of her. "The one that doesn't work?" she asked.

Libby nodded. Bernie flipped the ON switch up. Nothing. She remembered going prospecting for "treasure" with her grandpa on the Jersey Shore when she was six. They'd found five nickels and two quarters, and her grandpa had let her keep the two quarters. She'd promptly spent them on penny candy, all of which she'd eaten in one day, to her mother's chagrin.

"Do you think Darius was really looking for wreckage?" Libby asked.

Bernie shrugged. "Sure. Why not?"

"How much value could it have?"

"A lot if the find was archeologically significant."

"I wonder if he found anything. He did give Mrs. Randall's metal detector back to her."

"Well, if he did, it's not here," Bernie said as she studied the space in front of her. Aside from the take-out bags, the only evidence that someone had lived here was some books on the coffee table. She went over and took a look at the pile. There were three tablets of ocean charts; a book by someone named Sven Brighton, about his experiences crossing the Atlantic in a sailboat by himself; a copy of *Kon-Tiki*; and three paperback mysteries by someone Bernie had never heard of.

"Maybe he was planning on taking a sailing trip," Libby said as she looked at the books Bernie handed her, then put them back down on the table. "A long sailing trip."

"Maybe," Bernie said as she and Libby moved to the kitchen.

All they found there was a handful of groceries that were going bad in the fridge. In the bathroom, they discovered dandruff shampoo and body wash in the shower, and toothpaste, a toothbrush, a bottle of aspirin, and a tube of Bengay in the medicine cabinet. There were some underwear, socks, and a couple of flannel shirts in the dresser in the bedroom, and three pairs of old frayed pants and a pair of mud-encrusted sneakers in the bedroom closet.

"I guess he hadn't finished moving in yet," Libby observed. "There's no TV. No laptop."

"Maybe he was a low-tech kinda guy," Bernie suggested.

"Yeah. But even I watch TV," Libby told her.

"True," Bernie said. "We should take a look in his Park Avenue place. It might give us a little more."

"Such as?"

"If I knew that, we wouldn't have to go see, would we?"

"Fine. And how are we going to get in?" Libby asked.

"Don't worry. I'll figure it out."

Libby didn't ask what her sister had in mind, because she didn't want to know. Instead, she went over to the window in the living room, reached up, grabbed on to the plant hook, and pulled. It didn't move. "I wonder what kind of plant Darius was going to hang on this."

"A big fern, I imagine," Bernie replied, not that it mattered now. "Be careful," she warned when Libby leaned out the window.

Deep in thought, Libby just nodded. "It would be hard," she said, reenacting the crime in her head.

"Hard to do what?" Bernie asked.

"To get a rope over someone's neck, attach it, and throw him over. You'd have to be really strong and fast." Libby thought back to last night's scene. "Darius's feet weren't kicking."

"No. His neck was already broken," Bernie said quietly, remembering.

"Maybe it was broken before he went out," Libby suggested.

"Maybe," Bernie agreed. "I'm guessing it would be hard to tell."

And then the murderer did what? Libby wondered. The only way he could have gotten away was through the same window he threw Darius out of. He would have had to climb out of it and onto the metal railing of the small balcony and jumped. Assuming he didn't break his leg, he could have run away.

But he would have had to jump after he'd pushed Darius out, and since all eyes had been on the window, someone would have seen him. Libby tapped her fingers against her thigh. Or maybe not. Maybe the murderer had counted on all eyes being on Darius. It was taking a big chance, she thought as she leaned back into the room.

Or maybe, Libby thought, trying to work things out, Darius's killer had crossed over to the side of the balcony closest to the wall and had jumped from there. That way he wouldn't have landed in full view. He would have to have an excellent sense of balance to do that. Like a circus performer walking a tightrope. Libby could never have done it. She was thinking about that when Bernie nudged her.

Libby startled.

"What are you thinking about?" Bernie asked.

Libby explained.

Bernie leaned out the window and studied the railing. What Libby was suggesting was possible, but the person doing it would have to be extremely athletic. Then she noticed a small whitish mark on the railing. It looked as if the black paint had been rubbed off. She took off her stilettos, sat down on the windowsill, and pivoted around till her feet were touching the metal bottom. She pushed her right foot down and then her left. The small balcony creaked. She leaned forward so more of her weight was on it. The balcony groaned. She sat back.

"That thing is designed to hold plants, not people," Libby observed.

"No kidding," Bernie said as she leaned out the window and rested her chest on the metal railing. She heard another groan. "Hold my ankles," she said to Libby.

"Are you nuts?" Libby demanded as the metal railing let out a deeper groan. "Get off of that thing."

"I'll be off in a minute. What I want to see isn't that far."

"That noise is telling you not to do this," Libby said. "I'm not holding your ankles."

"Fine," Bernie told her. "Don't. If I fall, it's on your head."

"Don't try to guilt me. Anyway, I can't hold you if the balcony gives way," Libby replied. "I'm not strong enough."

"It won't give way, and I'm not going to fall. This is just a precaution," Bernie told her.

"Then why ask me?"

"I'm doing you a favor."

"A favor?" Libby was incredulous. "How's that?"

"Because if anything did happen to me, you wouldn't be able to live with yourself."

Libby stomped over and grabbed her sister's ankles. "Happy now?"

"Yes," Bernie said as she wiggled forward another couple of inches. "Actually, I am."

There was another, louder groan.

"Maybe this wasn't such a good idea," Bernie conceded, reversing her course. "Do me a favor," she told Libby when she was inside the window. "Find Manny and see if he has a tall ladder we can use."

# Chapter 15

It was a little after eleven at night, and Bernie, Libby, and Libby's boyfriend, Marvin, were camped out at RJ's, rehashing yesterday's and today's events. Since it was a weekday, RJ's had emptied out a little before nine, leaving the jack-o'-lanterns and the zombies hanging on the walls with no one to scare.

There were only three groups of people left in the place. A noisy group of eight twenty-something-year-old men and women sitting at one of the round tables in the back, taking selfies, and drinking Jack Daniel's; a group of five men, also in their twenties, who were drinking beer and having a raucous game of darts; and two women and a man dressed as pirates, who were shooting pool in the back and sipping Irish coffees.

Libby, Bernie, and Marvin were the only people sitting at the bar. They were sipping their beers, while Brandon was standing behind the bar, polishing glasses and listening to Libby and Bernie's story.

"So you think this . . . ," Brandon said when they were done.

"The killer," Bernie said, finishing his sentence for him.

"The killer used a rope to shinny down from the second floor?"

Bernie nodded.

"Then why wasn't the rope still there?" Marvin asked. He'd been following the conversation closely.

"He used a slipknot," Bernie explained. "Then all he'd have to do is give it a jerk and the rope would untie itself, and he'd be good to go."

Brandon turned down the sound of the TV behind the bar and came back. "How come nobody saw this?" he asked. "Everyone was looking out the window. I know that I was. I didn't see anybody. Except for Darius, of course."

"Libby and I figure he went down the narrow side of the balcony," Bernie replied. "That way if he went to the left, he could go around to the parking lot, and the guests wouldn't see him."

Brandon shook his head. "I don't know," he told her. "Offhand, it sounds pretty far-fetched to me."

Bernie ate a pretzel from the bowl sitting next to her. "Okay. Then what's your theory?" she challenged.

Brandon wiped another glass as he thought it over. "I don't have one," he admitted.

"So you think he killed himself and we're on a fool's errand?" Bernie asked.

Brandon looked sheepish. "Actually, I do."

Marvin took a sip of his beer and put his glass down on the coaster. "Remember Sam Otis?" he asked.

"The kid who made Mrs. Diver crash her car into her fence when he hung himself from the lamppost in front of her house?" Libby replied.

"Yes, that one," Marvin replied.

"And then he started talking to Mrs. Diver from the lamppost, and she ran screaming down the road," Brandon said. He started laughing at the memory.

"What's your point?" Bernie asked Marvin.

"My point is that maybe that's what Darius had intended to do," Marvin said. "And he made a mistake with the knots on the rope and killed himself."

Bernie reached over, took another pretzel, and broke it into little pieces. "My dad told me Sam had a harness under his shirt," Bernie said as she began picking each pretzel piece up with the tips of her fingers and eating it.

"Darius wouldn't be that stupid," Brandon said.

"You'd be surprised how stupid people can be," Marvin said. As the son of a funeral director, he'd seen some unbelievably dumb stuff.

"Then how do you explain the scuff marks on the railing?" Bernie asked him.

"They were probably there before," Marvin said, hazarding a guess.

"The maintenance man said they weren't," Libby replied. "We asked him. He told us he'd painted the railings a week ago. Plus, that balcony is really loose, unlike the other two. The bolts on that balcony are almost coming out of the wall."

"Of course they would be, given the fact that Darius Witherspoon hung from it," Marvin said.

Libby corrected him. "Darius hung himself from the plant hook."

One of the dart players caught Brandon's eye. "Excuse me," Brandon told Libby. Then he went over to the taps, pulled five glasses of Guinness, and set them on the bar. "You know," he said to Bernie and Libby after the dart players had paid for and collected their drinks, "if what you say is true, whoever killed Darius Witherspoon had to be incredibly fast and strong. And agile."

"Too bad the circus hasn't come through here," Marvin noted as he reached over and took a handful of pretzels out of the bowl and proceeded to pop them in his mouth. "Then you'd be all set suspect-wise."

Brandon reached under the counter, picked up the bag of pretzels, and refilled the bowl. "He or she—notice I'm being diverse here—could be a rock climber or a gymnast."

"True," Libby said as she stifled a yawn. The day was catching up with her. "Maybe the killer strangled Darius first," she suggested. "If he pressed on his carotid artery, Darius would have been unconscious in seconds. Or maybe the person he was eating with slipped something in his drink."

"We didn't find a glass on the table," Bernie reminded her sister.

"Maybe that's because whoever killed Darius took it with him," Libby countered.

Brandon looked from Bernie to Libby and back again. "A tox screen will settle that, won't it?"

"It would," Bernie replied, "but the powers that be have already declared Witherspoon's death a suicide. They'd have to reverse that to order a tox screen, and they're not going to do that."

"They'd have to move pretty fast if they wanted one," Marvin said.

Libby raised an eyebrow. "How's that?"

"Because the coroner is releasing the body to us tomorrow, and it's going to be cremated," Marvin told her.

Libby leaned forward. "You're kidding."

"Nope," Marvin said. "My dad was in touch with Witherspoon's only living relative, and that's what she wants done. In order to stop that, you'd need a court order."

"Maybe I can talk to her," Bernie said.

"Good luck with that," Marvin replied. "She's eighty-eight years old, hard of hearing, and lives in an assisted-living facility somewhere down in Florida." He looked at his watch. Pretty soon he had to go home and make sure his pet pig hadn't destroyed the house. "Frankly, I don't think a tox screen would matter, anyway."

"Why do you say that?" Libby demanded.

"Because," Marvin replied, "from what I'm hearing, I'm inclined to say that Darius Witherspoon killed himself. Sorry. But that's what it sounds like to me."

"Me too," Brandon said, shrugging apologetically. "But, hey, I could be wrong. It's happened before. Occasionally. Once in a really long time."

"But what about the money and the note?" Libby asked.

Marvin scratched his head. "Honestly, I don't know."

"It's the fly in the ointment, the bug in the bed, the mouse poop in the rice," Brandon sang out.

Bernie shot him a look, and he shut up.

"Sorry," he murmured. "I got carried away."

"It always comes back to the note," Bernie continued. "Why would Darius leave us so much money if he didn't think that someone was going to kill him? If he didn't want his killer caught?"

"Because he was loony tunes," Brandon suggested.

"He didn't seem that way to me," Libby said.

"Just because he didn't seem that way doesn't mean he wasn't that way," Marvin protested.

"True," Libby said.

"I mean, what was he involved in that would make someone go to that much trouble?" Marvin asked.

"That is the question, isn't it?" Bernie agreed.

"For all practical purposes, our killer could have just strangled him and left him in his apartment. Throwing him out the window was definitely overkill. Get it?" Brandon asked.

"A two-year-old would have gotten it," Bernie told him. "Can we be serious for a moment?"

Brandon lifted up his hands. "Fine. Then maybe it was a message. Or a warning."

"Yeah, but to whom?" Libby asked.

"Maybe to someone at the party," Marvin replied, slipping on his jacket. As he buttoned it up, he realized there was a hole on the right side. He'd have to buy a new one soon. Winter was going to be here in the not too distant future.

"The killer was most likely one of the guests," Brandon said, deciding to play the what-if game with Bernie and Libby. "Possibly someone Darius cheated out of money or some guy who had just found out Darius was carrying on with his wife."

"Why are you saying that?" Bernie asked.

"Because murder's always about sex or revenge," Brandon replied. "Or both together."

"Or money," Bernie added. "Don't forget money."

"But, on the other hand," Brandon said, continuing with his line of thought, "if that was the case, why invite that person to your party? I know I wouldn't."

"Because Darius wanted to lord it over him," Bernie said, hypothesizing. "Or because Darius didn't know that this person hated him."

"How about the people on the guest list?" Marvin asked. "Have you tried Googling them? Maybe there's something there."

"I would if I could," Bernie said. "Unfortunately, I don't have the guest list. We didn't send out the invitations. We just got a head count."

"I don't suppose you can get the list?" Brandon asked.

"I wish," Libby replied.

"It was probably on his computer," Bernie added. "Which I'm sure the police have, given that it wasn't in his Berkshire Arms apartment."

"Here's another thought," Brandon said. Now that he

was thinking about it, he wondered if Bernie might be right about the cause of Darius's death, after all. "I wonder if Darius's wife's disappearance had anything to do with his death."

"As in someone wanted them both out of the way?" Bernie asked. "As opposed to him killing himself out of grief."

"Exactly," Brandon said.

"Interesting thought," replied Bernie, who had been wondering about that herself. She tapped her fingernails on the bar. They made a *rat-tat-tat* noise on the copper.

"Isn't it, though?" Brandon poured himself a cup of coffee from the pot behind the bar and added three sugars. "Boy, I gotta tell you," he said, thinking back to Darius's death. "That's not the way I'd want to go."

"Me either." Bernie clicked her tongue against her teeth while she thought. "If what we're saying is true, then Darius's killer is a very clever man. . . ."

"Or woman," Brandon said.

Bernie gave him a look, and he shut up. She continued. "He made sure that Darius's death would be treated as a suicide and dismissed." Bernie swiveled on her bar stool and looked out RJ's window. The shops in the strip mall RJ's was in were shuttered. The parking lot was practically empty. There were no vehicles on the street. Everyone was home. "It's an efficient—if that's the right word—approach to a problem," she mused.

"But if Darius knew this man was coming for him," Libby objected, "why didn't he go to the police?"

"Maybe he was involved in something shady, and he didn't want the police around," Brandon suggested. "Or maybe he thought he could handle the situation himself and there was no need to involve anybody else."

"That would be a guy thing," Bernie said.

Brandon smiled. "Indeed, it would be."

Libby leaned forward. "Then here's another question. If Darius knew who his killer was going to be—and he had to have had some suspicion—why didn't he tell us? Why didn't he write it in the note he left us? There isn't even a hint pointing us in the direction we need to go."

"Good point," Marvin said, eating another handful of pretzels.

Libby ran her finger around the edge of her glass. "I mean, he must have suspected something was going to happen. Otherwise, why leave us the money?"

"Maybe," Marvin said slowly, exploring possibilities, "Darius didn't really believe it. Maybe he was just leaving the letter as an insurance policy. To make himself feel better."

Bernie nodded. That made sense to her. "I guess we'll find out the answer when we find out who killed Darius . . . if anyone did."

Marvin finished off the last couple of inches of beer in his glass and put it down on the coaster. He opened his mouth and closed it.

"What?" Libby said.

"Nothing."

She frowned. "That's so annoying when you do that, Marvin."

"Fine," he said. "I was just thinking about your father's motto."

"Which one?" Libby asked, since her dad had a long list of them.

"The one about the simplest explanation usually being the correct explanation. All of these permutations we're discussing . . ." Marvin waved his hand in the air.

"Nice word choice," said Bernie, complimenting him.

"Thank you, Bernie," Marvin said.

"What about them?" Libby inquired.

"It's just too complicated, and we haven't even gotten to the why yet, let alone the who," he said. Then, before

Libby could answer, Marvin bent down, gave Libby a kiss on her cheek, told her he'd see her tomorrow, and headed for the door.

Ten minutes later Bernie and Libby left, as well, but instead of going home directly, Bernie took the long way round and ended up on Peck Hill, one of the highest points in Longely. She killed the engine and sat there. The fog had lifted, and looking down, she had a clear view of the Berkshire Arms. It reminded her of a malevolent spider squatting on its kill.

"What are you thinking?" Libby asked her sister after a couple of minutes had passed.

"I'm thinking that you can remodel that school as much as you want," Bernie said, turning toward Libby. "It's not going to matter. Something bad will always happen there."

"Bad juju," Libby said.

"*Cursed* would be another word." Bernie turned the engine back on. "Let's go home," she said to Libby. "We're going to have a long day tomorrow."

# Chapter 16

Sean Simmons walked into Harry's market a little after ten the next morning, after having snuck in a smoke, something that was getting harder to do with Michelle in the picture, and headed straight for the office, where his friend Mitch Comitsky was waiting for him. He shook his head the way he always did when he came through the front door, because he could never get used to how big the store had gotten. He kept seeing it the way it was in the old days.

The place had started off as a hole-in-the-wall coffee and doughnut shop, and slowly through the years it had grown and grown, until the store took up half a block and had so many departments, you needed a map to find anything in it. Now Harry's sold things Sean had never heard of and wasn't much interested in learning about, either.

He'd liked it better when he was on patrol and stopped by for coffee and doughnuts. Then you asked for coffee and all you had to specify was whether you wanted medium or large. Now you had to say whether you wanted a pour over—which sounded to him like a bad hairdo—or a French press, and that was just for starters. He supposed his annoyance was a sign that he was getting old and cranky, but really, why did everything have to be so complicated these days?

He stopped for a minute and watched two store employees take down the skeletons, ghosts, and jack-o'-lanterns in the windows and put up pilgrims and turkeys, while a couple of other clerks were arranging mounds of pumpkins and smaller piles of decorative corn near the store's entrance. The older he got, the faster time seemed to go, he reflected. He was thinking about why that was when he heard someone call his name. He turned around. Mitch was standing right in back of him. The man was built like a fireplug, Sean thought, and like the shop he managed, he seemed to get a little larger every time Sean saw him.

"Long time no see," Mitch said, giving Sean a hearty slap on the back.

Mitch was ex-NYPD and had retired and come up here when he'd been clipped by a speeding car while he was giving someone a ticket on the East River Drive. They'd never caught the person who'd nailed him, but Mitch said it was just as well. He'd needed a change of scene, anyway.

"I understand you've been keeping busy these days," Mitch said, winking at him, as he walked Sean to his office. He slapped Sean on the back again.

"I'm doing okay," Sean said, pretty sure that Mitch was referring to Michelle, but hoping that he wasn't.

Mitch winked again. "Don't be modest. I've seen her. Not bad. Not bad at all."

"I don't know," Sean confessed.

Mitch stopped walking and gave him an incredulous look. "What's not to know?" he demanded.

"I'm beginning to have second thoughts," Sean confessed.

"Why?" Mitch asked.

"It's the whole marriage thing," Sean allowed.

"She wants to?"

"Absolutely. I had a good thing going with Rose, but I'm not sure I want to do it again."

"But you haven't told her that?"

Sean shook his head, then moved out of the way as a shopper went by him with her cart.

"And you think she'll book if you do?"

"Well, she's pretty determined to get what she wants."

Mitch nodded and started walking again. "Aren't they all, though? What does she want with you, anyway?"

"Damned if I know," Sean said, keeping up with him.

Mitch automatically reached over and straightened a bunch of bananas as he and Sean passed by the display. "I tell you what," he said. "If things don't work out, you can always pass her on to me."

Sean grinned. "I'm sure Peggy would be so pleased," he said. Peggy was Mitch's wife, and she ran him and the household.

Mitch laughed. "I don't think I can do two woman any-more, anyway. I don't think I have the energy."

"Sad, isn't it?" Sean said as he followed Mitch into his office.

The place was a cubbyhole with enough space for two chairs, a small desk, and a file cabinet. Four ghosts and one witch, remnants of Halloween, had been shoved behind the file cabinet. There were papers stacked every-where.

"You should get some shelving in here," Sean commented as he moved a pile of papers off of the chair by Mitch's desk and put them on the floor. "Neaten stuff up a tad. I don't see how you find anything in here."

"Neither do I," Mitch said, lowering himself into his chair. "But somehow it works. So what is this about?" he asked as Sean sat down.

"It's probably a fool's errand," Sean replied, and he ex-plained about Darius, Darius's note, and the coleslaw, the bread, and the pears Bernie had found in Darius's living room.

"You can't be serious," Mitch said.

"I wouldn't be here if I wasn't," Sean told him.

"Do you know how many people go through this shop each day?" Mitch asked.

"A lot," Sean said.

"And how many employees we have? We're open from seven in the morning till nine at night. Who's going to remember something like that?" Mitch snorted. "Please."

"I know," Sean said. "I'm just trying to dot the i's and cross the t's for my girls."

"How are they doing?" Mitch asked. "I keep meaning to go over there, but with the hours I put in here, well . . ." He turned his palms up.

"I'm sure they'd love to see you when you have a moment," Sean replied.

Mitch leaned forward. "So you think this Darius was really killed?"

Sean consulted the ceiling for a moment before he answered. "Probably not. But"—he brought his thumb and his forefinger together till they were about an inch apart— "there is a small possibility. The note bothers me. I can't find a reasonable explanation for it."

"I'll ask around," Mitch promised.

"That would be great," Sean said.

"Just don't expect anything."

"Believe me, I'm not," Sean said. "This is harder."

Mitch cocked his head.

"The girls, solving this kind of thing," Sean explained. "They can't rely on a badge to get answers. They have to be cleverer than we were."

Mitch laughed. "This is true. You like that your daughters are involved in this kind of thing?" he asked, suddenly turning serious. "I know I wouldn't be happy if Erin was."

Sean consulted the ceiling again while he thought about his answer. Mitch waited, the sounds of the store drifting into the office.

Finally, Sean said, "I'm proud of them."

"But," Mitch replied, prodding.

"I do worry." Sean frowned. "I can't tell them what to do, though."

Mitch laughed. His daughter was the same age as Bernie. "Tell me about it. Not that Erin's shy about sharing what she thinks I should be doing."

Sean chuckled. "Ain't that the truth?"

"I'll tell you one thing, though," Mitch said, changing subjects after another minute had passed.

Sean waited.

Mitch picked up a pen and tapped it on the desk. "Moran is probably pretty happy."

"Really?" Sean leaned forward, interested. "I would have thought the opposite. This can't be good for rentals."

"No, it isn't," Mitch agreed, putting the pen down. "But sometimes vengeance trumps money."

"You're saying William Moran had a reason to kill Witherspoon?"

"No. I'm saying he most likely wasn't shedding any tears about his death."

Sean leaned back in his chair, waiting for Mitch to continue, but his friend didn't say anything.

"Are you going to tell me or not?" Sean asked after a minute had gone by, unable to control his curiosity any longer.

"Guess," Mitch said, a big grin on his face, having won phase one of this particular game.

"Don't be a jerk," Sean told him. "I'm not in the mood."

"You're getting grumpy in your old age," Mitch observed.

"I always have been grumpy," Sean reminded him. "Now give."

Mitch bounced up and down in his chair like a five-year-old needing to pee. "One guess."

"Fine," Sean grumbled. "Some sort of business deal gone bad."

Mitch's face fell. "How did you know?"

Now it was Sean's turn to smile. "I didn't. But it was either that or some sort of sex thing gone south. So are you going to tell me or not?"

"Not," Mitch said. "Just kidding." He took a sip from the bottle of water on his desk. "You're going to like this," he promised as he put the bottle down.

# Chapter 17

Sean's eyes got wider as he listened to what his friend had to say. "Wow," he said when Mitch was through. "How'd you hear about that?"

"Come. I'll show you." Mitch got out of his chair and beckoned for Sean to follow him. They stepped out of Mitch's office and walked over to the checkout lines. "You see that girl over there?" Mitch pointed to the girl standing behind the cash register in the second line. She was tall and thin, with blond hair in a bun, big hoop earrings, and bright blue eye shadow that made her eyes look small and hard. "She told me."

"How did she know?"

Mitch's grin was so wide, it threatened to split his face. "She's the daughter of Moran's son's ex."

Sean took a minute to process that. "Okay," he said. "Go on."

"Well, evidently, Moran's son Gus invested in some scheme that Darius Witherspoon was running—something about finding the original ark."

"Gee, I thought they did that in *Raiders of the Lost Ark*."

"And gave him hundreds of thousands of dollars."

"So I guess he's pretty rich?"

"Not anymore, he's not, if he ever was. In fact, he's fallen behind in his child support payments—I hear he's about to file for bankruptcy—which is why Serena, who, by the way, is anything but, is working here."

"And she told you this?" Sean asked.

Mitch shook his head. "I overheard it. She was telling one of the other cashiers. She and her mom had to move from their fancy house out in Hayden to one of those apartment complexes by the train station."

"That would be quite a comedown," Sean observed.

"I'll say," Mitch agreed. "I lived in one when I first came up here with Peggy. I was afraid the roaches were going to eat us alive."

Sean thought for a moment. "Okay. Then if what you're telling me is true, why did Moran sell to Witherspoon? I certainly wouldn't have if I was him."

"I don't think he knew," Mitch said. "Evidently, he out-sources that side of the business. Lots of people do these days. And the same could be said for Witherspoon. I'm sure he wouldn't have bought a place from the dad of one of the people he screwed if he knew. Or maybe he would. Maybe he was that kind of guy, the kind of guy who likes trouble."

"I know a lot of those," Sean commented.

"My stock in trade," Mitch said.

"So where does this son live?" Sean asked.

Mitch rubbed his hands together. "That's when it gets even better. In the Berkshire Arms."

"Interesting," Sean said.

Mitch nodded. "Isn't it, though?"

"Think Serena will talk to me?"

"You can try, but I doubt it."

"I think I'd like to give it a shot, anyway," Sean said.

Five minutes later, Mitch brought Serena into his office,

introduced her to Sean, and stepped out and closed the door, leaving the girl alone with his old friend.

"That's a nice name," Sean began, but he could have forgotten about the pleasantries, because Serena gave him the stink eye.

"You a cop?" she asked.

"Why do you say that?" Sean asked.

Serena rolled her eyes and sighed a sigh that suggested the question was too obvious to answer. She did, anyway. "Duh. Because you look like one," she told him as she curled a tendril of hair around her finger.

*You never lose the look*, Sean reflected as he told her that he was. A slight lie. He had been one. He'd been the chief of police. Once. After all, what was a little misinformation among friends? Well, he could be arrested for impersonating an officer. There was that. Which would not be good. A major understatement, because he'd never live it down. On the other hand, if he'd told her that he wasn't, he knew she would have turned around and walked out the door.

He watched Serena wiggle around, looking everywhere but at him. Obviously, she was guilty of something.

"Have a seat," he said, gesturing to one.

Serena shook her head. "I'll stand. If it's about those packs of gum and the Snapples," she began, "I was going to—"

Sean held up his hand before Serena could go on. "I don't care about that." He saw Serena's body collapse in relief.

"Then what?" she asked, getting her defiance back. "Because I don't know anything about Richie, either."

"It's not about Richie," Sean told her as he wondered what Richie had done. Probably stealing stuff or selling dope out in the alley or both. He made a mental note to tell Mitch about him.

Serena put her hands on her hips. "Then what?" she demanded. "I've got to get back to work."

"Actually," he said, "I want to talk to you about your dad."

Serena bristled. "That loser!" she exclaimed. "I hope you arrest him!"

Sean smiled at her. "I don't know if I can do that, but I do have a few questions I was hoping you could answer for me."

"What do you want to know?" Serena replied, taking the seat Sean had offered her before and leaning forward, anxious to cooperate. "He deserves whatever he gets. You know, my mom didn't know what he was doing." She bit her lip. Her voice rose an octave, quivering in indignation. "He used her money, too. All her money. Our money. He didn't even ask her. He just gave it all to this stupid company."

"Do you know the name?" Sean asked.

"Treasure Hunters, LLC. Or something like that. Isn't there a law about doing what he did?"

And Serena went on talking, the words spilling out in a torrent. Sean just sat down in Mitch's chair, folded his arms across his chest, leaned back, and listened. Three-quarters of an hour later, when Serena had finished and gone back to work, Sean pulled out his cell and called Bernie.

"You know what that LLC means, don't you?" he asked Bernie after he'd told her what he'd found out.

"It means Darius wasn't personally liable for any of the debts his business incurred," Bernie replied.

"Makes for bad blood," Sean remarked before he hung up.

# Chapter 18

*Indeed it does*, Bernie thought as she put her cell down on her desk. She clasped her hands above her head and stretched, trying to work out a kink in her back. Then she stretched again and typed in "Treasure Hunters, LLC" on her laptop. A moment later the screen was filled with articles about the company, none of them complimentary.

According to what she was reading, Darius had led three archeological expeditions: one to find the precursor to Noah's Ark, the second to find a sunken Spanish galleon filled with golden coins that went down off the coast of Florida, and the third to locate the lost treasure of the Knights Templars.

Evidently, all three expeditions had failed miserably, and all of them had been the object of numerous lawsuits against Darius Witherspoon, charging him with everything from incompetence to outright fraud. None of the lawsuits had had a happy outcome for the plaintiffs, the judge ruling in all three cases that treasure hunting was an inherently risky business. *No kidding*, Bernie thought as she poked around some more. She found a Web site on the expedition to find the Spanish galleon.

It certainly looked legitimate, she thought as she scanned

it, but then she started reading the comments. They were scathing. Comments like *Witherspoon should be shot. The putz didn't even show up, left us stranded* abounded. She scrolled down, and near the end she came across a comment from Gus Moran. Yup. Just like her dad had said. Not that she had ever doubted him.

Now the son was living in the Berkshire Arms, as had Darius. Of course, Gus Moran had moved in considerably earlier. Mitch was probably right. Darius must not have known. Bernie was willing to bet it had come as an unwelcomed surprise when he found out. And why had William Moran sold to Darius Witherspoon in the first place?

Her dad said that Moran hadn't known. That a separate part of the company handled the mechanics of that aspect of the business. Bernie could see that. After all, more and more companies outsourced stuff. But what if that wasn't true? What if Moran had sold to Darius Witherspoon because he wanted to set him up? Was this a case of a father and son bonding over a murder?

She added them to her list of possible suspects. After all, even if William and Gus Moran hadn't been invited to the party, that didn't mean they weren't there. The father worked there, and the son lived there. Given that it was a masked costume party, it had been impossible to tell who was who. And afterward, given the commotion, it would have been equally easy to slip away. She certainly wouldn't have noticed anything, and neither would Libby.

Bernie reached for her coffee, took a sip, and made a face. She was trying out a new blend she was contemplating using in the store—a South American blend she'd gotten from Joe's Beans—but it was too acidic. She stirred in another lump of sugar and took a bite of her sandwich—grilled cheddar cheese, candied bacon, and avocado—and thought some more. So where had Gus Moran been at the time of Darius's party?

For that matter, where had William Moran been? She could ask him and his son, but she was certain neither one of them would tell her. Why should they? It was not as if she had the power to compel them to. But it might be fun to try.

She swallowed and took another bite of her sandwich, savoring the crunch of the bread and the bacon against the smoothness of the avocado and the cheese. She could see where the son would be angry enough to try to kill Darius, but would the father? Well, if he was a certain kind of man, he might, she thought, thinking of the men who attacked the refs at their sons' Little League games when they thought the call was bad.

Bernie flicked a bread crumb off of her pleated plaid skirt and thought about how she was going to go about getting the information she needed. Maybe it would pay to talk to Gus's ex first, before she talked to Gus. After all, the more information one had, the better the questions one was able to ask. She ate the rest of her sandwich, wiped her hands on a napkin, logged out of her laptop, went out of the office, and told Libby what she'd found out.

Libby looked up from the piecrusts she was rolling out and listened as Bernie spoke, nodding once in a while to show she was paying attention. But her mind was half on what Bernie was telling her and half on the pies. She had to make four apple for Mrs. Watson, six apple and cranberry for the monthly meeting of the Longely Book Club at the Longely Library, and three raspberry for a meeting of the Committee to Restore Longely's Original Train Station.

A couple of minutes later, Bernie went out front to straighten out a credit card snafu—the new machine they'd gotten really sucked—and Libby started thinking about what Bernie had told her. Then, after a few minutes, her mind drifted back to Halloween Eve. To the crows and the woman she could have sworn she'd seen on the roof of the Berkshire Arms.

Libby knew that Bernie had seen her too, even though her sister hadn't wanted to admit it. She had thought she was imagining things. So had Libby at the time. Now she wasn't so sure. She'd thought she had seen a ghost, but now she wondered if what she had seen was a real person. If, in fact, she'd seen Darius Witherspoon's murderer.

And maybe, just maybe, the "woman" she'd seen was a man dressed up as a woman. Maybe it was this Gus Moran whom Bernie had been talking about. Okay, so the scenario she was conjuring up *was* slightly far-fetched, but then everything about this case was. She and Bernie hadn't been up on the roof yet. Maybe it was time they took a look. Maybe whoever had been up there—if anyone had been— had left something behind. She was thinking about when they could go up there when Bernie walked back into the prep room.

"Penny Moran-Engels wants to meet with us," Bernie told her.

Libby put her rolling pin down. "And she is . . . ?"

"Guy Moran's ex."

"And we want to talk to her why?"

"Because she says she has something to tell us," Bernie replied. She turned and yelled to Amber that she'd be there in a sec, then turned back to her sister. "I told her we'd meet her at her place at five." Then she was gone with a swish of her skirt and a clack of her heels.

"I don't suppose she gave a hint about what it's about?" Libby called after her sister. "No. Of course she didn't," she grumbled to herself when Bernie didn't answer.

"What did you say?" Bernie asked, popping back in.

"Nothing," Libby replied. What was the point?

She sighed, picked up her rolling pin, and got back to work. The pies had to be done and boxed by four, when everyone was going to pick them up. After she'd put the pies in the oven, she carefully wiped off the rolling pin with a clean cotton dish towel and placed it in its drawer.

The rolling pin had been her mother's, and Libby always felt as if her mom was watching over her when she used it. In this case, though, she hoped that wasn't true, because her mother would most certainly not approve of what she was doing. At all. Well, not the baking part. She would have liked that. The detecting part, on the other hand, not so much.

In fact, her mom had never allowed her dad to talk about his cases at dinner. That was how strongly she felt about "bringing that kind of thing into the house." Not that that had stopped Bernie and Libby. They'd just waited until their mom was downstairs, in the shop, getting ready for the next day, before they pestered their dad into telling them what he was working on. It had been their little secret.

# Chapter 19

The sun was setting over the Hudson, and Penny Moran-Engels was exiting her Kia when Libby and Bernie pulled into the parking lot of the Longely Apartments. The apartments were a series of beige brick, two-story, one- and two-bedroom rentals targeted toward the lower-income inhabitants of the town. The apartments weren't awful; they weren't great; they weren't anything. They were simply there. What they weren't was quiet, since they were a little less than a block away from the train tracks.

"I just got home from work," Penny Moran-Engels explained as she strode toward them.

She was wearing a black leather jacket, an expensively cut dark blue suit, and blue suede wedges, and she had a Louis Vuitton bag slung over her shoulder, making her look, Bernie reflected, as out of place here as a side of beef in a vegan's freezer.

"How do you know who we are?" Libby asked, wondering.

Penny smiled. Her teeth were perfect.

*Expensive caps*, Bernie thought.

"Your name is on your van. And I've been in your shop.

I love your mint double chocolate fudge bars and your red ginger chicken."

Libby thanked her.

"I'd go there more often," Penny continued, a wistful tone in her voice, "but Serena and I are on a ramen budget these days." And with that observation, she turned and led the sisters into her apartment. Bernie instinctively ducked under the cobwebs hanging from the ceiling and the cardboard ghosts dangling from the overhead fan.

"Serena likes keeping them up," Penny informed the sisters without being asked. She shrugged off her jacket and threw it on top of the bookcase in the hallway. Libby and Bernie did the same. "Halloween is her favorite holiday."

"It was mine, too," Bernie told her. Which was true. She'd loved being out and about at night with her friends. Knocking on people's doors. Giggling. Yelling, "Trick or treat!" Getting candy. What was there not to like?

"I'm sorry, but I haven't gotten around to furnishing the place yet," Penny said as she walked into the living room, with Libby and Bernie right behind her. "I just can't bring myself to. Then it would mean that this is permanent."

They looked around. The only things in the room were a tired-looking tweed sofa, two matching armchairs, a cheapo coffee table made out of laminate, and a large flat-screen TV, which hung on one of the white walls.

"It's all Salvation Army," Penny said, sitting down on the sagging sofa. "Except for the TV. That came from the house. That's all I can afford," Penny explained as Bernie and Libby sat down in the armchairs. "He lives up there." Penny pointed in the direction of the Berkshire Arms. "My ex," she said, clarifying, in case Bernie and Libby didn't get it. "And *we* live down here, on the wrong side of the tracks. Literally."

Penny worried one of her nails with her teeth. Bernie noticed that they were all bitten down to the quick. "Serena had to give up her dog because they don't allow pets here, but this was the only thing I could afford."

"It must be tough," Bernie told her, thinking about the discrepancy between Penny's clothes and where she was living.

"You have no idea." Bernie could hear the rage in Penny's voice. She watched her take a deep breath and get hold of herself. "I heard you two were investigating Darius Witherspoon's death," she said when she had. "My daughter said her boss told her you guys think he was murdered. Well, I think my ex could have done it, and I want you to tell the police that."

"Why don't you?" Libby asked her. It was not, she thought, an unreasonable question.

"Because Gus scares me," Penny said after a pause. "He and his dad are really good with the words. But they're not right in the head. They do things when they get mad." She stopped talking.

Bernie leaned forward. "Like what?" she asked.

Penny bit her lip and studied her hands.

Bernie sat back and waited. A freight train rumbled by. She could feel the vibrations through the floor. "It can't be easy living here, especially given where you came from," Bernie said, playing the sympathy card.

Penny's eyes grew misty. She blinked the tears away. "Our house in Hayden was quite nice. Lovely really."

"I bet it was," Bernie said. Hayden was old money. All the houses up there were stone mansions, interspersed with horse farms.

"You know what really gets me, though?" Penny continued, looking up from her hands. "It's that Gus used our money. His and mine. All our money, and he can't understand why I'm so upset. He keeps saying if the expedition had been successful, I wouldn't feel this way. That's not the point." She slammed her hand down on the coffee table.

"That's not the point at all. The point is that he didn't talk to me about it first." She paused. "Are either of you married?" she asked Bernie and Libby.

They both shook their heads.

"Well, when you get married, keep your money separate," Penelope told them, her eyes flashing. "Whatever you do, don't have a joint account."

"I understand what you're saying," Libby replied. "But we're not divorce lawyers. There's nothing we can do about what happened to you."

Penny sat up straighter. Her eyes flashed. "There certainly is. You can put that son of a bitch in jail."

"Your ex?" Bernie asked.

Penny nodded. "Who else are we talking about?"

"In jail for what?" Libby asked.

"What do you think? Are you dumb or something?" Penny looked from Bernie to Libby and back again.

"How about you assume that we are and spell it out for us?" Libby told her with what she thought was admirable restraint.

Penny studied her hands again. Then she looked up at the ceiling, as if searching for the answers there. "You know Gus has a terrible temper, especially when he thinks he's being made a fool of," she said, speaking to the overhead lights. Then she stopped again.

Libby looked at her watch. She knew she should be more sympathetic. Obviously, this woman had been traumatized. But couldn't she speed things up a little? This was taking forever.

Penny started speaking again. "He does things," she said, looking everywhere but at Bernie and Libby.

Bernie and Libby waited some more.

"Like when he was in college, there was this guy Mike in a bar who was making fun of him, and two nights later someone set a fire in his room. Mike nearly died."

"I take it you think that Gus did it?" Libby asked.

Penny waved her hands in the air. "I know he did it, because he told me he did."

"And yet you married him," Bernie couldn't stop herself from saying.

"I . . . I thought he was saying that stuff to impress me, you know. I didn't believe him . . . but then there were other things. Accidents. Like this kid who sold Gus some bad sound stuff and got attacked one night with a baseball bat. Or the contractor who did a lousy job on the new bathroom in our house in Hayden and had his workshop flooded out and the windows in his truck broken. Everything was a total loss."

Bernie nodded to show she understood. "And the authorities never questioned Gus about these incidents?" she asked, making a note to ask her dad if he knew anyone in Hayden they could talk to.

Penny shook her head. "There were other things that happened, too. But Gus is really convincing, and his dad is really rich, and he gets away with whatever he wants."

"So you think he killed Darius Witherspoon?" Libby asked.

Penny nodded emphatically. "Witherspoon made a fool out of him," she said. "Killing him that way would be something that Gus would do."

"Okay. I get it," Libby said. "Thanks for letting us know. We'll put him on our list."

"I can do better than that," Penny said, and she got up, went to her bag, opened it, and pulled out a key. "Here," she said, handing it to Libby.

"What is it?" Libby asked.

"The key to Gus's apartment," Penny explained. "He's at work till six. I figure you can let yourselves in and take a look around. See if you can find anything that ties him to Witherspoon's murder."

"How did you get this?" Bernie asked.

"My daughter copied his key when she was over there."

Bernie raised an eyebrow.

"She hates him, too," Penny said. "Look," she continued, more urgently this time. "All I want you to do is go in and look around. If you find some sort of proof that Gus killed Witherspoon, then you can figure out how to take it to the police, and if you can't, then I'll figure out something else."

"And what's in it for you?" Bernie asked Penny.

She clenched her fist and brought it down on the coffee table again, harder this time. "I want to see that SOB fry. That's what's in it for me."

"It's nice seeing a loving family working together," Bernie commented as she and Libby walked toward their van.

"So what do you think?" Libby said.

Bernie looked at her watch. It was almost six. They had to get back to the store. "I say when we get home, we ask Dad if he knows anyone in Hayden, then visit Mr. Moran's abode tomorrow afternoon."

"The whole thing seems too pat to me," Libby observed as she jumped in the van and started the vehicle up.

"You think Penny's setting us up?" Bernie asked.

"The thought had crossed my mind."

"Have you ever heard the expression *Don't look a gift horse in the mouth*?" asked Bernie.

Libby grimaced. "Have you ever heard the expression *If it's too good to be true, then it* is *too good to be true*?"

"All the time, Libby, all the time," Bernie replied, thinking of her past dating life.

# Chapter 20

Yesterday the weatherman had predicted a storm blowing in today, and it seemed as if the weatherman had
been correct, Libby thought as she looked outside and saw
the rain splattering on the sidewalk. She sighed, put on her
hoodie, and slipped her yellow slicker on over that.

"By all means, be inconspicuous," Bernie commented as
Libby went by her. "That's what the well-dressed burglar
always wears."

"Well, excuse me if I'm not wearing my fancy-schmancy
French raincoat," Libby retorted.

"It's Italian, and it's black. Which is the whole point."

"Being Italian?"

"No, doofus. Being black."

Libby folded her arms across her chest. "This is what I
have, and this is what I'm wearing. Or I could just stay
here."

"Jeez," Bernie said, and she went back to the office, lifted
one of her old raincoats off the coat tree, and handed it to
her sister. "Put this on."

"This is the one with all those frills and stuff. I'll look
like a ruffled shower curtain," Libby protested.

"A dark, navy ruffled shower curtain, but at least you won't look like a bumblebee," Bernie pointed out.

"This slicker isn't that bad," Libby protested.

"It's fine if you're on the ocean, fishing for marlin," Bernie shot back, letting her inner snark out.

"We shouldn't be doing this, anyway," Libby grumbled as she put on Bernie's coat. "Or at least, we shouldn't be going until we finish up the Blitman job."

"We have plenty of time." Bernie gestured toward the clock on the kitchen wall. "It's two, and we don't have to be there until six, which leaves us four hours to pull together the appetizers, salad, and vegetable. We'll be in and out of Moran's place in no time."

"So you say."

"Yes, I do. You know what your problem is, Libby?" Bernie countered.

"I'm sensible."

"Your problem," Bernie continued, "is that you worry too much. Everything will be fine. And, anyway, I don't think this is about the Blitman job. I think you're using this as an excuse to chicken out."

"No, I'm not." Which was not true. "We just can't afford to lose the business."

"We won't." Bernie raised her right hand. "I swear."

Given Bernie's track record, Libby was not comforted.

As they set off for the Berkshire Arms, the sisters were silent, each wrapped up in her own thoughts. It was not a hospitable day. It was the kind of day in which one wanted to be home, in front of a fire, eating grilled cheese sandwiches and sipping tomato soup, yet here they were, going back to a place neither of them wanted to return to. Ever.

The Hudson was shrouded in gray, and the streets of Longely looked cold and lonely, the few people out hurrying along with their heads down, trying to avoid the rain. The road up to the Berkshire Arms was foggy again, and the trees nodded in the wind as the skeletons hanging from their branches swung back and forth in time to a rhythm Bernie and Libby couldn't discern. "Welcome, welcome," they seemed to whisper.

"I wish they'd take those damn things down," Libby groused as they drove up and up, rounding one curve after another. She shivered. "They give me the creeps." She looked up at the Berkshire Arms and saw a flash of what on the roof? A person? Something else? A something else she didn't want to entertain. It was probably a trick of the light, she told herself. Only she couldn't quite convince herself of that. "Did you see it?" she asked her sister, even though she hadn't been going to say anything.

"See what?" Bernie turned to glance at Libby. *She looks pale*, Bernie reflected. *She needs to get out in the sun more.*

Libby swallowed. "Nothing."

"Obviously, it was something."

Libby rubbed her eyes. She wasn't sleeping well these days. "I think I'm going nuts," she confessed, the words falling out of her mouth before she could take them back.

"No. You're not *going* nuts. You already *are*," Bernie assured her.

Libby laughed in spite of herself. "That makes me feel so much better."

"Tell me what you're thinking," Bernie commanded.

Libby did.

Bernie listened carefully. "We should look on the roof," she said when Libby had finished. "Maybe there *is* something up there besides the ghost you think you keep seeing."

"We can't. It's alarmed," Libby reminded her.

"True. But if it wasn't . . ."

"But it is."

"Maybe there's a way to short-circuit the alarm."

Libby snorted. "I think breaking and entering is enough for one day."

"We're not breaking. We're just entering. Remember, I have the key."

"I still think going into Moran's apartment is a bad idea," Libby protested.

"If we get caught, it'll be a very bad idea," Bernie agreed. "But we're not going to be."

"You don't know that," Libby challenged. "Anyway, I don't think it's worth the risk," she huffed.

"Obviously," Bernie said. "But I do. Gus Moran is on our suspect list. This is a chance to cross him off. Or not."

"What do you expect to find?" Libby grumped.

"I don't know," Bernie replied. "That's the fun."

"Not for me," Libby told her, then retreated into brooding silence.

Five minutes later they arrived at the Berkshire Arms. Another thought occurred to Libby as she looked at the parking lot.

"Where are you going to park Mathilda?" she asked Bernie. "It's not as if our vehicle is inconspicuous." She indicated the lot with a wave of her hand. Three cars were parked there. That was it. "Or," she went on, "that there are a lot of vehicles in the lot. Most of the people who live here are at work."

"No kidding. That's the whole point." Bernie gestured to the far side of the lot. There was a wide path that led to a toolshed. "We can park on the other side of the shed. No one can see us there."

"What if we get stuck?" Libby demanded.

"Why would we get stuck? It's paved."

"But let's suppose we do."

"And let's suppose a meteor comes down and wipes out all life on Earth," Bernie said.

"It could," Libby muttered, slumping down in her seat. "Look at the dinosaurs."

Bernie ignored her.

Libby rooted around in her bag for a piece of chocolate—a chocolate Hershey's Kiss—and popped it in her mouth. So far the day had not gone well. She wished it would reverse its present course, but she wasn't hopeful.

She ate another chocolate Kiss. Just thinking about the day gave her agita. First, the credit card machine was still malfunctioning; then she'd had to throw out a batch of burnt cookies, shortly after which Mrs. Veldman had come into the store, insisting that she'd ordered a carrot cake when she hadn't, and had been placated only with the gift of a caramel swirl pumpkin cheesecake; and last but not least, Goodman Produce had messed up their order. It was Mercury retrograde at its finest.

But she didn't say that to Bernie, because her sister had forbidden her to utter that phrase in her presence. So Libby just sat there, not watching the woods, as Bernie drove over the lot, because she felt that if she did, she'd catch a glimpse of someone watching her. Another thing she wasn't going to discuss with her sister. When they got to the shed, Bernie backed the van onto the square of asphalt that butted up against the building.

"We'll be able to get out faster if we need to," she explained to Libby.

"Let's hope we don't," Libby replied.

The motion upset the crows roosting in the branches of the oak tree next to the shed, and they came flying down, cawing and beating their wings at the intruders.

"Why don't we just announce our arrival with a bull-horn?" Libby said as the cawing rose to ear-piercing levels.

Bernie turned off Mathilda's engine. "They'll settle down soon enough."

"Well, I'm not getting out until they do," Libby announced, watching the birds hopping around on Mathilda, their beady eyes staring at her. "I've seen *The Birds*."

"According to Mrs. Randall, the crows are our friends," Bernie replied.

Libby folded her arms across her chest. "Why am I unconvinced?"

Bernie grabbed the half-eaten bag of animal crackers sitting on the dashboard.

"Perfect," she said as she put the hood on her raincoat up.

"What are you doing?" Libby asked.

"Feeding them on the 'You never know when friends will come in handy' principle."

"And that did Darius so much good," Libby muttered. Then she rolled her eyes. "And I'm the one you're calling crazy?"

Bernie didn't answer. She got out of the van, took handfuls of the animal crackers, and threw them in the air. The crows responded immediately, beating their wings, cawing, and flying around her. She instinctively ducked, at which point her cell slipped out of her raincoat pocket and fell in a puddle.

She waved her hands in the air. "Go away," she yelled at the crows. They cawed and flew up onto a branch overlooking the van. "Sons of bitches," she cursed as she bent down to retrieve her phone.

"That went well," Libby commented from inside the van.

"I don't want to talk about it," Bernie said as she reentered the van. She took down her hood, wiped the rain off her face, and tried her cell. Nothing. She waited a couple of moments and tried again. Still nothing.

"You need rice," Libby said.

"Do you see any here?" Bernie snapped, giving in to cell-phone panic. She felt as if half of her life had been erased.

"We can go home and get some."

"No, we can't." Bernie pried the back off her phone with the nail file she'd tucked in her pocket and forgotten to take out, wrapped the battery in a paper towel, dried the rest of the phone off with another towel, and put everything in the glove compartment. "We're not going back until we do what we came to do."

"You make it sound as if we're storming the barricades," Libby complained.

"In a manner of speaking, we are." Then Bernie put her hood back up, stepped out of the van, and made a run for the entrance to the Berkshire Arms. Libby followed, the cawing of the crows mocking her as she ran.

"It's miserable out there," Bernie observed, throwing off her hood once she and Libby got inside.

Even though she was dry, her sneakers were wet, and she was not happy to see that they were making marks on the marble floor. Hopefully, the marks would dry soon. She and Libby hurried up the stairs to the third floor, glad that the lobby had been deserted. The last thing that they needed was witnesses. A couple of minutes later, Bernie and a slightly out of breath Libby were standing in front of Gus Moran's door.

Bernie nodded to Libby. "Here goes nothing," she said as she fished the key Penny had given her out of her tote. She was about to slide it into the lock when she decided to knock first. Just to be on the safe side. Which she did. Her hand closed on the knocker, and she knocked three times.

"I'm coming," a voice from inside answered.

Bernie and Libby looked at each other.

"I told you this was a bad idea," Libby mouthed.

"It'll be fine," Bernie mouthed back. She'd just tell Gus Moran that they'd made a mistake and knocked on the wrong apartment door. No big deal, or as Brandon would say, "No harm, no foul."

# Chapter 21

A moment later the door opened, and a man Bernie assumed was Gus Moran stood in front of her. She would have known who he was even if she'd seen him on the street, because he was the spitting image of his dad. A little taller, a little stockier, but he had the same brown hair, the same hazel eyes, the same slight cleft in his chin, the same air of casual authority.

"It wouldn't have worked," he told Bernie before she could tell him they'd made a mistake and knocked on the wrong door.

"What wouldn't have worked?" Bernie asked, confused.

He nodded toward her tote. "I saw you palming the key and slipping it back in your bag. My ex gave it to you, didn't she?"

"I don't know what you're talking about," Bernie told him with as much indignation as she could muster.

Gus Moran laughed. "Don't bother lying. It isn't worth it, but you can tell her for me that I changed the locks." He leaned forward a little. "The problem with teens like Serena," he confided, "is that they think all adults are idiots. That we're half blind."

"Your daughter—" Libby began, but Gus Moran interrupted, correcting her.

"She's not my daughter." A teakettle whistled inside. "Come in. You look as if you can use something hot to drink."

"That does sound attractive," Libby admitted. Her feet were sopping wet, and somehow she had drops of rain trickling down her back.

"Irish breakfast tea and cinnamon toast," Moran said, smiling charmingly. "How can you say no?" he asked, gesturing for them to come in.

Bernie and Libby stepped inside. Gus Moran relieved them of their raincoats and wet shoes, put all the things in the bathroom so they could drip to their heart's content, as he put it, and handed towels to the sisters. After they'd dried themselves off, he led them through the living/dining area and into the kitchen. Bernie recognized the high-end Italian hypermodern sofa, chairs, and coffee table from some of the more exclusive furniture stores she'd been in over the past couple of years.

"Nice," she said, giving an appreciative nod.

"They should be, given what they cost," Gus said. He indicated an intricate antique Persian carpet on the floor and two more smaller ones hanging on the walls. "I don't need much, but I like excellence in what I do own." Then he said, "Penny sent you, didn't she? It's all right." He shut off the burner, put some loose Irish breakfast tea into a teapot, and slowly poured the water from the kettle over the leaves. "I don't believe in tea bags," he explained.

"Neither do we," Libby said.

"It's nice to know some people still adhere to standards," Gus said. The sisters watched as he turned on the oven, got out a baking sheet, then opened the red bread box on the counter, took out a large loaf of French peasant bread, and began to cut off thick slices of it. Then he went to the fridge, got out a round container of butter made from the cream of pasture-raised cows, lavishly spread it on the bread, and then arranged the bread slices on the baking sheet. "I bet she told you she thinks I killed Darius Witherspoon, and she wants you to find proof that I did, hence the key. Is that about right?"

"I told you," Libby said, turning to Bernie.

Bernie didn't say anything. She was thinking about what to do next.

Gus smiled at Bernie. "What? No answer?"

"None that I care to share," she replied.

He chuckled as he reached under the counter and brought out the sugar and cinnamon. "A lot or a little?" he asked.

"A lot," Bernie replied.

"Ditto," Libby said, seconding this.

"My kind of women," Gus remarked as he sprinkled an ample coating of sugar and cinnamon on the bread, then opened the oven door, shoved the baking sheet in, closed the door, and set the timer. "I bet my ex told you I was violent and she was afraid of me," he said, straightening up. "She told you I had done things in Hayden, bad things that I'd never been prosecuted for."

Libby nodded.

"Something like that," Bernie conceded.

Guy Moran pointed to himself. "Call up anyone you like and ask them. Hell, I'll give you the number of anyone you ask me for, and they'll tell you what I'm telling you. Penny's just selling her usual brand of lies. Look at me. Do I look violent to you? Do I look like the kind of man who would do what Penny told you I did?"

"No," Libby replied. "You don't, but that doesn't mean—"

Moran interrupted. "Do guys that are violent make cinnamon toast?"

Bernie and Libby couldn't help it. They laughed at the non sequitur.

"Of course they don't," Gus Moran continued. "Plus, you girls look as if you have pretty good instincts. I don't think you'd have agreed to come in here if you thought I was that violent. You'd have to be nuts to do that, and you two don't seem nuts to me. Anything but."

"You're good," Bernie said, complimenting him on his line of chat.

Gus bowed his head. "Thanks. I try." He wiped his chin with his fist. "I'm hoping you'd like to hear my side of the story now that you're here."

"Love to," Bernie told him as the smell of cinnamon wafted out of the oven. God, was there a better scent?

"Excellent," Gus said. He nodded toward the teapot. "Cream? Lemon? Sugar?"

"Sugar, please," Libby said.

"Lemon in mine," Bernie told him.

"I think I can do that," Gus said.

Bernie and Libby watched as Gus Moran put the teapot, the sugar bowl, a dish of lemon slices, mugs, small plates, forks, teaspoons, and napkins on a tray. "I used to be a waiter," he told them as he carried the tray out to the living room.

"Start," he said, putting the tray down on the coffee table. Then he went back into the kitchen. Bernie and Libby heard the timer ring. A few minutes later, Gus came out bearing a blue earthenware plate piled with the cinnamon toast.

"Wonderful," Bernie said after she'd bitten into a piece.

"Amazing how the simplest things are always the best," Gus Moran commented.

"True," Bernie said after taking a sip of her tea. Indeed, this was the perfect snack for this kind of day. "So," she said, beginning what she and Libby had come here for, "you're telling me that you're not violent and you didn't kill Darius Witherspoon."

"That's exactly what I'm telling you," Gus Moran replied. "And why should we believe you?" she asked.

"Gut instinct?" he answered.

Bernie took a sip of her tea and watched the rain turn to drizzle. Over to the east she could see the outline of the Hudson River. "Okay, then explain to me why your ex said what she did."

Gus Moran took another bite of his cinnamon toast and wiped his hands on a paper napkin. "That's simple. Because she's pissed. She's pissed that she signed a prenup and she's not going to get anything now that we're getting a divorce, not that I have anything at the moment, and she wants to get back at me. And I know she comes off as the poor downtrodden one, but believe me, she's not. Anything but. What she is, is a psychopathic liar who can convince anyone of anything." He pointed to himself. "But the person who is downtrodden here is me. The only thing I'm guilty of is making poor choices."

Bernie listened to Gus while she continued to sip her tea and watch the sky lighten up. At this rate the sun might even come out. "I'm guessing that Penny is your bad choice."

Gus Moran grinned, stirred his tea with a teaspoon, and put the spoon back on the tray. "See. I knew you would get it. Penny is scary. She seemed like the nicest, sweetest person imaginable when I married her, and then *boom*"— he clapped his hands together—"she turns into a full-on psycho. She buys all these expensive clothes and goes out and has her teeth fixed and her boobs done."

"That doesn't necessarily make her crazy," Libby pointed out. "Maybe greedy, but not crazy."

Gus Moran held up his hand. "That's the least of it. I would have said yes, if she'd asked. But she didn't. She lied to me about it, and then, when I confront her, she goes nuts. She slashes my car's tires, she threatens me with a knife, and she tells me that if I don't give her everything she wants, she's going to tell everyone I raped and beat her. She hacked into my e-mail accounts."

"Okay. So she *is* nuts," Libby agreed. "If what you say is true."

"It's true, all right."

"Is that when you divorced her?" Bernie asked.

Gus looked abashed. "I wish I had, but I'm ashamed to say I didn't."

"Why in heavens not?" Libby exclaimed.

"Good question." Gus Moran shook his head and studied the sky for a moment before settling on an answer. "Let's just say that it was the wrong time to get into a pissing match with her."

"You were doing something you shouldn't have been doing?" Bernie asked, intuiting this from the expression on Gus's face.

Gus rocked his hands back and forth. "Some people might see it that way."

"What was it?" Bernie asked.

"Not relevant," Gus said. He inspected his fingers before looking up. "All you have to know is that it was easier to let things go."

"I know how that is," Bernie remarked.

Gus Moran flashed her a thankful smile. "But then, when my thing with Witherspoon went south and I'm flat broke, you know what Penny did?"

Both Bernie and Libby shook their heads.

"She went ballistic and threatened him! She demanded that he give our—note the pronoun—money back, or she was going to make him pay."

Libby finished off the last of her cinnamon toast. "How was she going to make him pay?"

"No idea," Gus Moran told Libby. "She said she had something on him, but I'm damned if I know what it was."

"So what did Witherspoon do?" Bernie asked.

"He told her to bugger off."

Bernie took a sip of her tea. "And did he lose her money, as well? Did you give Witherspoon her money, as well as yours?"

Gus Moran snorted. "What money? She was working part-time at the checkout counter at Gristedes, for heaven's sake, when I met her. She had no money. She was getting food stamps."

"And Serena?"

"I think her dad is in jail."

"You know his name?"

Gus Moran squinted while he thought. "Alan Burns. Byrnes, Briar. Something like that. Why?"

Bernie shrugged. "No reason, really."

Gus Moran got up off the sofa. "I want to show you something," he said, beckoning for Bernie and Libby to follow him into his bedroom. Sitting on top of his dresser was a thirty-gallon terrarium. Gus Moran went over, took the top off, carefully set it down, lifted out a turtle, and brought it over to Libby and Bernie. "This is Daisy," he said.

The turtle looked at Bernie and Libby, and Bernie and Libby looked back at the turtle.

"I'm starting over again with Daisy," he explained.

"Pardon?" Libby said.

"It's simple, really. Penny was my third failed marriage, and the absolute worst of the bunch, so I've decided to start at the beginning. If I can maintain a good relationship with Daisy, I'll go on to the next level and then the one after that. Eventually, hopefully, I'll graduate to a dog, and if we do well, I might get back to women. But for right now Daisy and I are it." He carefully put Daisy back in her terrarium and replaced the lid. "And as for Darius Witherspoon, despite what my ex says, I had nothing to do with his death."

"Even though, according to Penny, he cost you all your money?" Bernie asked.

Gus Moran shrugged. "Hey, when you go treasure hunting, risk is the name of the game. I've been down before. I'll be back up soon. In fact, Witherspoon had some new project going on, something he was really excited about."

"What was it?" Bernie asked, sensing a possible lead.

Gus Moran shook his head. "He wouldn't tell me. Said he wasn't ready yet for full disclosure."

"So he wasn't depressed or anything?" Libby asked, trying to clarify the issue.

"Hell no," Gus Moran said, leading them back into the living room. "He was stoked. He said whatever he was working on was going to earn him international fame. It was going to be like King Tut's tomb all over again. So I sure as hell wouldn't kill him. Why would I when he promised me a place on his next expedition?"

"But you told us you're broke," Libby pointed out. "Don't you need money to buy in?"

Gus rubbed his hands together. "Ordinarily, yes, but Witherspoon was going to let me in for free. To make up for the last time."

"Nice of him," Bernie remarked dryly.

"Yes, it was. Don't believe me if you don't want to," Gus Moran said, sitting down. He noted the expression on Bernie's face. "I don't care." He shook a finger at her. "But I didn't kill him. I was out of town." And he got up, went to his desk, and produced a boarding pass. "See?" he said, sticking it in Bernie's face. "I was in the air over Ohio then."

Bernie looked. "So it would seem."

"But I'll tell you this," Gus continued. "You want to know who killed Darius? Who wanted him gone? You should try his partner or his receptionist. They'd be my candidates of choice."

"Receptionist?" Bernie echoed.

"The big Swedish blonde. At the gallery. Now, she was really pissed at him. She threatened to kill him."

"And why would she say something like that?" Libby asked.

Gus Moran ran his hand over the top of his head. "Evidently, he was sleeping with her and promised to marry her, and then he reneged, and if that wasn't bad enough, I think she's here illegally, and he told her he was going to call immigration. Something like that."

"Something like that, or is that what actually happened?" Bernie asked.

"That's what one of the baristas at Nell's told me." He paused. "You know, Nell's," Gus repeated when he saw the blank look on Libby's and Bernie's faces. "The coffee place on Madison. The one that has the fancy Japanese coffee brewing system."

Both Bernie and Libby shook their heads.

"Well, anyway, I was right in back of her in the line when she got a phone call, and she answered it, and a minute later she starts screaming, 'I'm going to kill you!' into the phone and storms out, and then the barista and I exchange 'What the hell was that about?' looks, and then he tells me what he thinks is going on, which is what I told you."

"Any chance you have this guy's name?" Bernie asked.

Gus looked at her like she was crazy. "Why would I know his name?"

"Right." Bernie sighed. "What does he look like?"

Gus Moran shrugged as he sat down on the sofa. "He just looks like a regular guy."

Bernie gave up and moved on. "And Witherspoon's partner," she said. "What about him?"

"I got the feeling that they hated each other."

"How come?"

"I don't know, really." Gus took a sip of his tea. "Just an impression. I was at the gallery a couple of times when Peabody's name came up, and Darius made this face. You know, like he was smelling something bad. It was like he couldn't help himself."

"Did Darius say anything about him?" Libby asked.

Gus shook his head. "No, but Darius didn't talk that much. He kept to himself. He was a paranoid kind of guy, but I guess in this case he was right."

"So it would seem," Bernie observed.

"Yeah. What is it they say? 'Just because you're paranoid doesn't mean you're wrong.'" Gus Morgan shrugged. "Funny how things work out. And let's not forget my ex. I wouldn't put it beyond her to kill Witherspoon and then try to frame me for it."

"Because?" Bernie asked, thinking back to Penny. She couldn't see her for it, but she'd been wrong before.

"I told you. She blamed him for losing all my money." Gus Moran finished off the last of his cinnamon toast. "She really is a scary lady."

"Funny, but she says the same thing about you," Bernie remarked.

"Well, she's lying," Gus replied, his face flushing slightly. "Do you know she got up on the roof last month and tried to hit me with an apple pie when I walked out? I was lucky I wasn't seriously injured."

Libby giggled. "Store-bought or homemade?"

"It's not funny," Gus Moran snapped. "I was late for an important meeting."

"How did she get up there?" Libby asked. "I thought the roof was alarmed?"

"It's supposed to be," Gus Moran replied. "But the alarm kept malfunctioning, and they had to turn it off a couple of months ago. We're still waiting for the company to come. In fact, my dad's threatening to sue them if they don't get over here soon."

Bernie and Libby exchanged looks.

"Really," Bernie said as she glanced out the window again. It had stopped drizzling, and she saw a patch of clear sky over the river.

Libby sighed. She knew what was coming.

# Chapter 22

Libby checked the time on her watch as she and Bernie walked up the short flight of stairs that led to the roof. "I don't think we have enough time to do this," she said.

Bernie halted on the last step and turned toward her. "We have more than enough time."

"What if something happens?" Libby persisted.

"Nothing is going to happen," Bernie assured her. "We'll just look around and leave. This will take twenty minutes. At the most. And, anyway, I just want to see the roof. For my personal mental health."

"Okay," Libby said. There was no arguing with that, even though she would rather not do this. "I wonder why Moran senior lied about the alarm?"

"Because he wanted us out of here as fast as possible," Bernie answered.

"Yeah," Libby said, remembering. "He couldn't wait to get rid of us."

Bernie turned toward the door. She hesitated for a moment before opening it. After all, what was the worst that could happen? If the alarm had been fixed, it would go off and they'd have some explaining to do. Nevertheless, she took a deep breath before she pushed. The door groaned as it swung open, letting a blast of chilly air into the stairwell, but that was it. The only sound that Bernie heard was the sound of squabbling crows over by the shed where she'd parked the van.

Gus Moran had been correct. The alarm wasn't working. Bernie felt the tension flow out of her body as she straightened up. "Nice view," she said to Libby as her sister shut the door to the roof behind her. The door thudded closed, the sound drowned out by the crows. Still, Bernie waited for a minute to see if anyone had heard it and was coming up to check out what was going on. No one did.

Bernie rubbed her arms, wishing she were wearing a sweater underneath her coat, as she took in the view. The sun was going down, taking the day's color with it, but you could still see the tugs guiding the tankers down the Hudson, now a grayish blue ribbon threading itself between its banks; as well as the treetops, some still heavy with leaves, others already bare, the birds' nests they were hosting visible for all to see. Toward the right, Bernie saw a black storm cloud moving in their direction. The sliver of clear sky had been a teaser. It looked as if the rain wasn't over yet. They'd just gotten a short reprieve.

Libby saw the cloud, too, and shivered. It was damp, and the wind blowing off the river made things chillier, but that wasn't why she was shivering. It had just hit her that she really, really, really didn't want to be up here. She just hadn't realized how much she didn't want to be up on the roof until now.

"We should hurry," she said, swallowing the saliva that was building up in her mouth.

Bernie nodded. She knew the way Libby felt, because even though she wasn't going to admit it, she was feeling the same way. Jittery. Wanting to go back down. Ordinarily, she and her sister would have split up to search the rooftop—it would be faster—but now they silently agreed to stay together.

With no rooms to break up the area, the rooftop seemed larger than it was, and the six turrets, along with the parapets and crenulated walls, served to reinforce that impression. Bernie tried to convince herself that she was standing on the roof of a small castle or chateau somewhere in France, looking down at the Loire. It didn't work.

"Okay, let's do this," Bernie said, plastering a fake smile on her face.

Bernie and Libby started by walking around the roof's perimeter. Bernie ran her fingers along the edges of the roof wall. It was waist high. She imagined students from the Peabody School coming up here to sneak a smoke or a drink or to make out—now, there was an old-fashioned phrase—or just to get away from everyone and daydream about what their future was going to be.

"You know," Libby said, pointing at the toothlike crenulations cut into the wall, "it wouldn't be hard to fasten a rope around one of these things and rappel down from here to someone's window."

"Darius's window," Bernie said, finishing Libby's thought for her.

Libby nodded.

"No, it wouldn't be hard to do at all," Bernie agreed. "Of course," she continued, "the window would have to be open, and it has been on the chilly side for the past few weeks."

"True, but you *could* get in if the windows were closed."

"How so?"

"Think about it."

Bernie closed her eyes and pictured the windows in Gus Moran's place. The handles to open them were on the inside, but if a window wasn't completely locked, you could grab one of its edges and pull. "I guess that would work as long as the windows weren't locked."

Libby crossed her arms over her chest. "Which they probably weren't. After all, how often do we bother locking our windows?"

"Never," Bernie replied after taking a minute to think about it.

"Exactly," Libby said, bending slightly so she could get a better look at the crenulations. The odds of a rope leaving a mark on the concrete were slim, indeed. At least, she hadn't seen anything that looked like that so far.

"But why would the murderer pick that way to enter Darius's apartment?" Bernie asked, thinking out loud.

"Maybe this person wasn't planning on killing Darius. Maybe he was planning on stealing something."

"Something that he knows is there," Bernie said.

Libby nodded. "Maybe something to do with the treasure Darius was looking for and possibly found." She closed her eyes and visualized the scene. "So this person gets into Darius's apartment before Darius gets there, and he's going through Darius's stuff. Now he's planning to go out the same way he came in, but he can't, because Darius comes in early. This person runs into Darius's bedroom and hides, but Darius discovers him, and this guy has a rope, so he uses it to shut Darius up." Libby's voice trailed off.

"The rope Darius was hanging from was tied to the planter thingamajig," Bernie objected, pulling the collar on her coat up and sticking her chin as far down into it as she could. "He'd have to have two ropes."

"Minor detail," Libby said as she bent down and picked up a brick from the small pile that was sitting in the wall's shadow. She weighed it in her hand, then put it back down. "Good thing Penny didn't throw one of these things at Gus Moran."

"Yeah," Bernie replied. "And how." Her attention was

drawn to an empty box of Oreos and a can of soda. "Well, someone's been up here," she noted. "And it isn't a ghost, unless the ghost likes Oreos, that is. Maybe whoever it is just likes to come up here and look at the river. It is a nice view."

Libby had to agree that it was. "When it's warmer," she said, jamming her hands in the pockets of Bernie's raincoat. Boy, she wished she were wearing her own raincoat right now. Maybe her slicker was a bit too conspicuous, but it sure as hell was a lot warmer than Bernie's fancy French raincoat, not to mention that it was 100 percent waterproof. She hoped she wouldn't need it, but she suspected that she would.

"You know," Bernie said suddenly, "there's no reason why she would be mad at us."

Libby didn't need to ask for clarification. She knew who *she* was. After the last time they'd been here, she and Bernie had decided by mutual consent never to mention her name again, because as their mother had always said, naming things called them into existence.

"That's true," Libby replied. After all, they *had* solved her murder. Hopefully, she was resting now, preferably someplace in another dimension. Or universe. Or wherever people went after they died—if they went anywhere. Because after her last Halloween experience, Libby had become a firm believer in segregation. As in if the living stayed on their side of the wall and the dead stayed on their side, everything would be fine. It was just when they mixed that the trouble started.

"Here's a radical idea," Bernie continued. "How about we stop letting this place screw with our minds?"

Libby cocked her head. "Meaning?"

"Meaning that we need to get a grip on reality. Odds are the ghost that we saw on the rooftop the afternoon we were coming up here wasn't a ghost. Odds are that, that person, and I stress the word *person*, was Darius's murderer, and he was getting ready to rappel down to Darius's window."

"We both thought we saw a woman," Libby protested.

"Maybe it was a guy in drag."

Libby snorted. She would have rolled her eyes, but her eyelids felt numb.

"It could be," Bernie insisted. She held up her hand. "Okay. Okay. Okay. I'm going a little too far."

"Anyway, the timing is wrong," Libby pointed out. "Darius was up in his apartment until the time he went out the window. We know that for a fact. If someone rappelled into his living room, I'm sure he would have yelled or screamed or done something. I mean, it's not the way one would expect a person to enter your home. It would make me reach for a butcher knife, on the assumption that this person was up to no good, and there were no signs of a struggle anywhere in that apartment. Absolutely none."

"You're right," Bernie conceded. "There weren't." And even if Libby was wrong and she was correct, so what? Bernie thought. It didn't advance their case. It didn't give them the name of Darius's killer. So far the only thing being out on the roof was accomplishing was making her wish she wasn't there.

She and Libby spent the next fifteen minutes methodically crisscrossing the roof, but aside from the empty box of Oreos, the can of soda, and a bird's nest, they didn't find any signs indicating that anyone had been up there. By now the wind was kicking up, and Bernie and Libby could feel spits of rain blowing in their faces.

"Well," Bernie said to Libby, "at least now we can cross the roof off of our list."

"Good, because it's time to get out of here," Libby said, looking at the sky, which was growing darker by the second. "We should leave before the deluge comes. Besides, we need to get back to the shop and start getting ready for the Blitmans."

"Absolutely true on both counts," Bernie agreed as she turned and hurried to the exit. She was debating about whether she should add toasted slivered almonds and cranberries to the buttercup squash or not when she got hold of the door handle and pulled it toward her.

Nothing happened.

# Chapter 23

Okay, Bernie thought. She looked at the door handle and gave another tug. Again nothing happened. Could the blasted thing be stuck? she wondered. *Not a big deal*, she told herself. All she had to do was pull a little harder. So she planted her feet on the roof floor and yanked as hard as she could. Nothing. The damned door wasn't budging. Not even an inch. So much for her weight training at the gym. She rubbed her fingers where the door handle had cut into them.

But if the door was stuck, what was it stuck on? She couldn't remember anything on the landing that could be jamming it. *Stay calm*, she told herself. Too bad she wasn't listening to herself. She could feel panic beginning to bubble up inside her as she kept telling herself to cool it and go to her special place. Right. Too bad she couldn't think of one. But that sobered her up. She shook her head. One thing was for sure. This was not good. This was not good at all.

"What's happening?" Libby asked, coming up behind her sister.

"I think the door is stuck."

"You're kidding, right?" Libby said, thinking of the Blitman party they were supposed to be catering this evening. Oh my God. She knew she should have followed her gut. What if they couldn't get back to the shop in time? That would be horrible. They'd never get any more business. "That's not funny."

"Do I look like I'm kidding?" Bernie demanded, turning to face her.

Libby took in the expression on her sister's face and decided this wasn't her sister's idea of a bad joke. " 'We'll be fine,' you said," Libby told Bernie, imitating her voice. " 'You worry too much,' you said. 'You always make a big deal out of everything,' you said."

Bernie raised her right hand. "That one I didn't say," she protested.

Libby shook a finger at her. "But you thought it."

"I'm sorry. You want to stand here arguing or try to figure something out?"

Libby took a deep breath and let it out. Boy, did she wish she had some chocolate right about now. "Okay. Let me try."

Bernie moved aside and extended her hand palm outward. "Be my guest."

Libby took Bernie's place. She wrapped her hands around the door handle and pulled. It didn't move. She pulled harder. The door stayed where it was. "Goddamn it," she cried, cursing under her breath as she tried for a third time. It didn't move.

"What are we going to do if we're stuck up here?" Libby cried. "What are we going to do about the Blitmans?" She closed her eyes for a second. It didn't bear thinking about.

"We're not going to get stuck up here," Bernie assured her. "That's not going to happen. Let's try pulling together."

"Literally or figuratively?" Libby said.

"Both," her sister answered.

Libby moved over so Bernie had some space. Then they

both planted their feet on the Tarvia and pulled as hard as they could. The only thing they could feel moving was the door handle, which seemed to be loosening up. Not the result they were after. After the third time, they gave up. The only thing they were doing was hurting their hands.

Bernie straightened up. "Okay. There's only one thing left to do."

"Commit hara-kiri?" Libby asked.

Bernie snorted. "No, Libby. I was thinking more along the line of using the phone. You know, that thing that's replaced smoke signals. Give me yours, and I'll call Amber and tell her to prep the veggies and the salad and see if, worst comes to worst, she and Googie can run everything down to the Blitmans, after which I'll call Brandon and have him come and get us out of here."

"Why can't we use yours?" Libby demanded. As the words came out of her mouth, her guts started to twist, because of course she knew why they couldn't use Bernie's phone. She'd just conveniently forgotten about that small detail for a moment.

"Because it's in the van, drying out, remember?"

"I forgot," Libby lied. Then she added, "You're not going to like this." Which had to be the most massive understatement she'd ever uttered.

"I'm not going to like what?" Bernie asked impatiently. All she wanted to do was call the shop and then get in contact with Brandon, or Marvin, if she had to, and get out of here. This was just a blip, she told herself. No big deal. They'd be down on the ground in no time at all.

Libby had the grace to lower her voice. "I left mine in the bathroom at home."

Bernie stared at her. She didn't want to believe what she was hearing. "What did you just say?"

Libby repeated herself. "I said I left my phone in the bathroom at home."

"Tell me what you're saying isn't true," Bernie pleaded.

"It's true, all right," Libby replied, giving a sickly little grin. "I guess we can kiss our business good-bye," she said mournfully.

"The Blitmans will understand," Bernie said, even though she thought that there was a good chance that they wouldn't, considering this was a dinner in honor of their parents' fiftieth wedding anniversary.

"No they won't," Libby retorted. "I certainly wouldn't, and neither would you." She bit her lip. "I just don't understand how the door got stuck," she said, saying what Bernie had been thinking. "There was nothing for it to get stuck on."

"Not that I saw," Bernie said.

"So maybe it's not stuck. Maybe it's locked."

"That would be bad on several different levels," Bernie observed as Libby turned around and studied the door.

"Yes, it would," Libby agreed, brushing a drop of rain off her nose. She could see a few small wet spots on the roof.

"On the other hand, there's no sense leaping to conclusions," Bernie said. "Maybe the door really is stuck. Maybe that's why William Moran didn't want us up here. Maybe he was afraid we wouldn't be able to get back down, and he didn't want to call attention to the fact that the door needed to be fixed."

"Well, there's one way to find out," Libby said. "Give me one of your credit cards."

"Any particular one?"

"Somehow, I don't think the door is going to care," Libby informed her.

"Fine. Just asking. No need to get snippy," Bernie said as she reached in her tote, took her MasterCard out of her wallet, and handed it to Libby, who slipped it in the space between the door and the frame and slid it up to the lock. The card wouldn't go any farther.

"Yup, the door is definitely locked," Libby said after she tried to move the card by the lock a couple of more times.

"The lock is a dead bolt," Bernie said, apropos of nothing, as she visualized the mechanism.

"Who cares what kind of lock it is?" Libby cried. "Lock, smlock. The result is the same."

Bernie nibbled at her cuticle. She really didn't want to believe this. "If it's true . . ."

"It's true."

"Then the question becomes, who did this and why? This was not an accident. This was deliberate. Someone knew we were going upstairs, waited until we got up on the roof, and locked us up here."

"Gus Moran knew we were coming up here."

"He didn't really. We didn't say we were."

"He could have heard our footsteps."

"Now, that's stretching it," Bernie said, having rethought her original statement. "The door probably malfunctioned. You heard what Gus Moran said."

"It's a pretty convenient malfunction, if you ask me," Libby retorted.

"Why would Moran do something like that?" Bernie asked.

"Because he's what Penny said he was."

Bernie shook her head. "I just don't buy it." Although, really, at this point she didn't know what to think. Then a bolt of lightning split the sky, and she forgot about wondering who had put them in this situation and started concentrating on how to get out of it.

A moment later she and Libby heard a loud boom. Thunder. The storm was announcing its arrival. As Bernie looked around, she realized it had gotten very quiet all of a sudden. She couldn't hear the crows cawing or the birds singing. So this was what the expression "the calm before the storm" meant. She'd thought the expression was a metaphor, but it wasn't. It was the literal truth, and while she was thinking about that truth, another truth occurred to her. She realized that the person she wanted to kill right now was her sister.

# Chapter 24

The wind was getting stronger. Libby watched the tree-tops bending up and down as another streak of lightning cleaved the sky. The storm was almost on top of them. It would be beautiful if they were indoors, Libby decided. Sadly, they weren't. It was only a matter of minutes before they were going to be drenched to the skin. She was about to say something to that effect to Bernie when she caught the look in her sister's eye.

"Well, how was I supposed to know we'd get locked on the roof?" Libby demanded before Bernie could say anything to her. "Or that you'd drop your phone in a puddle?" Both of which, she thought, were valid points. She couldn't have known. After all, she wasn't gifted with ESP.

"Why don't you ever have your phone on you?" Bernie countered.

"Duh. Because you always have yours with you," Libby told her. Which was also true.

Bernie looked daggers at her. "You could have said something, Libby."

"You didn't ask, Bernie."

Bernie threw her hands up in the air. "I give up. There's no talking to you when you get this way."

Libby could feel her face flushing. "All I'm saying is that this is not my fault. And, anyway, having my phone up here wouldn't make any difference. We'd still be up here."

"Yes, we would be," Bernie agreed, working very hard not to call her sister a moron. "That's true. But at least we wouldn't be marooned up here. At least, we could have called Brandon or Marvin and had them come get us. Now we have to figure out how to get out of here by ourselves."

"I know," Libby said, looking utterly woebegone. "I'm sorry."

Looking at the expression on Libby's face made Bernie feel guilty. She reached over and gave Libby a quick hug, her anger vanishing as quickly as it had come. "It's okay."

"Too bad we don't have a parachute," Libby observed, taking a step back.

"Isn't it, though?" Bernie said. "But in lieu of that . . ." And she started going through the possibilities. "We could rappel down to the ground."

"Maybe you could, but I can't," Libby said. Just the thought of it induced stomach churning. "Anyway, we don't have a rope."

"We could jump," Bernie suggested. "Hopefully, we'd land in the bushes. Two stories isn't that high."

Libby raised an eyebrow. "It isn't that low, either. And we could break our legs—if we're lucky. Thanks, but no thanks."

"I read somewhere that cats can jump from seven stories and land on their feet," Bernie replied.

"Need I point out we're not felines," Libby replied. "But if you want to try, be my guest."

"It's too bad Cindy isn't with us," Bernie mused. "We could attach a message to her collar asking for help."

"And throw her off the roof?"

"No. Of course not," Bernie quickly replied. "Never. I

was just going through hypothetical possibilities. Anyway, the cats survived only if they fell out of windows seven stories or higher. Any lower and they didn't have time to right themselves."

"Michelle would do something like that," Libby noted, not having forgotten or forgiven her dad's fiancée for letting their cat out of their flat.

"Yes, she would," Bernie agreed. "But then, Michelle wouldn't be in this situation in the first place." She was silent for a moment. Then she said, "Okay, we'll just yell to attract attention. Someone's bound to hear us."

"It might be a while." Libby gestured at the empty parking lot. "Most everyone's at work." She consulted her watch. "And it's going to be a good two hours before people start coming home."

"I was thinking of the people in the building," Bernie said.

Libby shook her head. "Probably not. Mrs. Randall is a little deaf, and as for Gus Moran . . . somehow or other, I don't think he's going to hear us . . . even if he does."

Bernie didn't say anything. She didn't feel like arguing the point. "There may be other people here. We don't know that there aren't."

"I guess it wouldn't hurt to try," Libby allowed.

So they did. Five minutes later, their throats hoarse from screaming, they took a brief break. Then they tried again. The result was the same, so they quit.

"I don't think we can compete with the thunder," Bernie said after a minute of waiting to see if anyone would appear. No one did. She clutched her raincoat more tightly around her while she pondered what to do next. In truth, she was running out of ideas. "Last thoughts. We could try to throw a brick through Mrs. Randall's window."

"And give her a heart attack?" Libby said. "I think not. Anyway, that would mean one of us would have to lean all the way over the wall while the other person hung on to them by their legs so that they could throw the brick. The person throwing the brick would be suspended upside down. Who do you want to be? The person throwing the brick or the person holding the person who's throwing the brick? Frankly, I don't think I'd like to be, either."

"Okay. Scratch that," Bernie conceded, rethinking the practicality of her last idea. "My last thought. We can jump up and down. Maybe the noise and vibrations will attract the attention of someone on the top floor."

"This is a pretty solidly built building," Libby pointed out.

"At least let's try," Bernie urged. "Anyway, the exercise will keep us warm."

"Works for me," Libby said as a clap of thunder sounded directly overhead. A flash of lightning turned the sky white. *Lord preserve me*, she prayed as she started jumping up and down around where she figured Mrs. Randall's apartment was. Two minutes later she stopped. "I feel like a moron," she told Bernie. "And my ankles hurt."

"But you *are* warmer," Bernie said, trying to look on the bright side of things.

"Yeah, I'm sweating," Libby replied. "Which means my sweat will freeze, and I'll be even colder than I was before."

"You're always so negative," Bernie replied.

"No. I'm realistic." Libby went and huddled by the doorway. At least that would provide a minimum amount of shelter from what was to come. "Let me tell you—it's going to be a long two hours up here, especially if we're going to be out in the freezing rain. By that point, we're going to be Popsicles. We'll probably be suffering from hypothermia."

"Come on," Bernie said, trying to jolly her sister along. "So you'll get wet. So what? It's not as if we're marooned at the North Pole."

"Maybe that's where we'll have to live since we will have lost our business. The Blitmans will tell everyone what happened, and no one will want to hire us."

"Let's not overstate," Bernie told her. "I think we have enough drama to deal with at the moment, don't you?" Another zigzag of lightning lit up the sky, interrupting Bernie and making the air smell like their toaster had when it had shorted out. "But on the other hand," Bernie said as she realized that the strikes were now too close for comfort and the roof didn't have a lightning rod, "this might not be the best place to be in a lightning storm."

"No kidding," Libby said as she huddled against the door.

"You do know what that door you're leaning up against is made of, don't you?" Bernie asked her. "I'd move away from it if I were you."

Libby sighed. *Oh well.* She guessed it was better to get wet than fried. As she was trying to figure out where she could go, she turned and saw what had dug into her back. An idea began to form. *This could work*, she thought as she reached out and tapped her sister on the shoulder.

"I think I may have a way to get us out of here," Libby told her.

# Chapter 25

"You want to take the door off the hinges?" Bernie asked after she'd listened to what Libby had to say. Her sister nodded. "How hard could it be?"

"Not hard at all if you have the right tools," Bernie said. She vaguely remembered watching a YouTube video on the subject with Brandon. "Which we don't."

"Maybe we can improvise," Libby said.

"I sure hope so," Bernie told her as she went over and inspected the door.

It was connected to the door frame by three large hinges, and Bernie knew enough about the hinge mechanism to know that they'd have to take all the hinges off in order to remove the door. Bernie extended her hand and tried to screw off the ball that was holding in the bolt on the middle hinge, but she couldn't get the dratted thing to budge. Then she took a closer look and realized that the ball wasn't threaded, so it wouldn't twist off. You had to pry it off.

"So what do you think?" Libby asked as she looked over Bernie's shoulder. "Can we do it?"

"I think we have a shot," Bernie replied as she thought about what she was going to need to get the job done. "Get me one of the bricks we saw," she instructed Libby as she took her metal nail file out of her tote.

"What do you need it for?" Libby asked.

"You'll see," Bernie told her. While she waited for Libby to come back, she placed the end of the file underneath the ball—she was sure it had another name, but she didn't know what it was—that was holding the bolt on the hinge. A moment later, Libby was back with the brick. Bernie took it, placed it underneath the file, said a silent prayer, and began to tap the file with the brick, applying even pressure all the way around.

Libby leaned in closer to watch, her hair brushing Bernie's cheek. "Do you think that's going to work?"

"We'll find out soon enough," Bernie replied as she continued tapping the nail file with the brick.

"Why don't you hit it harder?" Libby asked.

"Because I don't want to damage the file. Now, could you give me room to work?"

"Sorry," Libby murmured, taking a few steps back.

Bernie nodded and returned to her task. After a minute, she could feel the metal ball moving a miniscule amount. Little by little, it began to come up. Then Bernie slid the nail file into the quarter-inch space she'd made and began levering the ball up. A couple of moments later, it came off with a pop and landed on the rooftop.

"Excellent," Libby observed.

"Yeah." Bernie pointed to the bolt holding the two hinge plates together. "Now all we have to do is get that thing out of there, and we'll be good to go." She tried using the point of her nail file to work the bolt up and out, but the file was too wide. She needed something long and thin.

"Now what?" Libby asked.

"A screwdriver would be handy," Bernie said. "Too bad we don't have one."

"Would a pen work?" Libby asked.

"Do you have one?" Bernie asked.

"No, I don't. I was hoping you did."

"Well, I don't."

Libby looked around. There had to be something they could use. Then she had it. Bernie's stilettos. "We can use those," she said, pointing to Bernie's shoes.

Bernie took a step back and crossed her hands over her heart. "You're kidding, right?"

She loved her shoes. They were her new favorite thing. They made her smile every time she put them on. She'd stalked them online for two months, finally paying four hundred dollars for them on sale, which was one hundred dollars more than she wanted to, and they were worth every cent. She loved them to death—especially the line of pink leather bows down the center of the shoe.

"No, I'm not," Libby said. "Those heels are long enough and skinny enough to get into the opening and push the bolt up."

Bernie slipped out of her stilettos and inspected their heels. She had to admit that Libby was right. Unfortunately.

"Would you rather be stuck up here?" Libby demanded.

"I guess not," Bernie allowed. "My feet are freezing."

"The faster we get the door open, the faster you can get your shoes back on."

Bernie sighed. Maybe Pete the Shoemaker could fix them, and if he couldn't, there had to be someone down in the city who could. "Fine. But the business is paying the repair bill."

"Agreed," Libby said. At that point she would have given away her firstborn—if she had a firstborn—to get out of there.

"And I don't want to hear another word about how impractical my shoes are, like, ever," Bernie told Libby.

"Okay."

"I mean it."

"And I agreed."

Bernie sighed. There was nothing for it. It was time to get to work. "Forgive me," she murmured to her shoe as she turned it upside down, placed the heel underneath the bolt, and pushed up. At first the bolt didn't move, but after a few more pushes, it did. When it was three inches above the hinge plate, Bernie grabbed it and pulled.

"Success!" she cried, waving the bolt aloft. Then she looked at the heel of her shoe. It had little indentations in the leather. She only hoped they were fixable.

"We have only two more hinges to go," Libby observed.

By that time her shoes would be unwearable, Bernie thought as she shook out her hands. Her fingers were getting cramped. Then she leaned down and rubbed her feet. They were freezing. The sisters took turns with the next two hinges. The bottom one wasn't too much of a problem, once Bernie realized that she practically had to lie down next to it to get the proper angle; the top hinge, however, proved to be a bigger challenge since neither sister was tall enough to reach it.

"I need to get on your back," Bernie told Libby.

"Why can't I get on yours?" Libby snapped.

"Do you really want me to say it?" Bernie said.

"Twenty pounds isn't such a big deal," Libby said.

"Not usually. But it is in this case. Look. Do you want to get out of here or not?"

"Obviously, I do," Libby responded.

"Then let me try."

"I don't know if I can hold you."

"Well, I'm figuring if you got down on your hands and knees, I can stand on your back."

"No way," Libby cried.

"Do you have a better idea? Because I'm willing to listen if you do."

Libby didn't. "Fine," she said. She got down on her hands and knees next to the door.

"Ready?" Bernie said.

"Ready," Libby said through gritted teeth. If she'd been cold and wet before, now she was sopping.

Bernie stepped up, Libby's back promptly buckled, and Bernie fell off.

"You did that on purpose," Bernie said after she'd picked herself up.

"I didn't. Honestly," Libby cried.

After two more tries, Bernie was finally able to stand up on Libby's back and get to work on the last hinge.

"I think I can just make it," she said to Libby.

Libby didn't answer. She was too busy concentrating on not collapsing. The third hinge seemed as if it took an eternity, even though it didn't.

"My poor shoes," Bernie said mournfully as she stepped down and put her shoes on. "They're never going to be the same."

"Neither is my back," Libby told her as she grabbed the door handle and yanked. "You're not as thin as you think you are."

"I never said I was," Bernie retorted while she supported the door with both hands.

There was a squeak, the hinges came apart, and the door swung toward them, nearly knocking the sisters over.

"I wasn't expecting that," Libby noted as she and Bernie worked frantically to steady it.

"Neither was I," Bernie admitted once they got the door under control. "How much do you think this door weighs?"

"Too much," Libby replied as she and Bernie attempted to position the door on enough of an angle so there would be enough space for them to crawl through to the other side. It took three tries, but they finally succeeded.

"Yes!" Libby cried as she carefully made her way through the opening they'd created.

Once both sisters were on the landing, Libby looked at her watch while Bernie took her shoes off and carefully inspected them before she put them back on. The heels on the stilettos were stripped down to what looked like some sort of plastic, but they were still firmly attached to the shoes, which was pretty impressive when you considered she'd been using them as a hammer. The good news was the bows on the front of the shoes looked fine, so maybe the shoes were fixable, after all. Maybe the heels could be a different color. Like pink. Pink wouldn't be bad at all. It would match the bows. And she could still walk on them, and that was definitely a good thing.

"How are we doing for time?" Bernie asked her sister.

Libby grinned. "Amazingly, we're doing okay. If we hustle, we have enough time to get to the shop, finish our prep, and get to the Blitmans." Libby shook her head. "Weird. It felt as if we were up on the roof for hours and hours."

Bernie nodded. "Didn't it, though? We should probably tell Manny about the door on our way out."

"We don't have the time. We'll call him as soon as we get to the store," Libby said. "Or text him if your phone is working. Or whatever." She stopped and looked around. "I never want to come back here again."

"You won't get an argument from me about that," Bernie agreed as she started down the stairs.

They ran down the empty stairwell and across the deserted parking lot. By now the storm had arrived in full force and the rain had become a curtain, the wind driving it in horizontal lines. The rain stung their eyes, and Libby and Bernie both looked at the ground as they ran, trying to keep the water out of their eyes as it cascaded down their hoods and worked its way through the seams of their raincoats and drenched their shirts.

Which was why Libby didn't see what was hanging from the branch of the tree next to Mathilda until she ran into it.

Then she opened her mouth and screamed.

# Chapter 26

"I guess we know why someone locked us on the roof," Bernie said as she looked at Penelope Witherspoon dangling from the tree branch.

Libby didn't say anything. She was trying to get over her shock.

"Well, one thing is for sure," Bernie added, blinking the water out of her eyes. "The lady isn't missing anymore."

"Are you sure it's her?" Libby asked, because she couldn't think of anything else to say. Her voice sounded hoarse to her. She drew her raincoat around her. Not that it was doing much good in these circumstances.

Bernie snorted. "Of course I'm sure it's her. There have been only ten million pictures of her in the newspaper."

"Three," Libby said, correcting her. "There have been three pictures. I wonder where she's been all this time."

"Good question." Bernie pulled her hood down farther over her head. "The other one being, why did she turn up now?"

"There is that," Libby agreed. "We should call Lucy."

"Should we?" Bernie asked her sister as she walked over to get a better look at Penelope. Just to make sure. Yup, it was her, all right. It was hard to tell, given the circumstances, but it looked to Bernie as if Penelope hadn't been dead for very long. Maybe a day at the most. Probably less.

"Of course we should," Libby answered. "What else would you suggest?"

Bernie turned around and faced her sister. "I'm suggesting we can tell him when we get to the shop."

"That's cold."

"True. But so are we. This way we'll get a chance to talk to Amber and Googie and tell them what needs to be done for the Blitmans." Bernie stifled a sneeze. She was wet and cold, and she needed to change her clothes. "I don't know about you, but I'm miserable, and I'd really like to get into some dry things and have something hot to drink before we call Lucy. Penelope Witherspoon is dead. What difference is another half an hour going to make to her? None. Zilch. Nada. *Niente.* But it's going to make a big difference to us."

Libby raised her hands. "Stop. I get it."

"Good," Bernie replied as she walked toward the driver's side of the van.

"You think Lucy is going to blame us for Penelope, don't you?" Libby asked, her tone incredulous. "You want us to go home first because you're afraid we won't have the chance otherwise."

"And the lady wins the prize. Exactly right. I think there's an excellent chance we're going to be sitting around the police station for six hours, and I'd rather do it in dry clothes, with the Blitman stuff sorted out," Bernie said as she opened Mathilda's door and got in. At least she and her sister could get out of the rain while they talked. "Someone went to a lot of trouble to lock us upstairs so they could plant this body down here, right next to our van. There has to be a reason."

"You don't know that the two events are connected,"

Libby told her, joining her sister in the van. Water dripped down her hair and into her eyes. She wiped it away with her hand.

"Yeah, I do," Bernie replied. She reached over and got her phone out of the glove compartment and tried it. It still wasn't working. "Logic says so."

"It could be a coincidence," Libby insisted. She started to sneeze.

"And the sun could start rising in the west and setting in the east," Bernie said as she started the van up. At least that was working. "Come on. Seriously. Why hang Penelope in this tree? Why do it now? Why not dispose of her body in the Hudson or bury her somewhere? No. Whoever did this wanted her found. More specifically, they wanted us to find her, or they wanted us to be found with her. Probably the second, but neither one is a good thing."

"No. They're not," Libby conceded.

"So we've agreed, we're going back to the shop and then making the phone call?" Bernie asked her sister.

"I guess," Libby said, even though she still wasn't sure it was the right thing to do. On the other hand, the idea of hot chocolate and dry clothes was a powerful lure. She was just about to say something along those lines to Bernie when she saw Michelle's van in the parking lot and Michelle talking to a couple, a couple Libby was fairly positive she'd seen in the common room after Darius's death. She pointed. "Bernie, is that Michelle?"

"Yes, it is." Bernie groaned. Michelle was the last person she wanted to run into at this moment. She was just trying to decide if she could back up when Michelle spotted the van and waved. Bernie cursed under her breath as she drove toward her. There was no other choice. When she got close to her, she stopped the van and jumped out.

Michelle's eyes widened. "Thank God I found you." She clasped her hands to her bosom. "We've been worried sick."

"We?" Bernie asked.

"Your dad and I. Amber got a phone call from the Blitmans, and when you didn't answer your phone, Amber went to talk to your dad. Then he tried to call you, and when you didn't answer, he got really concerned."

"I didn't answer because my phone fell in a puddle," Bernie told her.

"Well, that explains that," Michelle said.

"But you haven't explained how you knew Libby and I were here," Bernie demanded. She couldn't help it, but she was irritated to see that Michelle was wearing the perfect coat for this weather. It was black and made of some sort of rubberized material that repelled the water. The hood fit snugly, and the wrist openings were tight enough to keep the water out. Not only that, but her makeup was perfect. Talk about petty, but Bernie had to admit that she was. Especially since she and Libby looked like drowned rats.

"You told Amber, remember?" Michelle replied, raising her voice against the crash of thunder.

"I guess I did," Bernie allowed.

Michelle shrugged. "In any case, I offered to run over and see if I could find you, and thank heaven I did."

"Who are those people you were talking to?" Libby asked, having joined Michelle and Bernie.

"I don't know," Michelle replied. "I was just asking them if they'd seen you. Why?"

"They look familiar," Libby told her. "I think I saw them at the costume party."

Michelle shook her head. "Sorry, but I really have no idea." She looked Bernie and Libby up and down. "You poor dears, you're absolutely soaked to the skin. You must be freezing to death. What have you both been up to?"

Bernie was just about to tell her that someone had locked them on the roof, but she realized that Michelle's attention was focused elsewhere. She was staring over Bernie's shoulder. As Bernie turned to see what she was looking at, Michelle pointed to the shed.

"What's that?" she asked, gesturing to the hanging body of Penelope Witherspoon.

Bernie's heart sank. *So much for getting out of here,* she thought. "It's—" she began, but Michelle interrupted her before she could finish her sentence, which, Bernie reflected, was just as well, since she wasn't sure what she was going to say.

Michelle squinted. "Is it a leftover Halloween decoration? Because it looks awfully realistic," she said.

"Funny you should say that," Bernie replied. For a moment she weighed finessing the situation, but she really didn't see how she could, at least not in a way that wouldn't come back and bite her in the ass. Sometimes it did pay to be truthful. "That's Penelope Witherspoon, Darius Witherspoon's wife."

"And she's dead?"

"Well, she ain't hanging there for laughs," Bernie said, reflecting as she did that Michelle brought out the worst in her.

"Oh my God." Michelle's eyes widened. She put her hand to her mouth. "That's horrible."

"It certainly is," Bernie agreed. "We were just about to call the police," she lied. "Unfortunately, my phone still isn't working."

"Here, let me," Michelle said, being ever helpful as she took her phone out of her raincoat pocket.

*Great,* Bernie thought. *This just gets better and better.*

But before Michelle could make the call, a police car with red lights blazing and siren blaring drove up the path to the parking lot, shattering the quiet of the late October afternoon, the lights imparting a reddish glow to the fading day.

# Chapter 27

The three women turned and watched the black-and-white car approaching. The rain had tapered off to a fine mist, and Bernie and Libby could see the Longely chief of police in the driver's seat. Not a good sign, both of them knew. A uniform should have been the first responder. The fact that Lucy had come himself meant that the crime was a newsworthy event. Otherwise, he wouldn't have gotten out of his chair.

"What an amazing coincidence," Michelle trilled in a tone of voice that gave Libby and Bernie pause as she watched the patrol car coming toward them.

"Isn't it, though?" Bernie said dryly, wondering about the timing.

"Yes. Just ask the universe for something, and it will give it to you."

"I didn't realize the universe answered such specific requests," Bernie observed. "Kind of sounds like the universe is a DJ."

Michelle smiled. "Of course, you have to help yourself, but I asked the universe for a companion, and it gave me your dad."

"Lovely," Libby said, rolling her eyes.

"It is, isn't it?" Michelle said, purposely ignoring Libby's tone and expression. She turned to Bernie. "Don't you think so?"

But Bernie wasn't listening. She was watching the patrol car racing toward them. She jumped back as it squealed to a stop right in front of her, Libby, and Michelle. "Could you get any closer? Why don't you just run us over?" she yelled at Lucy.

"There's nothing wrong with my driving," Lucy yelled back as he shut off the engine.

Suddenly it was blessedly silent. Then he got out, slammed the door after himself, and strode over to where the women were standing

*There goes the day*, Bernie thought as she studied Lucy's face. He looked pleased with himself, which, in her experience, meant that he had the upper hand.

"We got a phone call," he announced, folding his arms across his chest. "Something about finding a body at this location."

Bernie pointed to Penelope Witherspoon. "Whoever called was probably talking about that one over there."

Lucy frowned. "She's hanging in a tree."

"Would it be better if she was lying on the ground?" Libby asked.

"It would be better if she wasn't there at all," Lucy snapped.

"It was a rhetorical question," Bernie said.

He squinted. "Is that who I think it is?"

"You tell me who you think it is, and I'll tell you who it is," Bernie replied.

"Why are you here?" he demanded, not answering his last question.

"How about it was a nice day for a drive?" Libby replied.

"I thought I told you to stay away from here," Lucy said.

Libby turned to Bernie. "Did he? I don't remember him saying that."

"Neither do I, Libby. I guess we're just getting forgetful in our old age." Bernie turned back to Lucy. "So who called? Anyone we know?"

He glared at her. "A concerned citizen."

Bernie rubbed her arm to get the circulation going. "Does the concerned citizen have a name?"

"That's something your lawyer can ask about," Lucy threw over his shoulder as he headed over to the body.

"Are we going to need one?" Libby called after him.

Lucy didn't bother to answer.

"Oh, dear," Michelle said. She touched a finger to her lips. "This sounds serious."

"Lucy's in a huff," Bernie told her. "It'll be fine."

Michelle shook her head doubtfully. "I don't know. Why do you bait him like that?" she asked Bernie. "It just makes things worse."

"Because we can," Bernie told her. "And it's fun."

"It doesn't seem very wise to me," Michelle observed.

"It probably isn't," Bernie conceded. "Listen, something tells me that we'll be at the police station for a while, so I was wondering if I could borrow your phone for a minute. I need to call Amber and Googie and get a couple of things straightened out."

"You mean the Blitmans?" Michelle asked.

Bernie nodded. "Yes. The Blitmans."

Michelle smiled again. "Don't worry about that. It's all taken care of."

"What do you mean, it's taken care of?" Libby asked very quietly. Was there a note of triumph in Michelle's voice? Libby thought there was, but she wasn't sure.

"Well, when I heard what happened at the shop—" Michelle began.

"What happened at the shop?" Bernie asked, interrupting, her heart beating faster, fearing the worst. "Was there a fire? Did someone hurt themselves?"

"Heavens no." Michelle chuckled. "Of course not. I was talking about the Blitmans."

Bernie restrained herself from putting her hands around Michelle's neck and squeezing the answer out of her. "What about the Blitmans?" Bernie asked instead.

Michelle waved her hands in the air. "Well, it wouldn't have been a big deal if you were at the shop, but you weren't."

Bernie could hear the implied criticism in Michelle's voice as she watched Lucy. He was standing in front of Penelope Witherspoon, talking on his phone. "What did they want?" she asked.

Michelle shifted her weight from her left to her right foot. "Evidently, the Blitmans invited three more people over, and they wanted to make sure there was enough food for everyone. . . ."

"There is," Libby said.

"And they wanted you to add a gluten-free dessert to the menu, because one of their new guests has a sensitivity to wheat."

"Not a problem," Libby said. "We can do baked apples."

"Anyway," Michelle continued, "when no one could find you, I called the Blitmans and told them not to worry, that I'd take care of everything. I hope you don't mind. I asked your dad, and he said it was fine."

"You did what?" Libby asked, not believing what she was hearing.

"I told them I'd take care of everything," Michelle obligingly repeated. "And I'm so glad I did. Otherwise it would have been terrible for you. Having to deal with that"—she waved her hand in Lucy's general direction—"and the Blitmans at the same time. I'm just glad I can help. You can buy me a massage as a thank-you if you want." She laughed. "Just kidding. I just want you to know I'm always there for you if you need me."

"How comforting," Bernie said.

Michelle smiled. "After all, that's what family is for."

"I think I'm going to puke," Libby muttered.

"What did you say?" Michelle asked, turning to her.

"Libby said she's so glad we have you," Bernie told Michelle as she watched Lucy coming back. His phone was still glued to his ear, and he had a grim expression on his face.

"He doesn't look happy, does he?" Michelle commented as she watched Lucy approach. She looked at her watch. "Oh, dear. I didn't realize it was so late. I'd better get going if I want to get the Blitmans' dinner ready."

"It is pretty much ready," Libby said, puzzled.

Michelle put her hand to her mouth. "Oh. I'm sorry. Didn't I tell you? I added a farro cherry salad and a baked salmon with black garlic, capers, and tomatoes." She patted Libby on the shoulder. "Now, don't you worry about a thing," Michelle chirped. "I'll be sure to convey your apologies. And now I think I'd better go over and tell the captain I'm leaving. That would be the smart thing to do," she said, emphasizing the word *smart*.

"She did it," Libby said as Michelle walked away. "She locked us on the roof and called the cops." She took a step after her, but Bernie grabbed on to her sister's arm.

"Don't be ridiculous, Libby."

Libby jerked her arm away. "I'm not being ridiculous."

"You are. You're saying she murdered Penelope Witherspoon so she could steal one of our clients? Come on."

Libby rounded on her. "Then why is she here?"

"You heard her."

"I don't believe one word she says."

"I don't like her, either. She may be many things, but a murderer isn't one of them. Gus Moran is the more likely candidate. You said it!"

Libby jutted her jaw out. "Well, I've changed my mind. I'm going with Michelle."

"What's her motive?" Bernie demanded.

"I don't know, but I'm sure going to find out," Libby retorted.

"Lower your voice," Bernie hissed. "Michelle and Lucy are coming back."

"Nice lady," Lucy commented as he watched Michelle walk toward her car. Then he nodded toward Penelope Witherspoon. "I think you two have some explaining to do, and I think you should be doing that explaining down at the station."

"I take it that's a request," Bernie said.

Lucy glared at her. "What do you think?"

Bernie smiled brightly. "I appreciate the invitation, but as long as you're asking, I think Libby and I would prefer to go home."

"Is that a fact?" Lucy growled.

"Well, you asked, so I'm answering. And as long as you mentioned the word *fact*, I think it would be good if you got yours straight before you jumped to a conclusion."

"And what facts are those, if I may ask?" Lucy inquired. He was starting to grow a mustache, and Bernie decided it looked like a caterpillar.

Libby stepped up to him. "For your information, someone locked us on the roof. We found Penelope Witherspoon like that when we finally came down."

"Really?" Lucy said, baring his teeth in a grin. "How convenient."

"That's not the way I would put it." Libby sneezed into

her arm. She needed to take zinc immediately. "And I think it's safe to say that whoever hung Penelope Witherspoon from that tree killed her and probably her husband, too, and is trying to frame us."

"And you know this because you're gifted with second sight?" Lucy asked.

"No," Libby said. "I know this because I'm gifted with common sense."

Lucy turned and pointed to the roof of the Berkshire Arms. "How did you get down from there?" He sneered. "Jump? Float down on a magic carpet?"

"Actually," Bernie informed him, stepping back into the conversation, "we took the roof door off its hinges."

Lucy laughed. "With the screwdriver you always carry."

"No. With a nail file and a brick, if you must know. And maybe, just maybe you should talk to the couple we saw talking to Michelle earlier."

"And why should I do that?" Lucy asked her.

"Because they were here when Libby and I came down from the roof," Bernie said. "And my sister is pretty sure they were at Darius's party, and I think they might have something to do with what's going on now."

"Well, I don't," Lucy declared.

"Let's find out," Libby said.

"Let's not," Lucy said. "Let's have a nice little chat. Just you, me, and your sister instead."

# Chapter 28

Bernie and Libby walked out of the Longely police station two hours later. It was dark out, and the wind had picked up, bringing the smell of winter with it. The wind made Bernie's damp clothes feel even colder on her skin, and she rubbed her arms as she mulled over the conversation she and her sister had had with Lucy.

He'd warned them to stay in the area, and Bernie had asked him to define the term *area*.

"Here." He'd gestured around him.

"So you want us to live in the police station?" Bernie had asked, all innocence. "Do you have a shower here? Because I need to take a shower every day."

"In Longely," Lucy answered through gritted teeth.

"How about to Costco? That's one block over in Harrison. Can we go there?" Bernie asked, enjoying herself.

Lucy scrunched his eyes up and glared at her. Bernie reflected that he seemed to be doing a lot of that lately. Maybe he needed glasses. "Keep it up and I'll have both of you arrested," he snarled.

"That's hardly fair," Libby told him. "My sister is just trying to understand what you're saying, and now you're threatening us."

"On what grounds?" Bernie demanded as she once again surveyed her shoes. She sighed. They really were ruined. "I think you're violating my constitutional rights."

Lucy leaned forward and put his face, which was now beet red, an inch away from Bernie's. "How about I book you on suspicion of murder?"

"Oh, dear." Bernie crossed her arms over her chest.

"Whom are we suspected of killing?" Libby asked.

"Obviously, Darius Witherspoon and his wife," Lucy replied. "Is there someone else I should add to the list?"

"And why did we do it?" Bernie inquired, taking a step back. "Refresh my memory."

"Gladly," Lucy said. "You were stealing money from Witherspoon, and he found out."

"Right," Libby said. "I knew that. And we were hiding his wife in our basement, just waiting for the opportunity to kill her and put her next to our truck. Makes sense to me."

Lucy turned to Libby. He had an ugly smile on his face. "Another sister heard from."

"Better than our lawyer," Libby replied.

Lucy lifted an eyebrow.

"You're harassing us," Libby explained.

Lucy smirked. "Somehow, I don't think that's how the DA is going to see it," he told her as he looked down at his phone.

"You know what I'd do if I were you?" Libby said. "I'd start trying to figure out Penelope's disappearance. I'm guessing there's a link there between that and her husband's death. How about you? Do you think so?" she said to Lucy.

He looked up from the text he'd been reading on his phone while Libby was talking. "Excuse me. Were you saying something? I didn't hear you."

"You really don't care who did this, do you?" Libby demanded.

"Oh, I care, all right," Lucy answered. He slipped his phone in his pocket. "I'm quite satisfied I have the correct suspects. Now it's just a matter of proving it. And I will. Don't you worry about that. I'm tired of having you two running around, getting in my way, thinking you're better than I am. Things are going to be different around here. I can tell you that."

Bernie snorted. "Get serious," she scoffed. "Your case, if you want to call it that, will never hold up in court. It's as thin as tissue paper."

"It doesn't have to," Lucy said sweetly. "You'll still be in jail, awaiting trial. And it can take a long time to work up a case and bring it to court."

"Are you threatening us?" Libby demanded.

"No. I'm telling you the realities of the situation," Lucy replied. "And by the way, I spoke to William Moran. He wants you two to pay to fix the door."

"We should be suing him for damages," Libby cried.

"How do you figure that?" Lucy asked.

"He should have a fail-safe mechanism on the door so what happened to us doesn't happen again."

"I'll let him know. I'm sure he'll run right out and get one." Lucy's smile got bigger. "Just stay away from the Berkshire Arms, or he'll put a restraining order out on you, and I promise you I'll be there to enforce it."

# Chapter 29

"I can't wait to get home and get out of these clothes," Libby said to Bernie as they hurried across the parking lot to their van and got in.

"We're not going home. We're going back to the Berkshire Arms to see if we can find out who that couple we saw is," Bernie told her as she leaned over, opened the glove compartment, took her phone out, and turned it on. It worked!

"Have you lost your mind?" Libby demanded as Bernie silently thanked the phone gods. "Didn't you hear what Lucy said? He meant it. Do you really want to get arrested?"

"We'll be in and out before Moran sees us. I'll be quick. I promise."

"That's what you said the last time, Bernie, and look what happened."

"We got cold and wet," Bernie said, having decided to take a more positive view of things.

"We also got framed for murder," Libby countered.

"Attempted frame, Libby, and it's a pretty weak one at that."

"But a frame, nevertheless," Libby reiterated. "And"—

she raised a finger—"let's not forget we could have gotten struck by lightning up there."

"But we weren't."

"We could have been. We could have been fried to a crisp."

"And yet here we are," Bernie replied as she tucked her phone into her tote.

Libby glared at her sister. Sometimes she just wanted to slap her. "Seriously, whoever locked us up there was sending us a message."

Bernie put the key in the ignition and started Mathilda up. "That's great if it's true."

Libby's jaw dropped. "Great?" Libby repeated when she'd recovered enough to speak. "You call what happened great?"

"I do. Because that means we're getting closer. We've obviously hit a nerve."

"Whose nerve?"

Bernie frowned. "That's the part we still have to figure out."

"Oh, goody." Libby clapped her hands. "I can't tell you how much better that makes me feel, Bernie. All I can say is, I'm never going up on the roof again."

"We're not going up on the roof, Libby. We're going into the building."

Libby crossed her arms over her chest and leaned back in her seat. "I don't care. I don't want to go anywhere near the place. I said it before, and I'll say it again. The place is cursed. Nothing good has ever happened there."

"Fine. Then you stay in the van, and I'll go in."

Libby turned her head away and studied the lights in the valley below through the side window. They were from the houses in the Orchard Estates development. Everyone snug in their homes. Like she and Bernie ought to be.

"I don't know," Libby said to her sister, still looking at

the view. "Maybe this time we bit off more than we can chew, metaphorically speaking."

Bernie reached over and patted her sister's knee. "We can solve this thing. We *will* solve this thing. This person has killed two people. He might be getting ready to kill a third. If we don't go now, those people will probably be gone."

"They probably are already."

"They might be," Bernie admitted. "But right now they're all we have."

"And the Blitmans?"

"We'll call tomorrow, apologize, and send them a box of cookies."

"I guess that makes the most sense," Libby reluctantly admitted. She raised her hand and checked the heat coming out of the vent on the dashboard. *Anemic* was the word that came to mind.

Bernie smiled. "You'll see. Everything will work out. We're practically there, anyway. And this will just take a minute," she assured Libby. She held up her hand. "I swear. And then we'll go home."

"No longer," Libby said as Bernie stepped on the gas and headed toward the Berkshire Arms. "You promise?"

"I just did. Okay then," Bernie said, and she reached over and turned on the radio. The sound of the Beatles filled the van.

Libby sat back and closed her eyes. She was drifting off to sleep when she realized something. "The rope," she blurted out, thinking of the hanging skeletons lining the road that led up to the Berkshire Arms.

"What about it?" Bernie asked, keeping her eyes on the road. They had just begun their ascent to the Berkshire Arms.

"Think about it," Libby told her. "The Witherspoons were hanged. That's an unusual way to kill someone."

"Penelope might have been killed another way and then strung up," Bernie said.

"You're being too literal. What I'm saying is that the use of the rope is symbolic. The fact that they were hanged has significance."

"The Hanged Man is a tarot card," Bernie said. She used to consult them when she was in college.

"What does the card mean?"

Bernie thought for a moment. "If I remember correctly, if the card refers to yourself, it means you're at a cross-roads, and if it refers to someone else, it means they are a traitor and you should beware of them."

"I wonder which one this symbolizes?" Libby said.

"The second one," Bernie guessed.

Libby thought so, too.

# Chapter 30

Bernie thought about what she and Libby had just discussed as she drove along the road. Could the manner of the Witherspoons' deaths be a clue to a motive? Was it just coincidence? No. It couldn't be. So obviously, the hanging did have some significance. But what was it? Was the tarot card interpretation valid? Now that she thought about it, it seemed like a stretch. She was about to tell Libby that when her attention was drawn to the lights ahead of her. As she rounded the final bend, she saw spotlights illuminating the shed where she and Bernie had parked.

"I should have figured the Longely CID would still be here," Bernie muttered as she took in the yellow tape and the scurrying people, who looked antlike in the blazing light that was turning night into day.

"The question is, did Lucy come back?" Libby observed.

"Doubtful," Bernie replied as both she and Libby scrunched down in their seats. "He's probably home, watching TV." Which was good, Bernie reflected; not that people wouldn't know who they were, considering their shop's name was emblazoned on their van. Luckily, no one looked their way. Bernie turned off the van's headlights to make them less noticeable and drove over to the far side of the parking lot. She parked in between two cars, killed the engine, but left the key in the ignition.

"I'll be back in a minute, five at the most," Bernie told Libby as she got out. She closed the door quietly and headed for the Berkshire Arms's main entrance. She had a slight wobble as she walked, and Libby was reflecting that one of Bernie's heels must be coming off—nothing like using it for a hammer—when she glanced at her rearview mirror and saw William Moran striding toward Bernie.

"You!" he screamed.

*I knew we shouldn't have come up here*, Libby thought as she watched Moran close the distance.

Bernie whirled around.

"You," he repeated, his face red.

"May I help you with something?" Bernie asked. That only got Moran angrier.

Moran pointed to the van. "Yeah. You can turn around and get back in your van, and then you and your sister can drive out of here right now."

Bernie put her hands on her hips. "Or?"

"Or I'm calling the cops, having you removed, and charging you with trespassing. Didn't the chief of police tell you not to come here?"

"He might have mentioned it in passing," Bernie lied as she put on her best smile.

"So what part of 'Don't go there' didn't you understand?"

"Oh, we understood," Bernie said, gesturing to her sister. "We just thought we should talk in person before we get lawyers involved."

Moran scowled. "Lawyers?" The word came out as a croak.

"They're usually involved in lawsuits," Bernie explained helpfully, warming to her topic.

Moran snorted. "You suing me? Right. When pigs fly."

"There are going to be a lot of them in the air soon then, because I'm being serious."

"And on what grounds do you propose to sue me?" Moran asked, curiosity getting the better of him.

"On the grounds that there should be some way to open the roof door from the outside."

"There's an alarm on the outside, which is supposed to deter unauthorized access."

"Which wasn't working," Bernie countered.

"It was."

"It obviously wasn't. I don't even think that's a discussable issue," Libby said. "The issue is, why did you lie to us?"

"I didn't," Moran insisted.

Bernie shook her head in mock disgust. "We have people who will testify to the contrary. At least respect us enough to tell us the truth."

Moran straightened his back. "Fine. You want to know?"

"Yes, we do," Libby answered.

"Because I had better things to do that night than take you on a guided tour of the building," Moran said.

"Like what?" Bernie asked.

"I don't have to answer that," Moran said.

"That's true," Bernie replied. "But it would be helpful if you did." Then she added a *please*.

Moran looked at her for a moment, then shrugged. "Ah. What the hell. Mostly, it was a liability issue. But the fact remains that you shouldn't have been up there in the first place. You had no business up there. None. You were trespassing. And now I have to have the door replaced. Do you have any idea how much that's going to cost me?"

"That's what you have insurance for," Bernie observed.

"I can't claim this," Moran said. "I just told you that."

"We can fix the door if you want," Bernie said.

Moran snorted at the idea. "Fat chance."

"We could have died out there," Libby observed, her voice floating out from the van. "We can sue you for negligence."

"Oh, please," Moran growled. "No one would take the case." He took a deep breath and stood up straighter. "This is a ridiculous conversation."

"I agree," Bernie said. "Let us fix the door for you as a way to make amends."

"I don't want you to make amends," Moran retorted. "I just want both of you out of here."

"Are you sure?" Bernie asked, baiting him. "It wouldn't take more than ten minutes at the most, especially if we can borrow your screwdriver."

Moran pointed to the road leading up to the Berkshire Arms. "I want you gone. You two are nothing but bad luck."

"No," Libby told him. "It's your building that's bad luck. Nothing good has ever happened here."

"Superstitious nonsense," Moran snapped. He pointed to the road again. "Now, get out of here and don't come back. You've caused enough grief."

Bernie noticed a uniform heading in Moran's direction out of the corner of her eye. "We're going," she told Moran. "No need to get upset."

Moran visibly relaxed.

"I just have one question," Bernie said before she turned toward the van. "Did you kill Darius Witherspoon, as well as his wife? I mean, you might as well tell us now if you did, because we're going to find out sooner or later."

Moran got red in the face again. "Out!" he yelled. "Get out now."

"Jeez. You know, you're really quite an emotional guy," Bernie observed as she turned and headed for the van. "I thought you were a cold fish, but I can see that I was wrong."

"That's it," Moran spluttered. "I'm having you arrested."

# Chapter 31

"He isn't very happy with us," Libby observed as she watched Moran talking to the uniform who had been walking toward him. Moran was waving his hands up and down and gesturing in their direction. Libby decided he wasn't saying nice things as Bernie slammed the van door shut. The lock didn't catch, and she had to close it again.

"No, he isn't, is he?" she replied.

"Do you really think he killed the Witherspoons?" Libby asked.

Bernie shrugged. "It's possible."

"Anything is possible," Libby noted. She looked at her sister, taking in her expression. "You don't really think he did it, do you? You just wanted to see how he was going to react."

Bernie turned and studied Moran. "Which is not very well. But you get people angry enough and sometimes they say things they don't mean to."

"Frankly, I wouldn't be happy either if someone damaged my property and then accused me of a double homicide," Libby pointed out.

"There is that," Bernie allowed. "However, he *was* at the Berkshire Arms the night Darius died."

"We saw him after Darius died."

"He was there pretty quickly, so he couldn't have been that far away."

"True," Libby said.

"So that's number one." Bernie touched the pinkie on her left hand with the ring finger of her right hand. "Number two. Getting the key to Darius's apartment wouldn't have been an issue since it would have been on file in management's office in case of emergency."

Libby nodded. That was true, too.

"Or," Bernie continued, "he could have knocked on Darius's door and said he had heard there was a problem with the pipes or something of that nature. Darius would have definitely let him in, and Darius wouldn't have thought twice if Moran had a coil of rope with him. He would just assume it was part of some job Moran was doing."

Libby nodded again. "Okay. So Moran had the means, and he had the access, but what would his motive have been?"

"Well, he does have a lot of money tied up in this building," Bernie said, hypothesizing. "Maybe Darius was doing something that jeopardized that in some way."

"How?" Libby asked.

Bernie had to admit she didn't know.

"And speaking of wives, how does Darius's wife come into your scenario?" Libby asked.

Bernie shook her head. "Honestly, I don't have a clue. Maybe the same person didn't kill both of the Witherspoons," she suggested, although that seemed highly unlikely to her. She stopped talking and watched the uniform turn his head and talk into the radio he was wearing on his shoulder. A minute later, he nodded, said something to

Moran, and began walking toward Mathilda. "I think it's time we left," Bernie said.

"I was thinking that myself," Libby agreed. She'd seen the uniform, too, and whatever he was planning to say to them wasn't going to be good.

As Bernie put the van in reverse, she saw Manny coming out of the Berkshire Arms. "He might know something," she said, nodding in Manny's direction.

"Hey, you!" the uniform yelled at Libby and Bernie. "I want to talk to you."

"Definitely time to go," Bernie said as Manny got into an old beat-up Chevy. She heard the Chevy's engine kick over and saw its lights come on. "We should follow him," she said to Libby as he started out of the parking lot.

Libby nodded as Bernie shifted into drive. By now the uniform was standing next to them. The cop rapped sharply on Bernie's window.

"You two, out of the car," he ordered.

Bernie rolled down her window and smiled sweetly. "We'd love to, Officer, but my sister has female troubles. Sorry, but we really have to go, otherwise things are really going to get messy around here," she told him. Then she stepped down on the gas. Mathilda jumped forward, and the uniform jumped back.

"Female troubles?" Libby repeated as they sped out of the lot. "I have female troubles?" Her voice rose. "Seriously?"

Bernie shrugged. "Sorry. It was the first thing that came to mind."

Libby leaned forward so she could see better. "I just hope we don't get arrested for not stopping," she said as Bernie started down the winding road that connected the Berkshire Arms with the rest of the town. "That would be the perfect end to the perfect day."

"Did he ask us to stop?" Bernie inquired as she saw the Chevy's taillights in front of them. It was a rhetorical question. "I didn't hear anything, did you?"

"Must be we have hearing problems, along with everything else," Libby observed. "You should do something about the waxy buildup in your ears."

Then she stopped talking because she was too busy watching out for deer running across the road, even though she knew the possibility of that was slim. It was dark out now, and deer usually came out to feed at dusk and dawn. By now they were bedded down for the evening. Unless, of course, something spooked them. Like a coyote.

But it wasn't the prospect of hitting a deer that was giving her a bad case of the cobble wobbles, Libby admitted to herself. No. It was the forest itself. Which was like the ones in the fairy tales. The trees on either side of the road grew so close together, they seemed to be crowding the road, wanting to obliterate it, while the curves were so sharp, you couldn't see what was coming around the bend. Whenever Libby went down or up this road, she always had the feeling that something in the forest was watching her, something old, something that had no place in the modern world, something that didn't wish her well.

But that was absurd. She knew that intellectually, but not in her gut. She snuck a look at Bernie. She seemed fine. If the road scared her, she didn't show it.

Ten minutes later, they reached the bottom of the hill, and Libby exhaled. Manny was nowhere in sight. There were three choices: they could either go straight, to the right, or to the left.

Libby turned to Bernie. "Which way do you think?" she asked her.

"Straight," Bernie told her, thinking she saw the reflection of taillights up ahead of them.

Libby nodded as Bernie sped up. A minute later, Manny's

Chevy came into view. Bernie slowed down again so as not to spook him. The road they were on, Route 230, or Ash Street, was a back road that cut through the bottom half of Longely, then dipped down and skirted a wildlife preserve, went by two dairy farms, and came up again in the town of Clinton.

Ash started out with large, well-kept seven-bedroom estates with rolling lawns that had been built in the twenties for the railroad barons escaping New York City, then gradually turned into an area with smaller three- and four-bedroom wooden colonials and ranches with two-car garages, which had been constructed in the sixties, their windows still decorated for Halloween and bikes and basketball hoops in the driveways.

Three miles before the town line, the building stock changed again, reverting to older houses that had been constructed in the twenties to house the people who worked at the estates. These houses were small shoe-box affairs. Some of them were well kept, others had flaking paint and sagging porches, while still others lay abandoned, plywood covering their windows, their lawns a riot of weeds. Five miles down the road, the houses ceased altogether, and a wire fence with a wooden sign in front of it announced the beginning of the Peterson Wildlife Sanctuary, a marsh where flocks of birds stopped on their annual migrations.

By now Mathilda and Manny's Chevy were the only vehicles out on the road. It was pitch black out, with no moon or streetlamps to lighten the night, and Libby was concerned that Manny would spot them when he checked his rearview mirror, but there wasn't much Bernie could do about it except hang back as far as she could.

For a moment, Bernie toyed with the idea of turning off her headlights, but then she nixed the thought. She wasn't familiar with the road, and her night vision had never been very good. Her mother had been right. She should have eaten her carrots. Unfortunately, she'd never been a big fan of them. And she still wasn't. Unless they were in carrot cake, of course.

"We're going to lose him," Libby told Bernie as her sister slowed down even more.

"No, we won't," Bernie told her. "He's going to the Roadhouse."

"How do you know that?" Libby demanded. "Maybe he's going to Clinton."

"I guess we'll find out," Bernie said.

"A buck says he goes to Clinton," Libby countered.

"You're on," Bernie told her.

Libby nodded and struggled to keep her eyes open. Right about now she'd give anything for a cup of coffee and a piece of warm apple pie with vanilla ice cream melting over its top.

# Chapter 32

The Roadhouse was a dive bar housed in a rickety-tickety structure that was built sixty years ago and had been threatening to fall down ever since. Every five years or so someone on the Longely Common Council would bring up a motion to tear the place down, but then someone else would remember that the Roadhouse straddled the line between two counties, and the motion would be tabled.

When Libby pulled into the Roadhouse parking lot, she spotted Manny's Chevy, bathed in the red light of a blinking neon OPEN sign. He'd parked near the door, along with a handful of other vehicles. The place filled up on the weekends with college kids, townies, and bikers but was empty most of the rest of the time. It had been years since Bernie had been there, but as soon as she and her sister walked in, she smelled the old familiar odor of stale beer and cigarette smoke, the Roadhouse being one of the few places in the area where the no smoking law wasn't enforced.

It seemed as if nothing had changed while she'd been away, Bernie reflected. License plates from Texas were still tacked up on the walls, the tube lights hanging from the ceiling were still crooked, the mismatched tables in the back still looked as if they had a layer of grime on them, and the picture on the TV was just as blurry as it had ever been.

Not that any of that stuff mattered, because the bands that the owner, Rick Henderson, booked were good, the dance floor was large, the beer was cold and cheap, and no one checked IDs. Yes, she'd had some good times here, Bernie recalled with a smile as she nodded her chin in Manny's direction. He was sitting at the far end of the bar, hunched over his beer and talking on his phone.

She held out her hand. "One dollar, please."

Libby extracted her wallet from her pocket, took out a bill, and slapped it in the palm of Bernie's hand. "With pleasure. At least we don't have to drive to Clinton," she told Bernie as she headed in Manny's direction.

"Were you following me?" he asked, putting his phone down, as Bernie and Libby sat down next to him.

"As a matter of fact, we were," Bernie replied. The bartender walked over, and she ordered two Blue Ribbons, one for her and the other for her sister. This was not the sort of place where you ordered a microbrew, not that Rick would be stocking eight-dollar beers, anyway.

Manny slid the bowl of peanuts over to Bernie and Libby. "I figured that might be you when I saw your van pulling into the parking lot."

"Yeah," Bernie remarked. "Mathilda might be many things, but inconspicuous isn't one of them."

"True," Manny said, pushing a handful of peanut shells onto the floor. Bernie watched them fall. The floor was clean now, but on the weekends she remembered crunching as she walked.

"I used to come here a lot," Bernie said.

Manny pointed down to a name carved into the oak bar. "Is your name here?"

Bernie laughed. "No. My name is on one of the tables in

the far corner." She'd done it with her friend's Swiss Army knife. That had been fifteen years ago. Fifteen years. It didn't seem possible. She wondered if the table was still there—it probably was—and decided to check and see before she and Libby headed out.

"My boss is not happy with you," Manny announced as the sisters started to shell and eat the peanuts.

"To put it mildly," Libby said, surprised at the depth of her hunger. She knew she was hungry, but she hadn't thought she was that hungry.

Manny took a sip of his beer and put the can down on the bar. No coasters here. "I heard him on his phone. He was screaming at the chief of police, telling him to arrest you. He called you menaces."

Bernie chuckled. "Menaces. I like that." She popped a peanut into her mouth. "Lucy did pull us in, so I guess he listened," Bernie allowed.

"Then how come you're here?" Manny asked, turning toward the sisters.

"Obviously, because there wasn't enough evidence to hold us," Libby said. "Anyway, Moran was lucky. It could have been worse."

"How do you figure that?" Manny asked. "I'd say having two corpses turn up on your property is not good for sales."

"Penelope Witherspoon could have ended up somewhere *in* the Berkshire Arms itself."

"This is true." Manny took another sip of his beer and put the can down. "I'm impressed with your work, doorwise," he told them after he'd reached over and grabbed a handful of peanuts out of the bowl. "What did you get it off the hinges with, anyway?"

"A brick, a nail file, and the heel of my shoe," Bernie answered.

"I'm doubly impressed," Manny said.

"So was I," Bernie told him.

Manny took a sip of his beer, glanced down at his phone, read a text, then looked back up at Bernie. "My cousin is meeting me here," he explained.

Bernie nodded.

"You know, Moran's banned you from the property," Manny continued.

"So he said," Bernie replied. She ate another peanut.

"What were you doing up there, anyway?" Manny asked.

"Trying to figure out how Darius Witherspoon's killer escaped."

"If there was a killer," Manny said.

"We think there was," Libby told him.

Manny leaned back in his chair. "Be that as it may, if you're smart, you won't come back to the Berkshire Arms. Moran will probably shoot you if you do."

"He's that upset?" Libby said.

"He's upset. The chief of police is upset," Manny told her.

"Why the chief of police?" Bernie asked.

Manny gave her a "Don't you know anything?" look. "He's an investor."

"Ah," Bernie said. Now she understood why Lucy was pressing to arrest them. An arrest would put the story to bed—at least for a while.

Libby took a sip of her beer and made a face. It was like drinking dishwater. "How did Moran and Darius Witherspoon get along?" she asked.

Manny killed his beer and ate another peanut. "They didn't. Moran was on Mr. Witherspoon about feeding the crows. . . ."

"Why would Moran care about that?" Libby asked.

Manny held up two fingers. "Noise and poop. And then Witherspoon was always walking around the grounds, muttering to himself and stopping and staring off into space. It gave everyone the creeps." He paused. "So," he said, changing the subject, "are you two going to tell me why you're here? It certainly can't be for the lovely atmosphere."

"Hey, watch what you're saying," the barkeep growled as he slammed a new bowl filled with peanuts down on the bar.

"I didn't realize you were such a delicate flower," Manny replied.

The bartender glared at Manny, and Manny glared back at him. But then the moment passed, and the bartender turned and walked back to the other end of the bar.

"We have a question we were hoping you could answer," Bernie said as she picked up the peanuts that had spilled on the bar and made a little pile of them next to her beer. "There was a couple that came out of the building when we were going in. Do you know who they are?"

"That was Darius Witherspoon's partner," Manny said.

"And the lady?" Libby asked.

Manny shook his head. "No idea."

Bernie leaned forward. "What did he want?"

"He said Mr. Witherspoon had left a package for him, but when I looked and told him it wasn't there, he apologized and told me that he'd forgotten that Witherspoon had said he'd leave it for him in his house." Manny shook his head. "But I don't know. . . ."

Libby reached over and took a peanut. "You don't know what?" she asked.

"I had the idea that he was fishing, that he didn't know where the package was."

"Why do you say that?" Bernie asked.

Manny shrugged. "Just the way he and the woman he was with looked at each other." He spread his fingers out. "It was kind of a knowing glance. You think they had anything to do with what happened to Mr. Witherspoon?" he asked.

"I don't know," Bernie said. "But I'd certainly like to ask them."

"I think I saw them milling around the ballroom after . . . you know. . . ."

"Darius's death?" Bernie asked.

Manny nodded. "But it's hard to be sure, given . . . everything."

"I understand," Libby said. When she thought about that evening, disconnected scenes flashed through her mind.

Manny didn't reply. He was looking over Bernie's and Libby's shoulders.

Bernie and Libby turned to see what he was looking at. A man was standing in the doorway. Bernie put him in his thirties, medium height, medium weight. He was wearing jeans, a T-shirt, a polar fleece, and a baseball cap. Mr. Average.

"My cousin," Manny explained as the man came toward them.

Manny's cousin put out his hand and introduced himself. "Hi. I'm Eduardo Rico-Perez. Manny's first cousin."

"Nice to meet you," Libby and Bernie said together. Then they shook hands, after which they excused themselves, got up, and left. It had been a long night, and they were anxious to get home, take hot showers, and get to bed.

# Chapter 33

Three days later, Bernie and Libby drove into Manhattan. They'd planned on going in two days earlier, but that hadn't happened, because Amber had been out sick with a sinus infection and the sisters had had to cover. Now Amber was back, and they were taking off at two o'clock, right after the shop's lunch rush was over. Bernie was dressed in her vintage Pucci dress, stilettos, and a purple leather moto jacket, while Libby was decked out in a plain black knit sheath, her mother's pearls, and two-inch black heels.

"I feel like Mom," Libby complained as she fussed with the French knot her sister had put her hair into.

"That's the whole idea," Bernie told her, briefly taking her eyes off the car in front of her to look at Libby. She'd done well outfitting her sister, if she had to say so herself. She looked . . . What was the term her mother used? Well bred. Although, Bernie had always thought that adjective applied to horses.

"How is this going to help us?" Libby asked. Like her father, she hadn't inquired into how Bernie was going to get them into Darius Witherspoon's apartment, because she didn't want to know. She'd come to realize it was better that way. Less stressful. Fewer arguments.

"It's all in how you look. That's the key," Bernie remarked cryptically as the car in back of her honked. "I'm going. I'm going," she yelled at the driver as she sped down Second Avenue. But she was smiling as she yelled. She didn't mind the traffic. She enjoyed jockeying for position with the cabbies. Even better, it was one of those magical fall days in New York City, when the air was crisp, but not cold, and the whole world was out and about.

Originally, Bernie and Libby had planned to go to Darius's gallery first and then to his apartment, but the gallery didn't open until four today—at least that was what the message on the phone had said when Libby had called—so they'd decided to reverse their order of business.

"Maybe we could have an early dinner at Esther's if we have time," Bernie suggested, braking as a taxi cut her off. "Hey, watch what you're doing!" she screamed.

"If the line isn't too long," Libby said, looking at the shop windows. Esther's was a new kosher Italian restaurant that was supposed to serve fantastic pizza. Usually, the line was out the door, with a minimum of a forty-five-minute wait, although today it might be kind of fun to stand in line and people watch.

Bernie nodded and looked at her watch. So far they were making good time. Coming down from Longely had taken half an hour, and the traffic was moving in the city. When she got to Seventy-Fourth Street, she turned in and started looking for a parking space. Ten minutes later, she found one between Madison and Park Avenues.

"This is starting well," Bernie said to Libby as she got out of the van and stepped onto the sidewalk.

"Let's just hope it continues that way," Libby observed darkly as she watched Bernie walk over to the parking station.

"Ah, always the optimist," Bernie noted as she paid. "I figure an hour at the most."

Libby nodded absentmindedly. She went back to studying the three-hundred-year-old antique rug hanging in the window of a shop located on the ground floor of a five-story brownstone. "I wouldn't mind having one of those," she mused.

"When we win the lottery," Bernie said.

"I can't imagine putting something like that on the floor."

"Somehow, I don't think that's going to be your problem," Bernie retorted, and she started walking. Three minutes later she and her sister had arrived at their destination, 800 Park Avenue. The entrance to the building was on Park Avenue and the doorman, decked out in his uniform, was standing under the green canopy, looking very official.

"Can I help you?" he asked in a thick Irish brogue as the sisters approached him.

Libby stepped back and watched Bernie give the doorman her most charming smile. "Possibly."

The doorman, a man Bernie judged to be in his mid-twenties, waited for Bernie to continue speaking.

"I know this is a little irregular," she confided, lowering her voice so the doorman was forced to lean forward to hear her. "I hope you won't think badly of me when you hear what I have to say."

"Now, how could I ever think that of a lassie as attractive as you are?" he asked, smiling.

"Thank you," Bernie said, taking a step closer. "That's very sweet of you." She waited for a fire truck on Park Avenue, siren blaring, to pass by. "You see," Bernie explained, "my sister is about to get married." She pointed at Libby. The doorman nodded encouragingly. "And she needs to find a place to live for her and her hubby, a place that her mother-in-law will deem acceptable." Bernie rolled her eyes. "Only certain buildings will do. She's very picky."

"Ach. Aren't they all?" the doorman replied, thinking of his mother-in-law-to-be.

"Well, a family friend told us about what happened to poor Mr. Witherspoon," Bernie went on.

The doorman shook his head. "Terrible. Terrible, that was. A real tragedy. Such a nice man, too."

"Yes, it was. He must have been so in love with his wife to not be able to live without her." The newspapers had reported Darius's death as a suicide, although Bernie had a feeling that was going to change soon.

"He *must* have been in love to risk his immortal soul." The doorman shook his head at Darius's folly. "And Mrs. Witherspoon, poor thing," the doorman solemnly intoned. "What a horrible way to go." Word of her death had made the news yesterday afternoon. "Who knows where she was all this time?"

"That is the question, isn't it?" Bernie said.

"Maybe she got a knock on the noggin that took her memory clean away," the doorman posited. "If only Mr. Witherspoon had waited. Maybe if God is merciful, they'll be reunited in heaven for all eternity."

"Amen to that," Bernie replied, trying for sincere. "I only hope I can find someone I love that much someday," she said.

The doorman sighed. "True love is a wonderful thing, t'isnt it?"

Bernie nodded. "Indeed, it is." She paused for a moment to give them both time to contemplate true love with a capital *T* and a capital *L* before continuing. "I know it's early, but my sister was wondering . . ."

"If you could have a peek at their apartment?" the doorman asked, finishing Bernie's sentence for her. This wasn't the first request like this he'd had since he'd taken the job last year, and he was sure it wouldn't be the last.

"Exactly so," Bernie said. "Just a quick one. What, with the occupancy rate in the city being so high these days, finding a place to live has become quite the ordeal."

"Ninety-eight percent," the doorman replied.

Bernie shot him a look.

"I take a wee peek at the *Wall Street Journal* before delivering it," he explained. "It helps when talking to the owners."

Bernie understood. She kept up with all of Longely's local news for that reason. She nodded in her sister's direction. "She's already been outbid twice. The whole thing is becoming such a nightmare. And she's a little on the shy side."

"Indeed, apartments are going like that." The doorman snapped his fingers.

"And this is such a good building," Bernie said.

"Ay. That it is. One of the best," the doorman said. "Not many like it left."

"So I was wondering if you could let us up to take a quick look-see. We won't be that long."

The doorman put his hand to his chest. "It would be my job if anyone found out."

"No one will," Bernie assured him.

"But what if one of the co-op board members wants to come in and take a walk-through? Or an agent? What do I say then?"

"Do you have a cell phone?" Bernie asked.

"What kind of a question is that?" the doorman asked indignantly.

"I'll give you my number and one hundred—"

"Two hundred . . ."

"Fine. Two hundred dollars. Just call and we'll be out

the back door in an instant." Bernie raised her hand. "I promise. Please. We've driven all the way down from Westchester."

The doorman thought for a minute. "Ach. What's the harm? I'd hate to disappoint two pretty ladies."

Bernie thanked him, sent him her phone number, then reached in her pocket, palmed four fifty-dollar bills that she'd taken out of the register, and put them in the doorman's hand. He briefly glanced at them before depositing the money in his coat pocket. He opened the door and held it for Bernie and Libby.

"Fritz," he called out to the man standing by the elevator, "will you please show these young ladies apartment 2C? They need to get something out of there." And he winked at Bernie and Libby.

"Not a problem. It will be my pleasure." Fritz went to a box located in the side hall, opened the door, removed a key, and returned to the elevator. "This way, ladies," Fritz said, giving a little bow as he stepped inside. When Libby and Bernie got in, he closed the gate with a flourish, and they took off. Bernie spent the short ride studying her reflection in the mirror mounted on the back wall and looking at the leather bench sitting in front of the mirror.

When they arrived at the second floor, Fritz stopped the elevator, opened the gate, and got out. "Here we go," he said as he opened the door to 2C. "Just ring if you want anything," he instructed as a bell inside the elevator started going off. A minute later, Fritz was gone, and Libby and Bernie were standing in the entranceway to the Witherspoons' apartment.

# Chapter 34

The apartment was one of two on the floor. The entrance hall walls were covered with light green flocked wallpaper, a large mirror encased in a silver frame hung on the wall facing the elevator, and each apartment had a receptacle for umbrellas sitting by its respective door. Other than that, apart from two large etchings of Roman ruins on the walls, the area was bare. The sisters quickly stepped inside the apartment. The place smelled stale, the way places did when no one had been in them for a while.

"How much did you give the doorman?" Libby asked as Bernie closed the door behind them.

"Two hundred," Bernie said.

"Nothing like overpaying," Libby observed.

"It's Witherspoon's money," Bernie reminded her. "You know what they say. Easy come, easy go."

"I think in this case it's *easy go*," Libby said, pointing to the open drawers of the chest that stood in the middle of the hallway and the opened closet door and the coats lying on the floor. "I think it's fair to say someone has been here before us."

Bernie sighed. "Indeed it is. I'm putting my money on Darius's partner."

"Me too." Libby stepped out of her shoes and wiggled her toes. Ah, sweet relief. Her feet were killing her, and she'd walked what? Maybe five blocks. How Bernie could wear the heels she did was beyond her. "After all," she continued, "he was asking Manny for a package at the Berkshire Arms. So maybe he came here first, and when he couldn't find what he was looking for, he went up to the Berkshire Arms and asked, hoping it would be there."

"Or," Bernie said, a new idea having occurred to her, "maybe Darius's wife was doing the looking. We don't know what she was doing during the time she was missing. After all, she'd been missing for a while, and I presume she had a key, so getting in here wouldn't be a problem."

"But then one of the doormen would have seen her," Libby protested.

"Maybe one did," Bernie told her as she looked around. "Maybe he chose not to say anything. Maybe Penelope paid him not to say anything. Maybe she went in the back way at night and used the service elevator. Usually, the delivery entrance is locked after nine o'clock because no one is on duty in buildings like these. You can't get in unless you're a resident."

"But the doorman would have seen Darius's partner come up," Libby pointed out.

"Assuming he didn't have a key, most definitely."

"Maybe they've both been up here."

Bernie nodded. "Along with God knows who else." She decided she had a few more questions to ask the doorman when they went back downstairs. She had a feeling he hadn't been as forthcoming as he might have been.

Libby bit at her cuticle. "The bigger question, though, one that the doorman won't be able to answer, is, what was in the package?"

"If there was a package."

"Why wouldn't there be a package?"

Bernie shrugged. "There probably was."

Libby gestured toward the mess in the hallway. "Because someone was obviously looking for something. But did they find it? That's the question."

"Since we don't know what whoever it was, was looking for, we don't know."

"We know whoever it was, was looking for a package."

"Not really."

"Of course we do," Libby said indignantly. "Let's not make things even more complicated than they already are."

Bernie held up her hand. "I'm not. We're assuming they're looking for a package on the basis of what Manny said, but whoever was up here could have been looking for something else."

Libby rubbed her forehead. She was getting a headache. "Like the answer to world peace?"

"You know what Dad says."

"I know," Libby answered, repeating her dad's mantra with Bernie. "Never assume. Assuming makes an ass out of you and me."

They both looked at each other and laughed.

"We have no idea what we're looking for, do we?" Libby said.

"No. None," Bernie replied as she retied her dress. She'd forgotten why she didn't wear the dress a lot. It always came loose.

"So how are we going to know if we find it?" Libby asked.

Bernie shrugged. "We might not."

"Nice to know we're on top of the situation," Libby observed.

"I think so, too," Bernie replied, turning toward the hall closet. It was as good a place to start as any.

# Chapter 35

Bernie and Libby went through the closet. They picked up the coats, went through their pockets in case there was something of interest in them, then dropped them back on the floor. One thing was undeniable, Bernie decided: The Witherspoons owned a lot of outer garments. Especially Penelope. Bernie counted three mink coats, two Burberry trench coats, and a couple of expensive ski parkas, not to mention seven leather jackets and a variety of in-between coats of one kind or another, as well as a multitude of high-end scarves and boots.

"You could feed a village for a year on what the stuff in here costs," Bernie observed as she and Libby went through the closet's top shelf. It was fairly empty, except for some hats, a few rolls of wrapping paper, and, inexplicably, a bag filled with lightbulbs. "One thing is for sure, Penelope definitely had expensive taste and the money to indulge it."

Which got Bernie thinking. She thought back to the clothes she'd last seen Penelope in. She was almost positive they'd been from Old Navy. Now that seemed very un-Penelope-like to Bernie, given Penelope's background and what was in the hall closet. Had Penelope bought new clothes when she disappeared? Cheap clothes? Most likely. The implications were interesting. Bernie would bet she'd done it because she needed something to wear and she'd had to use cash.

She couldn't use her credit cards, because credit cards could be traced. It was suggestive, but of what? Possibly of the fact that whatever had happened to Penelope had occurred suddenly. It hadn't been planned. She hadn't had time to pack. Otherwise she wouldn't have been wearing the clothes she'd died in. So maybe her disappearance was voluntary, after all. But what would make her abandon a palatial Park Avenue apartment in the blink of an eye? That was the question.

Bernie was still thinking about it when she and Libby turned their attention to the chest in the hallway. For openers, it didn't fit in with the rest of the furnishings in the hallway. In fact, it stuck out like the proverbial sore thumb.

The other furnishings in the hallway were expensive. They looked as if they'd come from a chateau somewhere in France, and maybe they had, given Darius Witherspoon's business. The mirror over the chest, like the one in the hallway, was ornately carved. *Probably eighteenth century*, Bernie guessed, as were the chairs flanking the chest.

"I'd hate to sit on these," Libby said, pointing to them. They were carved out of mahogany and upholstered in a light green satin. "They look really uncomfortable."

"I'd be afraid I'd break them," Bernie said. "People's asses must have been a lot smaller back in the day."

Libby laughed as Bernie rested her hand on the chest.

"The chest looks Shaker to me," Bernie observed. "Or Amish or something like that." She didn't know enough about furniture's fine points to tell the difference. However, the design was simple. She thought the wood was pine. The top was scratched and scarred, and there were a few coffee cup stains toward the center. It looked like something you'd find in a camp in upstate New York.

"I wonder what this is doing here," Libby mused. "Maybe Darius was selling it."

"Doubtful. It doesn't look like his kind of merchandise," Bernie noted. "Maybe it had sentimental value to him. Maybe it was his mother's or a close relative's."

"Maybe," Libby said as she and Bernie bent over it and studied the contents of the pulled-out drawers.

The top drawer contained pens, pencils, old subway tokens, about five dollars' worth of loose change, a couple of embroidered women's handkerchiefs, and five small notebooks with spiral bindings, which had been shoved behind a large leather-bound book. The title read *The Atlas of Implausibility*.

"I like the title," Libby said as Bernie took out the book, opened it up, and began to leaf through it. Libby watched over Bernie's shoulder.

The book contained a number of maps of imaginary places, yet there was something familiar about them, something that neither Bernie nor Libby could put their finger on.

"I always was bad at geography," Libby noted as Bernie put the book down and took out the first notebook and opened it up. It was filled with random doodlings. Dates, initials, street names. Some were written in pencil; others in pen. It was obvious the notebook had been written in over a period of time.

Three other notebooks were filled with similar jottings, while the remaining one was empty.

"What do you think?" Bernie asked Libby as she put one of the notebooks in her tote.

"Darius's aide-mémoire?" Libby asked. She used to carry around a small notebook like these to jot down random stuff she had to or wanted to remember. As a matter of fact, the contents looked a little like hers. She pointed to a four-inch square sheet of lined paper taped to the bottom of the drawer. The writing on it read PROPERTY OF EZRA POLAND, EXPLORERS CLUB. "Well, at least we know where the chest of drawers comes from."

"I didn't know there was such a thing as an Explorers Club anymore," Bernie said.

"Me either," Libby replied, picturing a brownstone with a drawing room full of leather armchairs, maps, globes, and bookshelves, populated by men sipping brandies and puffing on pipes. "I kind of like the idea," Libby added as she went through the next three drawers.

They were all empty. There was nothing in any of them. Not even a penny or a pencil. Or maybe there had been, and whatever was in them was gone now, Libby thought as she fingered her pearls. Under the circumstances, there was really no way to tell.

"We should talk to Ezra Poland," Libby suggested.

Bernie nodded. "Definitely."

"I wonder if the notebooks and the atlas are his."

"There's only one way to find out," Bernie said, and she scooped them up and stuffed them in her tote.

Libby turned and looked at the apartment. "Can you imagine living in a place like this?"

"Frankly, no," Bernie replied. "It would be like living in a section of the Metropolitan Museum of Art."

"It's so uninviting," Libby observed. "I'd be scared to touch anything."

"Well, it certainly isn't the kind of place that would make you want to curl up on a cold winter night in front of a fire and sip hot chocolate," Bernie agreed.

"For sure," Libby said.

The hallway she and Bernie were standing in was quite large. In fact, Libby reflected, it was as large as Bernie's first studio apartment down in the East Village had been.

No. It was larger. The floor was made up of black-and-white marble tiles; the walls were painted a pale yellow and were covered with seventeenth- and eighteenth-century American paintings in elaborately carved gilt frames.

An oriental rug that looked remarkably similar to the one that Bernie and Libby had seen in the store window a few minutes ago lay on the floor. To the left was the kitchen, and to the right was what appeared to be a bedroom, while a small dining room was situated off the hallway next to the kitchen and was connected to it by a swinging door. In the rear was what Libby and Bernie took to be the living room. The blinds were drawn so that even though it was three o'clock, the room was dark. They stepped inside it.

"It's like a tomb in here," Libby remarked, rubbing her shoulders. "A very fancy tomb."

"They must have noise-canceling windows," Bernie noted, thinking about how quiet it was. They were on the second floor, but they didn't hear the traffic going down Park Avenue. Then she realized she didn't hear any sounds at all. "You're right. It is like a crypt."

"Is that the same as a tomb?"

"I believe so," Bernie said.

Libby waved her hand in the air, indicating the apartment. "The difference between this apartment and the one in the Berkeley Arms is like night and day," she observed.

"Literally," Bernie said. "The apartment in the Berkshire Arms is light, while this place is dark. This place is furnished with expensive antiques, while the Berkshire Arms apartment is furnished with expensive modern furniture."

"True," said Libby. She pointed to the large oriental on the floor. "I can't even imagine how much that cost."

"Probably more than our building," Bernie said as she and Libby got down to work.

They opened and closed cabinet drawers, lifted up the cushions that were on the chairs and sofas, and peered behind the painting on the wall, but all they got for their trouble was dust on their hands. If there was anything there, Bernie and Libby didn't see it. Of course, Bernie thought it didn't help that they didn't know what they were looking for.

A couple of minutes later they walked into the dining room. They both studied the crystal chandelier, the inlaid dining table with its six pushed-in chairs, the matching sideboard with its blue-and-white Chinese pottery, and the landscape oils on the wall. Nothing had been disturbed, and after a quick look around, the sisters moved on to the kitchen.

"At least no one has been through here," Bernie observed, taking in the closed kitchen cabinets.

Unlike the rest of the apartment, the kitchen was clearly an afterthought. The appliances were old, the white enameled sink was stained, and the red speckled linoleum floor was scratched.

"I bet the housekeeper did all the cooking," Libby said as she opened and closed cabinet doors and peeked in the refrigerator. There was nothing there that she wouldn't have expected to find.

"And the Witherspoons went out on her day off," Bernie added. She'd just found the housekeeper's uniform hanging in the utility closet. She sighed as she and Libby finished up and went into the Witherspoons' bedroom. She hoped there'd be something of use in there, although she wasn't too optimistic.

The bedroom was a surprisingly small but luxuriously furnished room. The bed was a four-poster worthy of Marie Antoinette, with an array of gleaming white sheets, mounds of pillows, and a pale blue duvet, a duvet that harmonized with the color of the walls and the pattern of the brocade drapes on the windows.

Two marble-topped nightstands holding two matching

blue-and-white Chinese vases that had been converted into lamps stood on either side of the bed. Two books on navigation rested on Darius's nightstand. He really was planning on taking some sort of sailing trip, Bernie thought as she paged through the books, looking for notes or underlining and not finding any. She sighed and opened up Darius's nightstand drawer. A collection of reading glasses, cough drops, and packs of tissues presented themselves.

While Bernie was doing that, Libby was going through Penelope's nightstand. Her reading material consisted of the most recent copy of *Vogue* and a variety of expensive shelter magazines, while her nightstand drawer contained a bottle of Ambien, a tube of lavender skin moisturizer, and a pair of reading glasses.

"Boy, she was neat," Libby commented, thinking of what was on her night table at home.

Bernie just grunted and went over and opened one of the closet doors. There were two closets, and Bernie knew she'd picked Penelope's when the smell of Joy wafted out into the room. Even at a quick glance, Bernie could tell that Penelope's clothes were like the coats and boots in the hall closet. Expensive. She was about to take a closer look when her phone started ringing. She extracted it from her tote, glanced at the screen, and started talking.

"Time to go?" she asked.

"Definitely," the doorman replied. "You need to get out now. People are on their way up."

"Will do." She stared at her sister. "Come on, Libby," Bernie cried, hanging up and jamming her phone back in her bag. "We gotta leave. People are coming."

"I knew this would happen," Libby complained as she and Bernie headed for the back of the kitchen, which was where the service door was located.

They rounded the corner at a run, Libby managing to stop herself from crashing into her sister as Bernie stopped short. Bernie grabbed the handle on the door and pulled. Nothing happened. It took her a second to realize why. The lock on the door was a dead bolt, and you needed a key to open dead bolts from the inside, as well as from the outside. A key she didn't have.

She wanted to kick herself. Of course the door would be locked. Why hadn't she thought of that? More to the point, why hadn't the doorman thought of that? Well, one thing was for sure. There was no time to call him and have him come up and unlock it.

"What now?" Libby demanded.

"I guess we'll have to go out the front."

"But the people are coming up the front," Libby wailed.

"Trust me," Bernie said. "It's going to be fine."

"Trusting you is what got us in this mess in the first place. We're going to be arrested!" Libby cried as her sister turned and headed for the front door. Libby was right behind her.

"No, we won't," Bernie said as she opened the front door. "Just act like you belong."

"Belong where?"

"Here, Libby, here." Then she glanced down at Libby's feet. "Oh my God." She put her hand to her mouth. "Shoes, Libby!" she cried. "Get your shoes on."

Libby glanced down. Her feet were bare. She'd taken her heels off and forgotten to put them back on. She dashed back to get them while Bernie held the door open.

"Hurry," Bernie urged. She could hear the elevator starting its ascent. It would be on the second floor any minute.

# Chapter 36

Libby and Bernie were standing in front of the elevator, chatting amiably, when the elevator door opened. Three well-dressed middle-aged people, whom Bernie estimated to be in their fifties, stepped out. Bernie smiled and nodded to them, and the woman and two men smiled and nodded back. Bernie noted that the woman was holding a key in her hand as she and Libby went back to chatting about the party they were supposedly catering.

"Tossed or chopped salad?" Bernie asked Libby. "That's the question."

The woman's ears perked up. "Oh," she said to Bernie. "Is Madeline planning a party?"

Bernie smiled and nodded and got into the elevator. Libby followed, and Fritz closed the gate. The elevator door shut, and Libby let out an audible sigh of relief. Fritz didn't say anything, just kept his eyes facing forward. A moment later, they arrived at the first floor.

"Lobby," Fritz announced, opening the door.

"Thanks," Bernie said.

"For what?" Fritz replied, keeping his face expressionless.

Bernie smiled her answer, and she and Libby stepped out.

"People see what they expect to see," Bernie explained to her sister as they both walked through the lobby. "As long as things don't deviate from what people expect to see, they don't question it. I mentioned salad, and the woman assumed I was catering an event for the people next door."

"What if she knew those people?"

"She obviously did. . . ."

"And what if this Madeline was home, and she knocked on her door?"

"But she didn't."

"But she could have." Libby pointed down to her feet. "Or what if you hadn't noticed that my shoes were off?"

"That would have been more of a problem," Bernie allowed as they walked out to the street.

The doorman was where they had left him. "You gave me a wee bit of a scare," he said when he saw Bernie and Libby.

"Me too," Libby said.

"So what did you think?" he asked Libby in his thick Irish brogue. "Are ye interested in the place or not?"

"Well, someone is," Bernie told him.

The doorman looked at her as if he didn't understand.

Bernie explained. "Someone went through the hall closet and the chest of drawers in the hallway."

The doorman clasped his hands together, brought them to his chest, and raised his eyes to heaven. "Faith, begorra, lassie. Who would do such a dastardly deed?"

"Faith, begorra, indeed. Here's what else I think," Bernie said. "I think you should drop the accent."

He looked at Bernie. "Too much?" he asked.

"Way too much," she replied. "And for the record, you completely forgot your accent when you called me."

The doorman shrugged. "What can I say? I panicked and broke character."

"Anyway, *lassie* is a Scotch word," Libby said.

"No, the Irish use it, too," the doorman said. "So I take it you're not looking for a place," he observed.

"You knew that all along, didn't you?" Libby asked.

The doorman smiled. "I didn't know. I suspected."

"Because other people have been up there?"

The doorman shrugged. "I'm here only three days a week. I have no idea what goes on the rest of the time."

Libby didn't believe him, but she didn't say that. Instead, she asked him, "Why the accent?"

"Simple," the doorman answered. "I needed a job, and this building hires only Irish, preferably straight from the countryside. Anyway, I'm half Irish. The second half is Puerto Rican."

"You're an actor?" Bernie asked, guessing.

The doorman grinned and clicked his heels together. "Flynn O'Brien, at your service. I've been in two commercials and a crowd scene for an indie movie, *The Werewolf and the Maiden*. You may have heard of it? It won an award for best editing in Toronto."

Bernie and Libby both shook their heads.

"Sorry," Bernie said.

For a moment the doorman looked crestfallen; then he brightened. "I'm in another movie shooting in Dumbo next week. De Niro is in it. I actually have a line. *Watch out*," Flynn said in a loud voice. "No. Too angry. *Watch out*," he said in a softer voice. "Too wishy-washy. *Watch out*," he said in a more peevish tone. "I think that's it. This kid is about to run into me because he's not looking where he's going," Flynn explained. "He's De Niro's grandson."

"In the movie?" Libby asked.

Flynn nodded. He looked off into the distance, and Bernie wondered what he was seeing. Then he shook his head and returned from wherever he had been. "Okay," he said.

"Now that we know that I'm an actor playing the part of a doorman, whom are you two playing the part of?"

"Detectives. We're looking into Darius Witherspoon's death," Libby answered.

Flynn raised an eyebrow. "You don't look official. Far from."

"That's because we're not," Bernie said.

Flynn grinned. "Just concerned citizens."

"Caterers, actually," Bernie said.

"I like the term *concerned citizens* better," Flynn mused. "It has a nicer ring. Sounds as if it could have come out of a thirties B movie." He straightened his hat. "But I thought Mr. Witherspoon hanged himself. Am I wrong? Because that's what the papers said."

"We think he might have had help," Bernie said.

"I see," the doorman said. He stroked his chin. "And you're saying this why?"

"Because Darius left us a note asking us to look into the matter if he died . . . or words to that effect."

Flynn stretched out his arm and pretended to read a headline. 'Murder on Park Avenue'. I like it," he said.

"Probably more than Darius did," Libby observed tartly.

Flynn looked chagrined. "Well, there is that."

"And it was Murder at the Berkshire Arms," Libby said, correcting him.

"You're very literal, aren't you?" Flynn said to Libby. Then he went on before she could answer. "Of course, there was that thing in the papers about his wife. That's fairly freaky."

"Isn't it, though?" Bernie replied.

"Were you the people that found her?" Flynn said, guessing. "The article said something about her being found hanging from a tree."

"Unfortunately, we did," Libby answered. "I don't suppose you saw her around after she disappeared?"

"No, I didn't," Flynn replied. Libby decided he looked as if he was telling the truth, but he was an actor, so who knew? "Why," Flynn continued, "would she turn up here, where everyone knows her, if she wanted to disappear?"

"Maybe she wanted something," Bernie suggested. "Maybe she was the one who went through the hall closet."

"She must have wanted whatever it was pretty badly to come back," Flynn observed.

"It wouldn't have been that big a risk," Bernie countered. "She had a key. She could have come in at night through the service entrance. No one would have seen her then."

The doorman thought for a minute. "Yeah, it's possible. It's true no one is officially on duty, but the night staff is around. She'd have to be lucky not to be seen."

"Maybe she *was* seen," Libby suggested. "Maybe she paid someone to forget her."

Flynn lifted up his hands. "Hey, don't ask me. I'm not on at night."

"Of course," Bernie continued. "It could be someone else. Has anyone else been around?"

Flynn didn't reply. He studied a pigeon pecking around the bottom of a gingko tree instead. Then he shrugged. "How would I know?"

"Because you let them up," Bernie guessed.

The doorman remained silent.

Bernie took a step closer. "Maybe I should tell the co-op board you're doing a little business on the side."

Flynn remained unfazed. "Here's another explanation. Perhaps Mr. Witherspoon left the apartment that way when he went up to Longely. Maybe *he* was the one looking for something. Have you thought of that?"

"As a matter of fact, I have," Bernie told him. "So that's your story, and you're sticking to it?"

Flynn nodded. "Indeed I am."

"So you deny that you or one of the staff here let some-one into the apartment after Mr. Witherspoon left?" Bernie asked.

"And how would I be knowing that?" Flynn said, falling back into his brogue again.

"Because you're the doorman, and doormen see all," Bernie answered.

"But we don't tell all," Flynn replied.

Libby frowned. "We could go to the board," she told him.

"Threats are a poor man's game," Flynn replied.

"What does that even mean?" Bernie asked.

"Frankly, I haven't a clue. But two can play that game, you know."

"What game?" Libby asked.

"Threats. I could call the police and tell them you were trying to bribe me to let you into the apartment." He shifted his weight from one foot to the other. "Come to that, how do I know you didn't make that mess in the closet your-self?"

"I guess we're at a stalemate," Bernie told him.

"I guess we are," Flynn said.

# Chapter 37

"I've been thinking," Bernie said after Flynn had returned from hailing a cab for a mother with a three-year-old boy.

"Always a good activity to engage in," Flynn observed. "So few people seem to be doing it these days."

"We shouldn't be fighting," Bernie continued. "After all, we both want the same thing."

"What? A cuddle and a kiss?" Flynn asked.

"That, too, but I was thinking we might want something a little closer to home. We both want to go on doing what we've been doing, right?"

"I'm listening," Flynn said.

"Neither one of us wants to get involved with the authorities," said Bernie. "So how about we cooperate and you tell me—what would it take to get you to tell us what we want to know?"

Flynn rubbed his fingers together in the universal gesture indicating money.

"That's ridiculous," Libby huffed. "We already gave you way more than we should have."

"And I fulfilled my part of the bargain," Flynn told her. "I let you up. But now you want something different. That's extra. After all, you don't go into a restaurant, order dinner, then add an extra side and not expect to get charged."

"You really have no shame," Libby snapped.

Flynn laughed. "Look who's talking. You can save the moral outrage stuff for someone else."

"Twenty bucks," Bernie said, naming a low figure. She'd decided Libby was right. The two hundred had been too much, and she wasn't going to make that mistake again.

"Cheapness doesn't become you," Flynn said after he had opened the door for a couple coming out of the building.

"I'm not being cheap," Bernie protested. "I'm being frugal."

Flynn grinned. "A tad too thrifty if you ask me. One hundred. You're asking me to break the confidentiality agreement I had to sign."

"Thirty."

"I'd have to pay thousands if I got caught," Flynn told Bernie.

Bernie frowned. "Forty, and that's as high as I go."

"Ninety."

"Fifty."

"Seventy-five, and you have a deal."

"But that's all the cash I have on me," Bernie lied.

Flynn smiled. "That's why God invented ATMs."

"Fine," Bernie grumped. "But I still think this is highway robbery. You have my two hundred."

"And my acting coach thanks you for it. If it'll help, consider this your contribution to the arts," Flynn told her. "When I collect my Oscar for Best Actor, I will thank you right after my mom, my dad, and my wife."

"How sweet. I will await the occurrence with bated breath," Bernie told him with a smile. "So who did you let up?"

"Whom," Flynn said, correcting her.

"What are you? The grammar police?" Bernie asked.

"My mother is an English teacher," Flynn explained. "I can't help it." Then he stopped talking and pointedly looked at the pocket from which Bernie had extracted two hundred dollars earlier.

"How do I know you're telling the truth?" Bernie asked as she slid her hand in her jacket pocket to get the money.

"How do I know you're not someone from the co-op board sent to entrap me?" countered Flynn.

"You don't," Libby said.

"Exactly my point," Flynn said. "I guess we'll just have to trust each other."

Bernie sighed. "I guess we will," she said, handing over the seventy-five dollars. "So whom did you let up?"

"His partner," Flynn answered promptly. "I let Darius Witherspoon's partner up."

"How long was he upstairs for?" Bernie asked.

Flynn thought for a moment. "He was in there for about an hour."

Libby tucked a strand of hair back in her French knot. "When did he go up?"

"About ten in the morning. Right after I came on duty."

"No. I mean, what day did he show up?"

"The morning after Mr. Witherspoon died," Flynn said.

"Did he say anything?" Bernie asked.

"No. He just handed me fifty bucks and said, 'I need the key.' But then, he wasn't a very talkative guy. No chitchat."

"Fifty bucks!" Bernie cried. She'd always prided herself on her bargaining skills; evidently, they weren't as good as she had thought they were.

Flynn shrugged. "The market bears what the market bears."

"What does that mean?" Bernie challenged.

"It means you're not getting your money back."

"I kinda figured," Bernie told him. "But it never hurts to try."

"Did the partner come here a lot?" Libby asked.

Flynn shook his head. "Mr. Peabody? Hardly ever. And never when Mr. Witherspoon was here. I don't think they got along. At all." He turned to Bernie. "See, I'm throwing that nugget of information in for free, so you won't think I'm a complete dick."

"I don't. I think you're a prince among men," Bernie told him. But she couldn't help smiling.

"Why are you saying that about Darius's partner?" Libby asked him.

Flynn shrugged his shoulders. "No reason, really. Just a feeling I got."

"So then who did he go up there to see?" Bernie asked.

Flynn looked at Bernie as if she was stupid. "The wife, of course. He went up to see Mr. Witherspoon's wife."

"Interesting," Bernie murmured as she wondered whether that would be a motive for murder. It could be, but the timing was off. You'd figure if that were the case, then Darius would have been the one to kill his wife, but he'd turned up dead first, so then who had killed Darius's wife?

Darius's partner? Had Septimus Peabody killed the wife and the husband? Had he been in the apartment to look for something that would link him to the double homicide? Love letters? Although, people didn't write those anymore. Or maybe this was about something else altogether. Maybe he and Darius had been in the middle of some kind of business deal that he didn't want anyone to know about, a deal that had gone sideways in a spectacular fashion.

"So are you saying the wife and the partner were having an affair?" Libby asked, wanting Flynn to clarify.

Flynn nodded. "Yeah. That's exactly what I'm saying."

"And you know this how?" Bernie asked.

"It's obvious," Flynn replied. "I mean, why else would the partner be going up there?"

"There could be other reasons," Libby told him.

"Like what?" Flynn demanded.

"I don't know. Maybe they were planning a surprise party for Darius. Maybe they were working on a Web site for the business."

Flynn snorted. "Seriously?"

"It *is* a possibility," Libby argued.

"An unlikely possibility," Flynn countered. "In my experience, when the hubby's away, the wifey will play."

"Not everything is about sex," Libby told him.

"No. Not everything," Flynn replied. "Just most things."

Libby was just thinking of a comeback when Bernie tapped her on the shoulder and pointed to her watch. It was almost four. Time to find Septimus Peabody and see what he had to say for himself.

Bernie asked Flynn one last question. "Did anyone else go up to the Witherspoons' apartment?"

"Not that I know of," Flynn replied. He raised his hand. "At least not on my shift. Scout's honor."

"Were you a Boy Scout?" Libby asked.

"No," Flynn answered. "I just like the way it sounds."

# Chapter 38

The Caldwell Gallery was located off of Eighty-Eighth Street and Madison Avenue, on the ground floor of a prewar apartment building. It was fifteen blocks from Darius Witherspoon's co-op to his gallery—a walkable distance, a walk Darius had taken twice a day, every day, since he was a man of regular habits. Bernie had wanted to walk there as well, but Libby had put the kibosh on it.

"Absolutely not," she said, pointing to her shoes.

Bernie let out the sigh of the long-suffering, but she turned around and headed for Mathilda. "Just don't blame me if we have to drive around for an hour looking for a parking space for the van," she grumbled. "It's not like she's small."

"Don't blame me," Libby retorted. "How about 'Don't blame you!' You're the one who made me wear these heels. You should have let me wear my flats."

"You can't wear those flats in public," Bernie declared.

"Because the fashion police are going to come and take me away?"

"No. Because they're a disgrace. They're held together with Shoe Goo," Bernie told her.

"That's a slight exaggeration."

"Not by much," Bernie told her as she got in Mathilda.

But as it turned out, the parking gods were kind, and Bernie found a spot for the van half a block down from the gallery. What kind of offering does one give the parking gods? Bernie wondered as she paid the meter and headed for the Caldwell. A can of high-test? An air freshener? A super-luxe detailing?

A tall, ash-blond-haired receptionist glanced up from her cell phone when Bernie and Libby walked through the door. There was something familiar about her, Bernie decided. She was positive she'd seen her before. Recently. She just couldn't remember where. But it would come to her eventually. It always did.

Bernie estimated the receptionist's age to be early twenties, but between the heavy foundation she was wearing, the bright pink eye shadow, and the black-rimmed eyeliner, it was difficult to tell. As she looked at her, Bernie's impression was one of angularity, and the heavy silver and turquoise necklace and matching cuffs the receptionist was wearing reinforced that impression, as they made the receptionist's arms and neck seem even longer than they were, and emphasized her knife blade–sharp cheekbones.

The slate-gray metal desk the receptionist was sitting behind echoed her angular lines. The desk was an ode to minimalism—not a good thing in Bernie's mind. In fact, Bernie decided, the desk looked like the stainless-steel prep tables they used in the kitchen, although she was willing to bet that this one was a lot more expensive than the ones she'd bought from the restaurant supply house. The desk's surface was completely bare except for a bulbous-shaped black metal lamp and a small metal nameplate. As Bernie looked around, it crossed her mind that she'd seen operating rooms that were cozier than this place was.

"Astrid," Bernie said, reading the receptionist's name off

the nameplate. "Is that Swedish?" It never hurt to start off pleasant.

Astrid's cell phone pinged. She held up a hand, then looked down at her cell, read the text, and began to type in an answer. Obviously, Bernie's question wasn't worth answering.

"Is Mr. Peabody in?" Bernie inquired, wondering as she asked if she'd been this obnoxious when she was in her twenties. Probably yes. The phrase *too cool for school* echoed in her head.

"You want to talk to him?" Astrid asked, not bothering to raise her eyes from her phone.

"No. I want to have wild, passionate sex," Bernie replied.

Astrid kept texting and didn't look up.

"An orgy."

Nothing.

"A threesome."

Still nothing.

"Yes, I want to talk to him," Bernie said, conceding defeat.

"He likes people to leave messages," Astrid informed her, still texting, her tone suggesting that only morons who were totally out of touch with the universe didn't know that.

"That's not going to work for us," Bernie replied.

Something in Bernie's voice penetrated Astrid's consciousness and made her glance up.

Bernie thought she saw a flicker of recognition pass over Astrid's face, but then it was gone, and Bernie didn't know whether she'd imagined it or not. "We need to talk to him," Bernie explained, trying to control her temper. "We have something he's going to want to see, something he's going to want to buy."

Astrid shook a stray lock of hair out of her face. "He's not acquiring anything right now," she announced, a smug tone in her voice. Unsaid was, "How could someone like you or your friend have anything my boss would be interested in buying?"

"I'm pretty sure he's going to want to see this," Bernie told her. She could see from Astrid's expression that she was not convinced.

"Like I said, I'll give him the message," Astrid replied, looking down at her cell phone again.

Libby stepped in and took over. "This is a time-sensitive matter," Libby told her.

Astrid frowned. "I said I'd tell him, didn't I?"

Libby was sure Astrid wouldn't do anything of the kind. On general principles. "How about writing it down?" she said.

Astrid gave her a blank look.

"The message. On paper," Libby said. "With a pen."

"We're paperless," she announced as she went back to her texting.

So far the exchange had definitely gone in Astrid's favor, Libby noted. She took a deep breath and let it out. "Do you have the back of a sales receipt I can use?" Libby asked, trying and failing to get the advantage back.

"We e-mail our receipts," Astrid informed her, not looking up from her phone. "Everyone does these days."

"Not everyone," Libby told her. "We don't."

Astrid didn't bothering answering. As Libby watched her, she wondered how the Caldwell Gallery did business. Especially with Astrid acting the way she was. What did the gallery sell, anyway? She knew it was supposed to be antiques, but she couldn't see any on display. Well, that wasn't quite true.

There was the spotlight-lit ceramic bowl in a niche over on the left wall. Libby went over and looked. It had an octopus painted on it. Then she read the neatly typed card enclosed in plastic next to it. According to the information, the bowl was Minoan. Four thousand years old. Found on the island of Crete. Price on request. Of course.

"Four thousand years. That's pretty old."

Astrid sighed at the observation.

"How much?" Libby asked out of curiosity.

"More than you can afford," Astrid snarked.

"How do you know how much we can afford?" Libby demanded. "We could be ultrarich."

Astrid looked her up and down, lifted an eyebrow, snorted, and went back to texting. Evidently, Bernie hadn't done as well outfit-wise as she thought she had.

Now it was Libby's turn to sigh. To be fair, she supposed that Astrid had a point. Most people who came in off the street didn't buy a four-thousand-year-old piece of pottery, nor, for that matter, did they sell one. Maybe this place was like the ultraexpensive dress stores Bernie liked to browse in. The more expensive the store, the less merchandise they had on display.

Libby shifted her weight from her left foot to her right. One thing was for sure: She was glad they hadn't decided to walk down to the gallery, because even though the heels she was wearing were only two inches high, they were killing her. How her sister managed to walk around in her four-inch stilettos and tight skirts was beyond her.

"We need to speak to your boss now," Libby said in as forceful a voice as she could manage, ignoring her stomach's rumbling. It had been so busy at the shop, she hadn't had time to eat lunch.

Astrid lifted her head again. "Well, I'm sorry, but Mr. Peabody is not here," she said, her eyes betraying her as she glanced toward a door in back of the store. It was a quick glance, but it was enough to call the door to Bernie's and Libby's attention.

They hadn't seen it at first, because the door was unobtrusive, disappearing into the cream-colored wall. The only thing giving it away was a thin line and two hinges. It wasn't supposed to be noticed, and neither Bernie nor Libby had noticed it when they'd entered, a not-great commentary on their detecting powers, Bernie reflected. But now they had.

"Thanks," Bernie said as she started toward it.

"You can't go in there!" Astrid cried, but it was a pro forma cry, one without heat, Bernie noted as she opened the door and she and Libby stepped through it into a different world, metaphorically speaking.

# Chapter 39

If the space on the other side of the door was Zen, all space and light, designed to call attention to whatever was in there, the back of the store was tomblike, smelling of dirt and decay. Narrow and dark and crammed with stuff, it concealed by virtue of the sheer volume of the matter within the space. The walls were covered with cheap floor-to-ceiling plank shelving, and all the shelves, in turn, were filled with pieces of statuary and pottery in various states of disrepair.

There were Greek and Roman pieces sitting cheek and jowl with pieces of Egyptian papyrus, alabaster jars, and funerary objects. Olmec masks, jade cats, Aztec statutes, Tang horses, pieces of blue-and-white pottery, clay tablets with cuneiform writing, and fragments of Norse helmets were jumbled together like pieces on a garage-sale table. As Bernie and Libby walked down the narrow corridor, they frequently had to turn sideways to avoid marble hands with hacked-off fingers reaching out to them, noseless heads with blank eyes that seemed to stare at them, and feet with missing toes.

At the end of the room was a workbench, and over it sat a series of cubbyholes filled with various tubes and paintbrushes, rags, small tins, unlabeled bottles with liquids, tiny screwdrivers and hammers, and large drills and bits. Here the air smelled of glue and paint and epoxy, making Libby feel slightly dizzy.

Septimus Peabody was standing in the rear of the room with his back to them. Bent over the workbench, he was holding a piece of a marble pedestal in one hand while he dipped a small paintbrush into a bowl of a liquid on the workbench with his other hand and carefully applied it to the bottom of the pedestal. He had earphones clamped on his head and was listening to Beethoven, which was why he didn't hear Bernie and Libby come in. Bernie watched him for a moment, then went over and tapped him on the shoulder. Septimus jumped and whirled around.

"Jeez!" he cried, almost spilling the liquid in the bowl.

Bernie apologized.

Septimus was not placated. "What the hell are you doing here?" he demanded, removing his earphones from his ears and hanging them on a red hook sticking out of one of the bottom cubbyholes.

"We need to speak to you," Bernie explained.

"Make an appointment," Septimus growled, balancing the paintbrush on the rim of the small bowl.

"This will just take a minute," Libby said.

"I don't care if it takes a second. You shouldn't be back here. Astrid shouldn't have let you in here."

"It wasn't her fault," Bernie replied. "She told us not to come in, but we did, anyway."

"And now you can get out." Septimus pointed to the door. "I have work to do."

Bernie tsk-tsked. "So rude. How about a *please* with that?"

Septimus's eyes narrowed. "How about you do what I say before I call the police?"

"On what grounds?" Bernie demanded.

"On the grounds that you're making a nuisance of yourself."

Bernie leaned against a middle shelf. A blue-and-white piece of pottery started to wobble. "Sorry," she said, steadying it just before it fell.

"See?" Septimus cried, shaking a finger at her. "That's what I'm talking about. This is why I don't want you in here. Do you have any idea how much that vase costs?"

Bernie shook her head. "I don't."

"Thousands and thousands of dollars."

Libby intervened. "It's about your partner. . . ."

"Very tragic, but I'm busy," Septimus snapped.

"This will just take a minute," Bernie said.

"Nothing ever takes a minute," Septimus observed bitterly. He looked at his watch. "I have an appointment in twenty minutes."

"That will be more than enough time," Bernie said and smiled reassuringly.

Septimus shook his head. "I doubt it."

"Wouldn't you like us out of here?" Bernie remarked. "I can see where we'd make you nervous. Especially since the fumes are making me light-headed."

Septimus pressed his lips together. "Is that a threat?"

"No," Bernie said. "Not at all. It's an observation. I'm just worried I might fall against a shelf when I leave."

Bernie watched Septimus's face as he did the math. "Fine," he said after a minute had gone by. "You win. Happy now?"

"Yes, I am," Bernie told him.

"I suppose when all is said and done, speaking to you will take less time," Septimus grumbled. "My office is a better place. Less chance of an accident."

"I'm sure that Darius would be grateful to you if he were alive," Bernie told him as she turned and started toward the door.

"And for heaven's sake, watch where you're going," Septimus called after her.

"I'm trying," Bernie responded as she edged around a large Greek amphora.

Astrid smiled as he came out into the gallery. "I'm so sorry, Seth . . . Mr. Peabody. I tried to stop them, but . . ."

Bernie noted Astrid's slip, but before she commented, Septimus waved his hands. "It's fine," he told Astrid. "Just bring us three bottles of water and come into the office and get me in fifteen minutes."

Astrid nodded and got up. As she did, Bernie noticed her shoes. They were lime-green suede gladiators that should have been ugly but were stunning instead. Suddenly, Bernie remembered where she had seen her before.

"You were at Darius's party," Bernie said to her. "I saw you standing in the common room, waiting to be interviewed by the police. You were wearing a black lace half mask and a strapless gown."

Astrid nodded.

Bernie turned to Septimus. "She was with you, wasn't she?" Bernie said, guessing.

Septimus nodded.

Bernie closed her eyes and visualized Septimus. When she'd seen him, he'd been standing by the open window, staring out, not saying anything, a point of stillness in a room full of people chattering hysterically while they waited to be interviewed. She turned back to Astrid. "I thought you looked familiar when I walked in, but I couldn't place you. It was the shoes," she explained. "I recognized the shoes."

Astrid smiled at Bernie and Libby for the first time. It was, Bernie decided, a nice smile. "They are wonderful, aren't they?" Then Astrid's smile dimmed. "I wish I had never gone to the party." She shook her head. "First, Mr. Witherspoon and then his wife." Penelope's death had made CNN. Astrid gave a delicate shudder. "He had to have done something. Opened something. I warned him not to. . . ."

"Not to what?" Libby asked.

Septimus gently interrupted Astrid as she began to talk. "I'll explain it to them. Just bring us the water, if you wouldn't mind."

"Of course," Astrid replied, smiling.

*There's definitely something going on between them,* Bernie thought. Then she wondered if what Flynn had said about Darius's wife and Septimus was true, after all. Septimus sure didn't look like a player, more like a middle-aged accountant, not that that meant anything. Sometimes guys like that were better in bed than the lookers, because they had to try harder.

# Chapter 40

Bernie and Libby were surprised at how ordinary Septimus Peabody's office was. The place could have been an insurance office. It contained a desk, three chairs, four dark blue metal file cabinets that looked as if they could have come from an office supply store, cream-colored walls, light gray wall-to-wall carpet on the floor, and a large Toulouse-Lautrec poster on the wall.

"The first piece of art I ever acquired," Septimus explained, gesturing to it. Then he gestured to the furnishings in the room as he sat down. "I find their lack of character very soothing."

"How so?" Libby asked.

Septimus explained. "Except for the poster, everything in this room is one hundred percent replaceable. And cheap. Given the nature of the things I work with, I find that idea extremely refreshing."

"I can see that," Bernie said as Astrid came in with three bottles of water and handed them out. "You two have a thing going, don't you?" she asked after Astrid left.

Septimus Peabody blushed. "Is it that obvious?"

"Yeah. To me it is," Bernie replied.

"I know what you're thinking," Septimus said.

"Tell me," Bernie commanded.

"You're thinking she's hot and I'm anything but. She's young and I'm . . . older. But we understand each other. We do," he insisted.

"I didn't say you didn't," Bernie replied. "I guess I was misinformed, because I thought Astrid had something going on with your partner."

"Hardly." Septimus drew himself up. "My partner"— he curled his lip—"wanted to sleep with her, and when she said no, he threatened to report her to Immigration."

"So what did you do?" Libby asked Septimus.

"We got married." He gave a little laugh. "And that's when we discovered we really liked each other. So in the long run, I guess you could say that Darius Witherspoon did me a favor. For once in his life."

Septimus unscrewed the top of his bottle of water, carefully put the cap down on his desk, and took a sip. "So," he said. "What's so urgent that you had to bully your way in to see me?"

"I hardly think that *bully* is the right word," Bernie objected.

"Fine." Septimus looked at Bernie. "We can use the word *threaten* if that will make you feel better."

"I don't think that's particularly accurate, either," Bernie replied.

Septimus tapped the face of his watch with one of his fingers. "We can debate semantics or we can get to why you came here in the first place. Time's a-wasting."

"Okay then," Bernie said. "Let's get to it. We're here because someone went into your partner's apartment and went through his things."

If Bernie was looking for an "Oh my God, she knows" moment from Septimus, she didn't get it. Instead, he put his water bottle on the desk, leaned back in his chair, and rested his hands on his belly. "And this concerns you how?"

"He was supposed to have left a package for us," Bernie lied. "It wasn't there. But someone went through the hall closet and the chest of drawers. We think maybe they took it."

"You were up in his apartment?" Septimus asked, his tone of voice as bland as his office.

"My sister just said that," Libby replied.

"I see." Septimus swiveled his chair first to the right and then to the left. "May I ask how you got in?"

Bernie lied again. "As a matter of fact, your partner left us his key."

"Convenient," Septimus said, not bothering to hide his skepticism. "And I take it your package wasn't there?"

"Bernie just told you that," Libby said.

"Which is why you're here."

"Exactly," Libby said. "We wondered if you knew anything about it. Perhaps Darius changed his mind and left it with you instead and forgot to tell us."

Septimus swiveled the chair he was sitting on around with his foot; then he swung it back again while he considered his answer. "I'm afraid I can't help you," he finally said. "I hope the package wasn't too valuable."

"It was important," Bernie replied, ad-libbing, admiring Septimus's tone of fake sympathy.

"Perhaps," Septimus said, postulating, "the person who took your package was someone to whom Darius owed money or some objet d'art? He did that a lot."

"What?" Libby asked.

"Owed people things." Septimus coughed and took a sip of water. "Perhaps this hypothetical person took your package in lieu of what was owed him. Or her."

"Did he owe you anything?" Bernie asked, looking Septimus in the eye.

"My, you are a cheeky little bugger, aren't you?"

Bernie didn't reply. She squinched her eyes and fixed Septimus with a hard stare, the way PIs did in the movies. He didn't look intimidated. Far from. Bernie was considering the fact that her outfit might be sending the wrong message when Septimus started talking.

"That's my business, wouldn't you say?" Septimus replied.

*This is going nowhere*, Bernie thought, deciding to try charm and flattery instead. The truth was she and Libby just weren't the intimidating type. She took a sip of water. "Do you repair the things in the other room?"

Septimus laughed. His laugh filled the room. "No. I restore antiquities. One does not *repair* items like these."

"It must require a lot of talent," Libby said, following her sister's lead.

"And knowledge," Bernie added.

"It does," Septimus agreed. "I have an advanced degree in art restoration." For a moment, his fingers seemed to caress the air, as if he was still working on the pedestal . . . "That's really my passion."

"Was it Darius's, too?" Libby asked.

Septimus's face darkened. "No. He fancied himself an expert in other areas."

Libby and Bernie waited for Septimus to explain. He didn't.

"So you repaired his things, as well?" Bernie asked, trying to keep the conversational ball rolling.

"That I did not," Septimus replied. "He sold smaller objects. Ephemera. Coins. Things of that nature. We didn't overlap. Actually, if I had to characterize him, I'd say he was more of a treasure hunter and less of an art historian."

That squared with what Bernie had read online. She

leaned forward. "So none of the stuff in your workshop belongs to him?" she asked, trying to clarify the matter.

Septimus shook his head. "No. It all belongs to clients or museums. I not only sell antiquities, but I restore them, as well. It's actually my bread and butter."

Bernie took another sip of water. "I get the feeling you didn't approve of how Darius conducted his business."

"I didn't," Septimus told her. "That's no secret. Not to put too fine a point on it, my partner was a huckster and a charlatan."

"If you felt that way, why did you go into business with him?" Libby asked.

"He wasn't like that when we started out." Septimus cracked his knuckles. The sound echoed in the room. "And when he offered me a partnership in a gallery on Madison Avenue . . . well, it was a once-in-a-lifetime opportunity. I knew Darius had these theories. I knew that he had dreams of glory. I knew he was always looking to make the next big find, archeologically speaking. But I never thought he'd go down the direction he'd selected to the extent that he did."

Bernie and Libby nodded sympathetically.

"Or perhaps he was always like that," Septimus mused. "And I didn't see it, because I didn't want to. But at the time, in the beginning, I thought he was fundamentally sound. And then . . . I don't know. . . . After a couple of years he started going down this path. . . ." Septimus's voice trailed off.

"What path?" Libby asked.

Septimus took a long drink of water. Libby and Bernie waited.

"Does this path have anything to do with what Astrid was talking about?" Bernie prompted.

"In a way," Septimus said, resuming speaking. "You might say it's a by-product of it. Darius organized these big treasure hunts—finding Noah's Ark, looking for Incan gold in the Amazon basin, in short *Raiders of the Lost Ark* kind of stuff. Big and flashy." Bernie didn't say she knew that. She didn't want to interrupt the flow. "But most of his expeditions were smaller covert affairs." He gave Bernie and Libby a meaningful look.

"Are you talking about grave robbing?" Bernie asked, taking a guess.

"I wouldn't put it that crudely, but let's say that Darius's procurement policies were more than a little lax. Anyway, there's a big market among a certain group of people for things . . . fetishes . . . voodoo objects . . . things with power . . . old things. . . . I don't know how else to explain it."

"Is that what Astrid was talking about?" Libby asked.

Septimus nodded. "You might think I'm ridiculous, but I didn't want that kind of stuff around the gallery. I felt it brought bad luck. And I was right. Look what happened to Darius and Penelope."

"So where did Darius keep this stuff?" Libby asked. She hadn't seen anything like that in his apartment.

"To my knowledge, he'd sold off all his inventory and was concentrating on his next big thing—whatever that was. At least, that's what I heard, but I'm not sure whether it's true or not."

"So there'd be nothing that anyone would want in his house?" Bernie asked.

Septimus shrugged. "I'm afraid I couldn't tell you. We each kept track of our own inventory."

Bernie nodded. "I'm sorry to have bothered you. I guess the neighbor was wrong."

Septimus cocked his head. It made him look like a robin, Bernie decided. There definitely was something birdish about him.

"Darius's next-door neighbor," Bernie explained. No

reason, she decided, to get Flynn in trouble. They might need him again soon. "She thought she saw you getting off the elevator and going into your partner's apartment right before Penelope went missing."

"Are you accusing me of something?" Septimus inquired in a tone that seemed more amused than angry.

"Not at all," Bernie replied, even though she was implying it.

Septimus nodded. "Good. It's true I have been in there from time to time," he told Bernie. "But not recently. This neighbor of yours must have gotten her dates mixed up." He ran a finger around the edge of the water bottle. Bernie noticed that he had freakishly big hands for his size, hands that looked as if they were made to chop down trees, not wield small brushes. "Now, let me ask you and your sister a question," Septimus continued. "Why are you really here?" When Libby started to explain, he added, "And don't bother to tell me the story about the missing package again, because it makes no sense."

"I thought it was rather good on short notice," Bernie answered.

"Well, it wasn't," Septimus told her.

Bernie and Libby exchanged glances.

"Go ahead," Libby told Bernie. "You might as well tell him."

"Actually," Bernie said, "we heard you and Astrid were looking for a package that Darius had supposedly left you."

"So?"

"So we were wondering what was in it."

"First of all, we weren't, and even if we were, it's none of your business."

"Suit yourself." Bernie leaned forward. "I'll tell you what *is* my business. You and Astrid were at the Berkshire Arms the nights that the Witherspoons were killed."

Septimus raised an eyebrow. "Aren't you using the wrong word?"

"No, my sister is not," Libby replied. "And we think you might have had something to do with it."

"Really?" Septimus chuckled. "I've never heard anything sillier in my life."

# Chapter 41

Bernie adjusted her dress, sat back in her chair, and studied Septimus. This wasn't the reaction she'd expected. Or hoped for. "I'm glad you find it funny."

"I don't find your accusations funny. I find them ludicrous," Septimus said.

"And why is that, pray tell?" Bernie asked.

"Because according to the news, while Penelope's death was a homicide, Darius committed suicide."

"We don't think it was," Libby replied.

"Because?" Septimus inquired.

"Because Darius asked us to look into his death," Libby told him.

Septimus knit his brows together. "Funny, but you and your sister don't strike me as the type of people who attend séances."

Bernie sneezed. She hoped she wasn't coming down with a cold, especially since she and Libby were entering their busiest time of the year. "We're not."

"Then how could my erstwhile partner have asked you to look into his death when he's already dead? Unless, of course, he did a Lazarus and rose from the grave."

"Not quite," Libby told Septimus. "I guess I wasn't clear enough."

"I guess you weren't," Septimus said.

"Darius left us an envelope to be opened in the event of his death."

"How very Agatha Christie of him," Septimus sniped.

Libby ignored him and continued on. "After he died, my sister opened it, per his request. She found five thousand dollars and a typed note asking us to investigate his demise. In other words, he saw what happened coming."

"So you say," Septimus said, crossing his arms over his chest.

"Indeed I do," Libby replied.

Septimus shook his head and studied his water bottle for a moment. "Ah. Leave it to my partner to cause trouble even when he's dead," he muttered to himself. Then he looked up. "But I still don't understand what there is to investigate. He killed himself."

"His note said he expected to be murdered," Bernie said.

"Murdered? Don't be ridiculous," Septimus scoffed. Then he went off on a rant. "He killed himself. I saw it, God help me. I only wish I could unsee it, and I'm sure that everyone who was there feels the same way I do. I mean, why he couldn't have had the decency to go off in the woods and shoot himself is beyond me. That would have been the right thing to do. But, of course, Darius wouldn't do that. Of course, he had to kill himself in a way that caused the maximum amount of trouble to his nearest and dearest, which is the way . . . *was* the way . . . he usually did things. No. I think he gathered everyone together so he could have an audience. So he could have his fifteen minutes of fame."

"It's hard to enjoy your fifteen minutes of fame when you're dead," Libby observed.

"Some people have more of a sense of history than others," Septimus replied.

"Be that as it may," Libby shot back, "given what you said, I'm surprised he invited you to his party and even more surprised that you accepted his invitation and brought Astrid along."

"It's important to keep up a facade," Septimus told her. "Anyway, I really came to see what Moran had done with the building."

"Are you by chance related to the Peabody who founded the Peabody School?" Libby asked. The possibility had intrigued her when she'd first thought of it.

"Very distantly. My mom said he was a shirttail relative."

"Did you go to school there?"

Septimus shook his head. "Good Lord, no. There was always . . . strange stuff happening there. Or maybe I just thought that because I was young. But I always thought the place was creepy. I think Moran did an excellent job rehabbing it." He took another drink of water. "So you two really don't think Darius committed suicide?" he asked, changing the subject back to his partner.

"No, we don't," Bernie answered. "My sister and I," Bernie said, pointing to Libby and herself, "think he had help hanging himself."

Septimus snorted. "The police declared Darius's death a suicide."

"The presence of Darius's note seems to indicate otherwise," Bernie said blandly.

"Of course it would. You have no idea who you're dealing with. None."

"Then why don't you tell us?" Libby said.

Septimus checked the time on his watch, then looked back up at Bernie and Libby. "Indeed, I shall, because I don't want you or your sister under any illusions." He cleared his throat. "Hanging himself the way he did has all the earmarks of something Darius would do. He was all drama, all the time. He never had any regard for how other people fit into the equation. That's probably why Penelope ran off the way she did, poor thing. She couldn't take it anymore. She was thinking of getting a divorce from Darius, and I was advising her about the business aspect of things."

"Such as?" Bernie asked.

"She was a partner in Caldwell—actually, she had put up the capital—and I was trying to convince her to remove Darius from our partnership. Before she disappeared, we were discussing the legalities and ramifications of that course of action."

"Why would you want to do that?" Libby asked.

Septimus frowned. "Because my partner was getting worse and worse. In a business where your word is your bond, to lie is to court disaster, both literally and figuratively."

"What was Darius lying about?" Libby asked.

Septimus's frown threatened to bisect his face. "As I said, he was a treasure hunter, and he was very, very convincing about his projects. He even had his wife convinced that his next big trip—whatever that was—was going to be successful." He pointed to himself. "I was trying to convince her that this one would be no different than the others." Septimus leaned forward and tapped the desk with his index finger for emphasis. "Even though he led those trips under another name, their failures impacted the gallery."

"Gus Moran seems to think the expedition would have been a success."

Septimus shook his head. "I will never understand people. This was the person who marched in here in a homicidal rage and threatened to kill Darius, and now he's going on another trip with him? Unbelievable."

"And you couldn't get him to stop?" Libby asked.

"Don't you think I would have if I could? He was absolutely intransigent on the subject. Said I was just jealous. Truth be told, we hadn't talked to each other in ten years. I just couldn't deal with his shenanigans."

"Then how did you do business?" Libby asked.

"Simple," Septimus replied. "We alternated weeks. One week I was here, and the following week he was here. For all intents and purposes, we ran different businesses out of one store. We overlapped as little as possible. It was easier that way, although in retrospect, it wasn't such a good idea." He looked at his watch again. "My appointment will be here soon."

"One last thing," Bernie said, taking one of the notebooks she'd found in the chest drawer in Darius's apartment out of her tote. "Darius sent us this," she lied. "Do you know what it is?"

Septimus reached over and took it. It nearly vanished in his large hand. "No, I don't," he said, paging through it. "It's definitely his handwriting, though. I'd say he was taking notes of some sort. It has all the earmarks of his lack of a system." Septimus handed the notebook back. "Was there anything else with it?"

Libby shook her head. "Just more of the same."

"I wonder what happens to the business now that Darius is dead?" Bernie mused when she and Libby were back out on the sidewalk.

"And Penelope. Don't forget about her."

"I wasn't," Bernie said.

"Septimus must get it," Libby said. "After all, there's no

one else left, which is very convenient," she observed. "New wife, new business—metaphorically speaking."

"Do you think he was having an affair with Penelope?" Bernie asked.

Libby shook her head. "No. I did, but I don't now," she said as they headed for the van.

Bernie skirted a lady with a double stroller. "Well, he didn't seem too broken up about Penelope's death."

"That's for sure." Libby looked at the sky. The clouds had moved in. "So do you think he's our perp, to coin a phrase? Do you think he killed the Witherspoons?"

"I wouldn't rule him out," Bernie replied. "After all, he was in both places when each of the Witherspoons died, he has a motive, and Darius probably would have let Septimus into his apartment." She paused. "And then there's Astrid," she added.

"Indeed there is," Libby agreed. "After all, she was there, too, and if Septimus is to be believed, she had a good reason for hating him."

"Maybe Astrid and Septimus did it together," Bernie posited. "You know, the couple that slays together stays together."

"Although, I can't see her making that kind of effort," Libby observed. "That would be so uncool."

"Maybe she has hidden depths of emotion," Bernie said.

"Maybe," Libby said, although she didn't think so.

Bernie stifled a yawn. "We did stir the pot a little. Now let's see what happens." Bernie looked at her watch. If they hurried, they could get some pizza at Esther's. And a couple of beers. Definitely a couple of beers. "We're missing something."

"I know," Libby replied. She just had no idea what it was.

# Chapter 42

"I don't see why we're out here in the middle of the night," Libby complained as she stumbled over a tree root and nearly fell. It was the following evening, and she, Marvin, and Bernie were down by the edge of the Hudson River. Although it was fifty degrees out, the wind blowing off the water made it feel a lot colder.

"It's not the middle of the night," Bernie pointed out, wishing that she had a warmer jacket on. "It's eight o'clock."

"Well, it feels like the middle of the night to me," Libby carped. "We could have waited until the morning. We could be back at RJ's, shooting a game of pool."

"You don't like pool, Libby."

"Well, I like it better than freezing my tush off out here."

"Look at me," Bernie told her sister. "I'm wearing a silk shirtdress and a sweater, and you don't hear me complaining."

"If you want to dress inappropriately, that's your business," Libby snapped.

Bernie didn't reply, but she wondered if her sister was right—not about dressing inappropriately, but about being here now. What Libby had said was true. This could have waited until the morning, when they would actually be able to see what they were doing, instead of stumbling around in the dark with nothing but a couple of flashlights, and not great ones, either.

On the other hand, who knew what tomorrow would bring? There could be another crisis at the shop, and they might not get the chance to come out here again for a day or two. And Bernie had a feeling that they were going to find something down here, something that was going to help explain who had killed the Witherspoons and why. She was about to tell Libby that, but her sister spoke first.

"And Phil even admitted he was drunk. He was probably seeing things," Libby added for good measure. "I mean, he's, like, the official town drunk."

"Phil Craven *is* the official town drunk," Marvin said.

"What if he wasn't seeing things?" Bernie asked as she moved her flashlight over the ground. "What then?"

"But he probably was," Libby told her. "We're on a wild-goose chase."

"What does that expression mean, anyway?" Bernie asked. "Why a wild-goose chase? Why not a wild-rabbit or wild-bunny chase?"

Libby thought for a moment. "I have no idea, but that doesn't change the fact that Phil hallucinates."

"Not all the time."

"But sometimes."

"Okay. He does," Bernie replied. "I admit that. But again I ask, what if what he was seeing was real? Then what?"

"All I'm sayin' is that it's bad enough to be here during the day," Libby said, indicating the Berkshire Arms with a wave of her hand, "but at night . . ." She shivered.

"Don't wimp out on me now," Bernie told her. "We got down off the roof, didn't we?"

"What does that have to do with this?" Libby asked.

"Nothing. I'm just trying to bolster your self-esteem."

"My self-esteem doesn't need bolstering, thank you very much. All I'm saying is that this place is creepy."

"Libby's right. It is," Marvin agreed, jumping into the fray.

"I didn't think you believed in ghosts, Marvin," Bernie said.

"I don't," Marvin said. "I've never seen one, and neither has my dad, but that doesn't mean I like it down here. It's dark, and you can't see where you're going." There was something else, as well, but he couldn't put it into words. He rubbed his arms. The jacket he was wearing wasn't warm enough. "Can we get on with this before we catch pneumonia?"

He had been at RJ's, having a beer and listening to Bernie and Libby tell Brandon about yesterday's talk with Septimus Peabody and Astrid. They'd just finished their story when a host from one of those TV talk shows that dealt with the latest crime story had started yammering on about the strange circumstances of Penelope Witherspoon's death. That was how the commentator had put it. *The strange circumstances.* Libby had been about to comment on it when Phil Craven turned to them.

"I saw her, you know," he'd said, pointing at the TV.

"The commentator?" Libby had asked, turning her head away so she wouldn't have to smell Phil's breath.

"No. Penelope Witherspoon." Phil had crossed himself twice. "She was dead."

"She certainly is," Bernie said, remembering what Penelope had looked like when they'd last seen her. "No doubt about that."

Phil drained his glass and held it out for another shot of rye. Brandon filled it up. He'd learned a while ago that there was no point in cutting Phil off. If he did, Phil would just head over to another bar. At least this way Brandon had his keys and would drive him home at the end of his shift.

"No," Phil told her after he'd drained his glass again and wiped his mouth off with his sleeve. "This was before she was *dead* dead. I saw her at night. I saw her coming out of the water and going into the old place. She was glowing."

"Glowing?" Libby asked.

Phil nodded his head vigorously. "Her boobs. Like a zombie."

"Zombie boobs don't glow," Marvin told him. "It's a well-known fact," he said in answer to Libby's raised eyebrow.

Phil grimaced. "This one's did."

"When did you see her?" Bernie asked, although she knew her chances of getting an answer were remote.

Phil just stared at her, his eyes blinking.

"Did you see her before or after you got your welfare check cashed?" Brandon asked him.

Phil thought for a minute. "Before."

Brandon turned to Bernie. "You just have to know the right way to ask a question," he told her.

"She came out of the water, all wet and slimy. She was dripping." Phil's voice rose. "I thought she was going to kill and eat me."

"Only if she liked pickled meat," Bernie couldn't resist saying.

Brandon shot her a dirty look as he reached across the bar and laid a restraining hand on Phil. "Easy does it."

"But I did see her. I did," Phil insisted, his voice getting louder.

"No one said you didn't," Brandon told him in a soothing voice. He poured him another drink.

Phil picked it up and downed it. His hand was shaking so badly, he had trouble connecting the glass to his mouth.

"So where did this happen?" Libby asked.

"On the riverbank. Down below the haunted place. Near the old house. The brick one."

"You mean the house below the Berkshire Arms?" Bernie asked. "The one that's falling down?"

Phil nodded, his eyes wide with terror. "I saw her," Phil said again. He hiccuped. "I did. She was dead before they say she was."

"What did you do when you saw her?" Bernie asked. She had a feeling there was more to the story than Phil was telling.

"I passed out," Phil said. "I don't know what time it was, but it was light when I woke up."

"And then?" Bernie prompted.

Phil lowered his voice. "I heard this noise."

Bernie nodded.

"And I saw this guy going into the house."

"The one that's falling apart?" Libby said.

Phil nodded again.

"And then what did you do?" Libby asked.

"I ran," Phil said. "I ran as fast as I could."

"What did this man look like?" Bernie asked.

"He looked scary, and he was carrying something."

"What?" asked Bernie.

"One of those shopping bag kind of things."

"A tote?" Bernie asked.

But Phil didn't answer. He had put his head down on the bar and gone to sleep. A faint snore escaped his lips.

"Interesting," Bernie said, taking another sip of her beer. "We should investigate."

And that was the reason that she, Libby, and Marvin were mucking around near the Hudson.

# Chapter 43

"I don't know what we're looking for," Libby complained as she played her flashlight over the dirt. She could hear the sound of rushing water below.

"Neither do I," Bernie confessed.

"That seems to be the leitmotif of this case," Libby noted.

"Then why are we here?" Marvin asked. "Remind me."

"Because," Bernie said, speaking to him while she kept her eyes to the ground, "I think Phil saw something that scared the crap out of him, and I want to know what it was."

At the moment what she saw were beer bottles and cans and fast-food wrappers that people had left behind, pieces of plastic that had washed up from the river, fishing lures, a couple of old lifesavers, a couple of tires, charred pieces of wood from campfires, and a moldy old sleeping bag as she slowly made her way to the house Phil had mentioned.

It wasn't a house, actually. It was a cottage, and it had been there as long as Bernie could remember. Legend had it that a man from New York City had built it for his wife because she loved to paint the Hudson River. They'd come up often, but five years after he built it, his wife had taken their boat out on a summer's day. An unexpected storm had come up, the boat had capsized, and the wife had drowned, her body claimed by the river, never to be found. The husband, unhinged by grief, had never come back to the house, abandoning it to the mercy of the weather and the vines.

Later, when Bernie was in college, she'd learned the true story. A contractor down in New York City had actually built the house as an investment property, but the contractor had gone broke, and the property had lingered in bankruptcy hell until it was too late to salvage. It was still up for sale, but because of its proximity to the river, no one wanted it. In truth, though, Bernie preferred the first version of the story, so that was the one that she told.

Bernie and her friends had hung out there a fair amount when she'd been in high school and on her college vacations. They'd drunk beer and built fires, eaten hot dogs and told ghost stories. From the look of the garbage on the floor when Bernie stepped inside, she figured that the tradition was continuing. Libby and Marvin followed her in a moment later.

"You never came down here, did you?" Bernie asked Libby.

Libby shook her head. "I never saw the point."

"It was fun."

"Not to me," Libby replied.

"Is it safe?" Marvin asked as he took in the sloping floor, the leaning walls, and the hole in the roof where the shingles had rotted out.

"Just watch out for the rats," Bernie told him.

"She's teasing," Libby told Marvin.

"Actually, I'm not," Bernie said. "And the floor."

"What's wrong with the floor?" Marvin asked.

"Some of the boards are rotten."

"So I could fall through?" Marvin demanded.

"Yup," Bernie replied. "To the tunnels down below. Hopefully, the vampires won't get you."

"Har. Har. Har," Marvin replied. He took a step, and a floorboard groaned. He jumped.

"I was kidding," Bernie told him as she got busy looking around. "The floor is fine in here. The vampires are a little more problematic."

"Good to know," Marvin said, having resolved to stick to the room's outer perimeter. He was just here for moral support, anyway.

"It'll be fine as long as we keep to this room," Bernie told him. The floors in the rest of the house *were* pretty much gone, as she and her friends had found out when they'd gone exploring and one of them had fallen through to the basement.

"I'm surprised some developer hasn't torn this place down yet and built something else," Marvin observed as he moved an abandoned bird's nest aside with his foot.

"The asking price must be really high," Libby noted.

"But still," Marvin said.

Libby said, "And then there's flood insurance, which doesn't come cheap these days."

"No, it doesn't," Marvin conceded.

Bernie ignored their chatter while she played her flashlight over what had once been the living room. The middle of the space was occupied by a sofa, two chairs, and a coffee table, all of them contorted, mildewed reminders of what they had once been. The carpet had disintegrated into a remnant of its former self, as had the wicker rocker and table over by a glassless window through which a small weed tree was beginning to sprout.

The walls were covered with dusty cobwebs, while beer cans and food wrappers, bird droppings, and a sprinkling of cigarette butts littered the floor. Over in the far right-hand corner, Bernie spied what looked like a pile of some-thing—she wasn't sure what—sitting on the floor. She went over to investigate. As she squatted down beside it to get a better look, she heard a sharp crack. *Oh no,* Bernie thought. *I should never have teased Marvin. He's right. The floor is about to give way.* But then she realized she was still where she had been, and she continued her inves-tigation.

"What is it?" Libby asked, coming up behind her.

Bernie reached over, picked up a piece of fabric, and held it up. As she did, a large spider dropped off and scut-tled across the floor.

Libby screamed. She hated spiders.

"At least it wasn't a rat," Bernie observed.

Libby took a deep breath. *Focus,* she told herself. The sooner they looked through everything, the sooner they'd get out of there. "A dress?" Libby said, guessing, as she played her flashlight over it. It smelled of river water and mold.

"Definitely a dress," Bernie said, straightening up. She held the dress out in front of her with both hands. She couldn't tell what color it was now, but it was a knit, and she could see outlines of a zigzag pattern in the fabric. Patches of gray mold dotted the front of the dress. "You know," she said, thinking out loud, "you can get phospho-rescence from the ocean. I wonder if it occurs in the river, as well."

"Why do you want to know?" Marvin asked.

"I was thinking about Phil's story," Bernie answered. "He said Penelope's boobs were glowing. Maybe they were."

"I think that's a stretch," Marvin said.

"Maybe," Bernie said as she turned the neckline inside out to look for a dress label. "I think it's Missoni," she said. "See," she said, pointing out the *m*, the *s*, and the *i* at the end of the name, the rest of the letters having disappeared, covered over with muck.

"What's a Missoni?" Marvin asked.

"An expensive Italian brand," Bernie replied. She thought about the clothes in Penelope's closet. There had been two Missoni dresses hanging in there.

She squatted back down to see what else was in the pile. She came up with a bra, a pair of panties, and a shopping bag from Gristedes. There was a Gristedes close to the Witherspoons' New York City apartment, as well as one on the other side of Longely, and that one was near Old Navy. Bernie picked up the remaining items and stood up.

"You know what I think?" she asked.

"Enlighten us, O great one," Libby responded.

Bernie raised the dress. "I think this dress belonged to Penelope. I think you guys might owe Phil an apology."

"And why is that?" Libby asked.

"Because I think he was telling the truth," Bernie answered.

"I don't understand," Marvin said.

"I do," Libby replied as her sister took her cell out of her pocket and dialed Brandon.

"Phil is still there," she told Libby and Marvin when she was through talking. "Brandon's going to try to wake him up so we can talk to him." She turned to Marvin. "I'll explain everything on the way over." Then she turned to Libby. "We need to go back down to the city tomorrow."

Libby didn't argue. She had come to the same conclusion herself.

# Chapter 44

It was a dreary, blustery Wednesday afternoon when Bernie and Libby drove into Manhattan, the kind of afternoon that made you think about the winter to come. Libby found a parking space on Seventy-Third Street, between Lexington and Park, and pulled into it.

Bernie got out and buttoned up her coat against the wind—the coat was Italian, mohair, light blue, and she'd gotten it at Barneys on sale last spring—then bought an hour's worth of time on the meter. She didn't think her and Libby's conversation with Flynn would take that long. Either he would tell them what they wanted to know or he wouldn't, but it wasn't worth risking a parking ticket and having to shell out the fine.

The sisters spotted Flynn half a block down. He was standing in the street in front of his building, hailing a cab for two women. By the time Bernie and Libby reached him, he'd succeeded in flagging a taxi and settling the two women inside it. He was stepping back onto the sidewalk when he saw Bernie and Libby. He smiled. They didn't smile back.

"And what can I do for you two beautiful ladies today?"

he asked when they got within hailing distance. This time there wasn't a trace of a brogue in his speech.

"We have a question for you," Bernie said.

Flynn gave a quick bow. "Always happy to be of service."

"I don't think you've been entirely forthcoming with us," Libby said.

Flynn pointed to himself. "Me? You cut me to the quick. I am utterly desolate at your accusation."

Libby put her hands on her hips. "I just bet you are."

"But I am," Flynn protested.

"He is, Libby," Bernie said. "Can't you see the expression on his face?"

Libby mimed studying it. "You're right, Bernie. He does look penitent."

Flynn smiled another smile. "Penitent is my middle name. It comes from being raised Catholic. Now, what have I done to offend you two?" he said.

"It's what you haven't done that offends us," Bernie countered.

Flynn cocked his head. "Which is?"

"Tell the truth."

Flynn crossed himself with his right hand. "Cross my heart and hope to die if I haven't."

Bernie rolled her eyes.

"Ask me," Flynn said. "Ask me anything at all."

"Fine," Bernie said. "Your shift begins at five a.m., doesn't it?"

Flynn fiddled with a button on his coat. "May I ask why you want to know?" he inquired.

Bernie thought he looked alarmed, but she wasn't sure if she was reading him correctly. "So I take it that's a yes?"

"I didn't say that," Flynn said.

"You didn't not say it, either," Bernie pointed out.

"Why do you want to know?" Flynn shot back, all traces of good humor gone.

"What happened to 'Ask me, ask me anything at all'?" Libby demanded.

Flynn didn't reply.

"I didn't know it was a state secret," Libby observed.

"It's none of your business is what it is," Flynn told her.

Libby turned her collar up against the wind that was tunneling down the street. "Is that even an English sentence?"

Flynn snorted. "Stop with the shtick. You're not that good at it."

"I thought we were," Bernie said.

"Well, you're not," Flynn replied. "Now, tell me what this is about."

Bernie looked at Libby. "Do you want to explain, or should I?" she asked her sister.

"I will," Libby said. "In essence," she began, "this is what we think. We think that contrary to what you told us, you saw the Witherspoons leaving their apartment through the service entrance together early on the day Penelope supposedly disappeared."

"Supposedly?" Flynn said. "There's no supposedly about it. She was gone."

"Yes and no," Libby told him.

"Which is it?" Flynn demanded.

"A little of both," Libby said.

"What we're fairly certain of," said Bernie, taking over the narrative, "is that contrary to what Darius said, he and his wife both left here together, and the thing is, we think that you saw them going out."

"Because you have that shift," Libby put in.

"How do you know what my shift is?" Flynn inquired.

Bernie explained. "We have a friend called Eric who

works as a doorman in a building down the street. I called him yesterday. Evidently, he knows you, and to the best of his memory, you had coffee with him on that particular day."

"He could be mistaken," Flynn countered.

"Yes, he could be," Libby replied. "But given the way you're acting, I don't think he is."

"And even if I was here," Flynn added, "that doesn't mean I saw them. This is a big place."

"I also think," Bernie continued, ignoring Flynn's protests, "that Darius paid you *not* to say anything to anyone."

"I resent that," Flynn cried.

"Well, given the circumstances, it certainly doesn't put you in a very good light," Bernie allowed.

Flynn looked from one sister to the other and back again. "You're just guessing. You have no proof. No proof at all."

"That's true," Bernie told him. "We don't. But here's what we do have. We found Penelope's dress in an old house down by the river."

"So what?" Flynn demanded. "That has nothing to do with me."

"You know," Libby told him, changing the subject, "underneath everything, I think you're a pretty nice guy. I would think your conscience has been bothering you since Penelope Witherspoon disappeared. I'd think you'd want to know what happened to her."

"I know what happened to her," Flynn retorted. "Someone put a rope around her neck and hung her from a tree."

"Let me clarify," Libby said. "I'd think you'd want to know what happened to her *between* the time that she left here and the time of her death."

Flynn raised an eyebrow. "And you can tell me that?"

"We can guess at some of it," Libby answered. "We think we know part of the puzzle."

"Good for you," Flynn said. "I think you should leave now." And he turned to go inside.

"It's not your fault," Bernie called after him. "I'm sure Darius told you a convincing story."

Flynn disappeared into the lobby. Bernie watched the revolving door turn.

# Chapter 45

"Well, that was a waste of time," Libby observed as she stuck her hands into her coat pockets. One day it was warm and sunny; the next day it was just plain nasty. It made both menu planning and dressing difficult because it was impossible to predict what to expect.

"Not really," Bernie said. "Given Flynn's reaction, we know that our guess is correct."

Libby shook her head. "We know no such thing."

"He practically confessed, Libby."

"Then you and I were listening to two different conversations." Libby turned to go, but Bernie laid a hand on her shoulder.

"Give him a couple of minutes," she told her sister. "I think he's going to come back."

Libby snorted. "A dollar says he doesn't, Bernie."

"Make it two, and you're on."

"Done," Libby said. She looked at her watch. "Two minutes."

The minute hand on her watch was just making its second round when the side door opened and Flynn came out.

"Damn," Libby said, cursing under her breath.

"You never learn," Bernie said, holding out her hand.

"You're one to talk," Libby replied as she dug into her pocket and came up with a crumpled dollar bill and another dollar in change. "Here," she said, slapping the money onto Bernie's outstretched palm.

"Is that chocolate on the tops of those quarters?" Bernie asked, studying the money.

"M&M's. I can take them back if you want."

"No need," Bernie said as Flynn reached them.

"I didn't think it mattered, okay? I didn't think it was a big deal," he told Bernie and Libby.

"I think it may be," Libby said gently.

"I thought I was doing a good thing," Flynn explained, a pleading note in his voice.

"I'm sure you did," Bernie said. She reached over and patted his arm reassuringly.

A flicker of gratitude crossed Flynn's face and died. He rubbed his hands together and shook his head ruefully. "I wanted to believe him. Maybe I wouldn't have if my rent were cheaper."

"Maybe," Libby said.

"It's just that I really need every cent that I can get."

"I'm sure you do," Libby said.

Flynn shook his head again. "I can't believe I fell for his story. I can't believe I was such an idiot."

"If it's any consolation, I think Darius is—excuse me—*was* a pretty good liar," Libby told him.

"It's not," Flynn said. "I lie for a living. I should have spotted it."

"I wouldn't call acting lying," Bernie said.

"Maybe you're right," Flynn said, rethinking his previous comment. He broke off speaking and tipped his hat to a well-dressed man in a camel's hair coat and a teenage boy with his pants riding down around his butt as they came out of the building. A moment later, a chauffeur-driven black town car glided up to the curb. Flynn hurried over to the car and opened the door to the backseat. The man and the boy climbed in. Flynn closed the door, and the town car sped away.

"Stepfather and son. They're not getting along too well," Flynn explained as he, Bernie, and Libby watched the town car head toward Madison Avenue. "Having a stepparent must be rough—especially when you're a teenager."

"It can be rough at any age," Libby said, thinking about Michelle and her dad. "So what did Darius tell you?"

Flynn took a deep breath, let it out, and began. "He said that Penelope had been involved in a bad business deal and that she was going to disappear for a little while because the person she had done the deal with was really pissed."

"And then he gave you some money to keep quiet?" Bernie asked, guessing.

Flynn nodded.

"Why did you believe him?" Libby asked.

"Because a week before there'd been this really angry . . . man . . . who wanted to go up, and I called Mrs. Witherspoon to tell her, and she said I shouldn't let him up. This . . . guy . . . he had a fit. I mean a real fit. I thought I was going to have to call the cops."

"Who was he?" Libby asked.

Flynn didn't say anything.

"You know him, don't you?" Libby persisted.

Flynn pressed his lips together and looked away. He seemed embarrassed

"It was Darius Witherspoon's partner, wasn't it?" Libby guessed.

Flynn looked down at the ground.

"You should be embarrassed," Bernie told him. "You took money from Darius not to tell Septimus Peabody where he and Penelope were going, and then you let Septimus into Darius's apartment."

"Hey," Flynn said, the embarrassment now gone. "Don't try to guilt me. I kept my word in both cases. I had nothing to do with . . . with . . . whatever happened."

"Maybe not with Darius's death, but I'm not sure you can say the same about his wife's," Bernie observed.

"You can say whatever you want," Flynn shot back. "You have no idea about what happened, either. You're guessing."

"Maybe we are," Bernie said. "But that doesn't mean we're wrong." She continued. "So was what you told me about Septimus and Penelope having an affair true?" Bernie asked. "Or was that a lie, too?"

Flynn corrected her. "I said that's what people do. I didn't say whether or not it was true." Then he turned and went back into the building. A moment later, he popped back out. "Just because A happened doesn't mean it has anything to do with B. You're assuming a connection that might not be there."

"He's right, you know," Libby said after Flynn had gone back inside.

"I do know," Bernie answered, thinking about what her dad would say. "But, on the other hand, if it looks like a duck and quacks like a duck . . ."

"It's not a lion," Libby said, mangling the saying as she and Bernie set off in the direction of the van.

Bernie burst out laughing as Libby looked at her watch. "We have another hour and a half before we have to meet Justin," she noted.

"Maybe if we're lucky, we can catch up with Septimus at his gallery. I, for one, would be fascinated to hear what he has to say about what Flynn just told us."

"Ditto," Libby replied, picking up the pace.

As it turned out, they were lucky. Bernie was driving along Madison Avenue when Libby spotted Septimus walking down the street half a block before the gallery.

"Stop!" she cried.

Bernie jammed on her brakes. The driver behind her leaned on his horn. So did the one behind him. "What's wrong?" she asked Libby.

"There's Septimus, Bernie. See him?"

"No. I don't. Where is he?"

Libby pointed. "He's in front of the tree with the bike chained to it. Near the lady with the Irish wolfhound."

Bernie looked again. "Okay, now I see him," she said after a minute had gone by and the honking behind her had risen to a fever pitch. She moved over a lane and double-parked. There was no way she could stay here. "I'll try to find a parking space," she told Libby. "You go and talk to Septimus."

Libby nodded and jumped out of the van. A moment later, Bernie pulled back into traffic. Libby watched her go, wondering if she was going to find a parking space and thinking about what a pain it was to have a vehicle in Manhattan, before she turned and looked for Septimus. For a second, she thought she'd lost him, but then she saw him again. He'd paused to look in the window of an antique store.

He was half a block ahead of her. As she watched, Septimus started walking again. A moment later, he turned into a deli. Libby hurried in after him. By the time she entered, Septimus had gotten his coffee and a poppy seed bagel with cream cheese and had stopped to read the headline of the *New York Post*. Then he looked up and saw her.

"What are you doing here?" he demanded, frowning.

"And hello to you, too," Libby replied, wishing she had the line of chat that Bernie did.

"What do you want?" he asked.

"Maybe I don't want anything," she told him. "Maybe I just wandered in here."

"Good for you," Septimus said, heading out the door.

Libby stepped to the right to give him room to leave as a man and a woman entered, coming between her and Septimus. "Leave me alone," Septimus told her once they were back out on the street. "I want nothing to do with you or your sister."

"I will leave you alone," Libby said, "when you tell me what you and Penelope were fighting about."

"Who said Penelope and I fought?" Septimus asked as he increased his pace.

"The doorman," Libby replied, having decided that there was no longer any reason to lie about her informant. "He said you two had a big row. He said Penelope wouldn't let you come up to the apartment. Something about a bad business deal."

Septimus walked even faster. "He did, did he?"

"Yes, he did," Libby told him, trotting to keep up. "He said that he thought he was going to have to call the police to have you removed. You were that out of control," she added for good measure.

Septimus came to a dead stop. The man in back of him bumped into him. "Why don't you watch where you're going?" Septimus growled at him.

"Why don't you watch where you're stopping? You're in the big city now," the man growled back before hurrying on.

"What else did the doorman say?" Septimus asked, turning back to Libby. The venom in his voice made Libby take a step back.

"He said that Darius told him that you and Penelope had some kind of deal going, and that something happened and she was afraid you were going to hurt her, and that she decided it would be a good time to disappear for a while, which was why they were heading up to Longely. Not exactly the story you told us when we spoke to you before."

"Really?" Septimus took a step toward her. "And you believe him?"

"Shouldn't I?"

"No, you shouldn't, because he's a liar and a cheat."

"Darius?"

"Darius and the doorman."

Libby crossed her arms over her chest. People eddied around them. "Why should they lie?" Libby asked.

"That's simple," Septimus snapped. "Darius lied because, as the Brits would say, he was a bounder and a cad, and the doorman lied because he'll say anything for money." Septimus continued. "So tell me, did the doorman actually say this out-of-control person was me?"

Libby hesitated. Just for a few seconds. But it was long enough.

"He didn't, did he?" Septimus demanded.

"Not exactly," Libby admitted, now that she thought about it. Because he hadn't. Or at least he hadn't come up with the name on his own. She and Bernie had suggested it to him.

Septimus smiled triumphantly. "I knew it," he crowed.

"Maybe not, but he sure as hell implied it," Libby countered. She sighed. She should have been the one looking for a parking space, and Bernie should have been the one conducting this conversation. Things would have gone better.

"And even if, hypothetically speaking, it was me being slightly out of control, people tend to get that way when money is involved. It doesn't mean I killed the Witherspoons, for heaven's sake," he told Libby.

He went on. "I feel sorry for you. You and your sister are running around like chickens with their heads cut off, so I'll tell you this. Okay. It's true. Penelope and I were in the middle of having a big row about partnership percentages, and yes, I did yell at the doorman, but he hardly had to call the police. I have to say the boy has a definite flair for the dramatic. Maybe he'll make it as an actor, after all.

"But if you want to know who Darius really wasn't getting along with, you should talk to William Moran. It could prove to be an enlightening conversation. I'm also putting you on notice that I'm going to sue you and your sister for harassment and libel if you keep this up," he told Libby. Then he turned and stalked away.

People seemed to be saying that to her a lot lately, Libby reflected as she watched Septimus bulldoze his way down Madison Avenue.

A moment later, Bernie double-parked Mathilda in front of Libby and honked her horn to get her sister's attention. It looked as if her sister hadn't been able to find a parking space, after all, Libby reflected as she jumped into the van and they took off.

# Chapter 46

"Maybe Septimus is right about William Moran," Bernie said as they exited the FDR Drive. So far the traffic had been mercifully light, and they were making better time than expected.

Libby nodded and unzipped Bernie's old leather jacket. It was true. It did look better than her old barn coat. "We should try to talk to him. Septimus is the third person to have mentioned his name in connection with Darius. Not to mention he was around when both homicides were committed."

Bernie stopped for a jaywalker. "We don't know that."

"Well, he appeared pretty quickly, so he couldn't have been very far away."

"True," Bernie allowed. She'd looked up his office address a while ago. It was close to the place where they were supposed to meet Justin Poland. She glanced at her watch. "Let's see what the development business is like these days."

Libby nodded. "Works for me. The worst that can happen is that he's not there."

Ten minutes later, Bernie started looking for a parking space. She found one three blocks away from William

Moran's office. The office was located on the second floor of a prewar building on the corner of Third Avenue and Twentieth Street. The stairs going up were narrow, steep, and badly lit.

"Obviously, he doesn't get too many people up here," Bernie said when she and her sister reached the second floor.

Libby sniffed. "I smell bacon."

"Not a bad thing," Bernie commented as she spotted Moran's office. The sign on the door read BUILDINGS INC. Not exactly an original name, in her estimation. The closer she and her sister got to the door, the stronger the smell of bacon became. "Here goes nothing," she said to Libby as she put her hand on the doorknob, pushed, and went inside.

The reason why the hallway smelled of bacon became obvious. Moran was standing over a hot plate set on top of a file cabinet next to the window, spatula in hand, cooking bacon and eggs in a small frying pan.

Bernie clapped her hands. "Oh, goody. Eggs cooked in bacon fat. My favorite thing," she said as she took in the unmade airbed in the second, smaller room. "Can I have some?"

Moran turned around. He wasn't smiling. "How did you get here?"

"The usual way. We took the stairs," Bernie told him.

"No magic carpet?"

"Next time," Libby told him. "We have a few questions." She was standing by Moran's desk. It was piled high with stacks of papers and folders.

"I'm calling the cops," Moran said, putting the spatula down.

"Go ahead," Bernie said. "But you'd better clean up this place first, because I'm betting the landlord of this building doesn't allow cooking in it, let alone living here."

"And how's he going to know?" Moran demanded. "Not that I am."

"I'm going to tell him," Bernie said sweetly.

"He won't believe you," Moran said.

Bernie got out her phone and started snapping pictures. "Let's see, shall we? Considering that this area is in the middle of upscaling, I'm betting your landlord can rent this space out for quite a bit more than you're paying for it."

"This is just temporary," Moran told her. "I've been working night and day. I don't have time to go home."

"I'm sure he'll be very sympathetic," Libby said as she read the top paper on the closest stack of files on his desk. The word *foreclosure* was written in bold letters. She shifted her attention back to Moran. "So let's make a deal. You answer our questions, and your secret will be safe with us."

Moran briefly thought about Libby's offer and decided it wasn't worth risking his office space. "You don't mind if I eat while we talk?" he asked.

"Not at all," Bernie answered.

Moran picked up a piece of bacon and took a bite before putting the rest of the strip on a plate. "That place has been a nightmare since I bought it," he said as he sat down. Bernie assumed he was referring to the Berkshire Arms. "Nothing has gone right with it, and now it looks as if I'm going to have to declare bankruptcy. Well, if the bank wants the building, let them take it. I, for one, have had enough. The publicity over Penelope Witherspoon's death was the last straw." He ate some egg. "So," he said, looking from Libby to Bernie and back again, "let me guess why you're here."

"I'll play," Libby said. "Why?"

"Because you want to know what the fight I had with Darius was about?"

"The man wins the prize," Bernie said.

"It was stupid."

"Tell us, anyway," Libby instructed.

Moran finished his eggs and bacon, wiped his hands with a paper napkin, threw it on top of his plate, and sat back in his chair. "Fine. It was about two things. It was about his feeding those damned crows. Having one person doing it was bad enough. Two was impossible. All Manny was doing was cleaning up bird crap. And the noise. Good God. People come up to a place like that for peace and quiet. When those crows got going, it was worse than being on Third Avenue with the trucks going by."

"And the second thing?" Bernie asked.

Moran got two red dots on his cheeks. "My idiot son. He was becoming involved with that scammer again. After everything that happened the first time. Hundreds of thousands of dollars down the drain. And a lot of that was my money. And he's running all over the place, digging holes and looking for what? Some kind of cockamamie treasure. I told his mother years ago he needed to go to military school, but she couldn't bear to part with the little darling."

"So why did you sell the place to Darius if you felt that way?" Libby asked.

Moran pounded his fist on his desk. A file slid off the edge and landed on the floor. He bent over and started picking the papers up. "I didn't know," he told Libby when he was through. "If I'd known, you think I would have? I outsource my rentals. They do the security checks, collect the rents, and keep the records for a percentage of the take. Up until now it's worked really, really well."

"It seems to me you had a good reason for killing Witherspoon," Bernie suggested.

"Well, I may have wanted to kill him," Moran said, "but if I'd done it, I wouldn't have done it in such a public fashion. Why would I do something that would put my investment at risk when I could have done it quietly, away from the Berkshire Arms?"

Bernie had to admit that what Moran was saying made sense.

Moran got up. "And now, if we're through here, I have an appointment with my divorce lawyer."

# Chapter 47

"I think Moran's telling the truth," Libby said as they walked over to meet Justin Poland.

"I do, too," Bernie agreed. Which left them with what? Not much. Hopefully, Justin Poland could supply some answers.

After all, he was the son of the late Ezra Poland. When Bernie had called up the Explorers Club, looking to talk to Ezra, the person who answered the phone had informed her that Ezra Poland had died last year.

When Bernie had pressed, the woman had referred her to Justin and had given her his phone number. So she'd called him, and they'd had a chat. When she wanted to meet, he'd agreed. They'd set the time and the place, a coffee shop named King Java, located on Third, between Twenty-Second Street and Twenty-Third Street.

"So what do you think?" Justin asked the sisters when they walked into the place and introduced themselves.

Justin was tall and thin and wore skinny jeans, a buffalo plaid shirt, horn-rimmed glasses, and had a serious handlebar mustache. He was two shades away from being a hipster, Bernie decided.

"I like the place," Bernie said, telling the truth. "It has a nice vibe."

The place was tiny, with just enough room for the counter and ten small tables. Libby wondered what the place had been before. Maybe a small convenience store.

"Good color scheme, right?" Justin asked anxiously. "Not too Starbucksy."

"Not at all," Bernie assured him. The walls were painted a mint green, while the floor was green-and-white linoleum tile, and the tables were white Formica. Framed coffee ads covered the walls. "It's got a fifties feel to it."

Justin beamed and almost jumped up and down with delight. "That's just what I was going for. I own this place, you know."

"We figured," Libby and Bernie said together.

"I just opened up two weeks ago."

For the next twenty minutes, he and the sisters discussed the food business in general, and coffee sourcing and roasting in particular, while they sipped lattes and sampled Justin's baked goods as they crowded around a table in front of the window and watched the world go by.

"All your food stuff is good," Libby told him, gesturing to the plate on the table that was overflowing with samples of the chocolate chip cookies, brownies, blueberry scones, cranberry-nut bars, cake pops, and mini black-and-white cookies that Justin sold. "But I especially like the cheddar cheese corn muffin and the walnut short-bread," she noted. "Do you make everything yourself, or do you outsource?"

"My girlfriend does all the baking, and thanks. We're going to add more stuff, too. Like a couple of gluten-free options. And some dairy-free stuff."

"It's tough these days," Libby said, sympathizing. "So many people with so many allergies."

"It sure is," Justin agreed. "Of course," he said mournfully, looking around at the empty room, "it would help if we had some customers in here."

"They'll come," Libby said, trying to be reassuring. "The first year is always the toughest."

"Ninety-nine percent of restaurants fail during the first year," Justin noted, quoting a well-known statistic.

"But you're not going to be one of them," Bernie told him. "Social media," she suggested. She took another sip of her latte. "It really does help. Not that we do it," she admitted. "But my friends tell me it works. But then, you're probably doing that already." She felt foolish. Of course he was doing that. Anyone his age would.

"That I am," Justin told them. "At least my friends are coming," he added. "And we have a couple of knitting circles, a crocheting group, and two book groups that are interested in meeting here, so that's good."

"And they'll bring their friends, who in turn will bring their friends," Bernie told him. "The good thing about having a small place is that it doesn't take many people to fill it up. Then people walking by see you have a crowd, figure it must be good, and come in, too."

Justin smiled. "I never thought of that. And at night I've got some people coming in who are doing acoustic guitar. I'm thinking of getting a panini machine and maybe offering some cakes, as well."

"See?" Bernie said. "You're on your way."

"I hope so," Justin said. "I'd hate to see my dad's money go to waste."

"You did this with your inheritance from him?" Libby asked.

Justin nodded. "It took a while to get the will probated." His shoulders slumped as he thought about his father. "I really miss him. I guess I didn't think I'd miss him as much as I do, because when he was alive, all we did was fight." He straightened up. "But enough about me. How can I help you guys?"

"Your dad's chest of drawers," Bernie said. "We want to know about your dad's chest of drawers."

Justin finished off his corn muffin, brushed the crumbs off his shirt and into his cupped hand, and deposited them on the side of his plate. "Like I said on the phone, there really isn't that much to tell."

"Tell us, anyway," Bernie urged.

"But I already did," Justin protested.

"I know you did," Libby said. "But please tell us again. At this point any random shred of information could prove helpful."

"If you think it'll be of assistance," Justin said. He looked around and sighed. "It's not as if you're interrupting anything." Then he repeated what he'd already told Bernie about Darius Witherspoon getting in touch with him after his father died and asking if he could have the chest of drawers as a memento.

"Memento?" Libby asked. "That's rather odd, don't you think?"

Justin shrugged. "I don't know. I just assumed that Mr. Witherspoon wanted something to remind him of the trip he and my dad were on. He told me that they'd used that chest of drawers when they'd planned their trip to Paraguay."

"Really?" said Bernie, who was having trouble visualizing the scenario. "For what?"

"Mr. Witherspoon told me that he and my dad had used it as their command center. They'd stored things they needed for the trip in it and put a picture of the place they were going to on it to motivate themselves. So I said, 'Sure. Take it.' I was just going to sell the thing on eBay or Craigslist, anyway."

"They were on a trip together?" Bernie asked.

Justin nodded. "One of Mr. Witherspoon's treasure hunts." He frowned and sighed.

"And you didn't approve?" Bernie asked.

"I thought it was silly. Grown men looking for buried treasure." Justin pointed to himself. "It's not my bag, but my dad liked that stuff—he lived for it, in fact—and he got a chance to go on this one for free. It was a very big deal to him."

"How come?" Bernie asked.

"That he got to go for free?"

Bernie nodded. "Yes."

"He'd worked in that part of the world as a civil engineer, so he had contacts down there, and he was familiar with the area Witherspoon was set on exploring." Justin grimaced. "Which turned out to be a good thing. There's a lot of jungle there, and you can get lost pretty easily." Jason gulped down the last of one of the lattes he'd made for himself, Libby, and Bernie. "There are supposed to be gold caches all over the place. According to my dad, the locals spend a lot of time digging for Incan gold in the jungle. It's like their national hobby. Sometimes Dad said they even find some."

"So I take it he and Witherspoon didn't in this case?" Libby asked.

Justin shook his head. "Nope. It turned out to be a bad trip. One of those ones where nothing goes right from the beginning, and you'd be better off having stayed home in bed." He paused, and Libby and Bernie waited until Justin had finished off a piece of walnut shortbread and resumed his tale. "Evidently, there was one snafu after another. First, they missed their flight, and then the equipment wasn't there when they landed. And when it did come, some of it was broken, and they had to jerry-rig it, after which my dad came down with dysentery, and then, to cap it all off, one of the workers on the expedition died, and his village blamed his death on Darius Witherspoon."

"And was it Witherspoon's fault?" Libby asked.

"My dad was in town when it happened, so he didn't see it," Justin replied. "But Mr. Witherspoon told him the man was drunk, he was playing around, and he fell off a cliff and broke his neck. But the locals thought differently. Darius and my dad had to get out of town. Left all their equipment and most of their camping gear behind. I guess it was pretty scary."

"Okay," Libby said. "I get that. But what I don't see is why that would make Darius Witherspoon want a memento of your dad."

"That's because if it wasn't for my dad, Mr. Witherspoon probably wouldn't have gotten out of there. They couldn't go back to the village. It was too dangerous. So my dad and Mr. Witherspoon walked through the jungle for two days before they came to another village. Without my dad, Mr. Witherspoon would have died." Justin shook his head. "Ironic that after the life he led, my dad gets hit by some guy making an illegal right on red down on Canal Street, isn't it? He was real excited, too."

"About what?" Libby asked.

"About this new venture that he and Mr. Witherspoon were planning. He said it was going to be the find of the century, the trip to end all trips."

"I don't suppose you happen to know what it was?" Libby inquired.

Justin shook his head. "My dad wouldn't tell me. Said he was sworn to secrecy. Said he and Mr. Witherspoon had combined resources and had come up with something spectacular."

"And you don't have any idea what it was?"

"Nope. The only thing he said was that I'd be surprised when I found out where it was."

"Where it was?" Libby repeated.

"That's what he said," Justin told her.

"And you have no idea where he meant?" Bernie asked.

"Absolutely none." Justin scratched his chin. "My dad had a big collection of old maps and books and stuff like that. Maybe they found something in one of them."

Bernie leaned forward like a beagle scenting a fox. "What happened to the collection?"

Justin shrugged apologetically. "I was going to auction them off, but the guy who came by to give me a price on my dad's stuff said his books weren't worth anything, so I threw them in the Dumpster. Except for the atlas in the dresser. Darius asked me for that, as well."

"How come?" Bernie asked.

Justin shrugged again. "Same reason as the chest of drawers. Sentimental value."

Libby slipped out of her jacket and hung it on the back of her chair. "So it wasn't worth anything?"

Jason laughed. "Not at all. The atlas was my dad's. He found it in a used bookstore somewhere. He thought it was valuable, but actually it turned out this guy—I forget his name, but he was some sort of savant—had drawn all the maps and then had paid to have them made into a book and published. He just enjoyed looking at it, and I think Mr. Witherspoon did, too."

"And the notebooks?" Bernie asked after she'd explained about them.

Justin shook his head. "They must have been Mr. Witherspoon's, because my dad never took notes. He prided himself on his memory." He stood up. A customer had wandered into the store. Justin started walking toward the woman, who was reading the menu.

"One last question," Bernie said.

Justin paused.

"Do you happen to know how your dad and Darius Witherspoon met?"

"I think my dad wandered into Mr. Witherspoon's gallery one day and they got to talking. Some random thing like that."

# Chapter 48

"So maybe this whole thing is about a treasure hunt gone awry," Libby observed on her and Bernie's way back up to Westchester. "Maybe the atlas actually did contain a clue to the treasure's whereabouts, and maybe Darius actually found it, and one of his partners killed him for it."

"How very *x* marks the spot," Bernie said as she slowed down, then sped up again. "On the other hand, this whole thing could be about something else entirely."

"Like what?"

"I don't know. However, I think we're overcomplicating this."

"I think you may be right. We should start with Penelope's disappearance," Libby suggested as Bernie spotted the end of the roadwork and picked up speed. "After all, that's where everything began."

Bernie nodded. "Begin at the beginning," she said, quoting one of her dad's many maxims. "When you get stuck, go back to square one. The answer is usually there." Which she'd found was usually true.

Libby smiled. "Exactly. We just got swept up with all the other stuff."

"So what if we turn things around?" Bernie proposed after a moment of thought. "Let's say that Septimus was telling the truth—he had a fight with Penelope, but that was as far as it went—and that Darius's story to Flynn about Penelope being in mortal danger was a lie."

"Because?" Libby asked.

"Because he was covering his tracks."

"And he was doing that because he knew his wife was going to disappear," Libby said excitedly. "And he wanted an alibi."

"Precisely," Bernie continued. "And he knew she was going to disappear because he was going to make it happen." Bernie thought about the Missoni dress and the shopping bag she'd found in the cottage down by the river, the dress she was almost positive had belonged to Penelope Witherspoon, because you didn't just find those lying around.

Then she thought about what Phil Craven had said about seeing a woman coming out of the water. At first, she hadn't believed him, as his story was too fantastical, but now she was inclined to. "Okay. This is a big leap, but let's suppose that Darius wants to kill his wife—"

Libby interrupted. "Motive?"

Bernie took her hand off the wheel and made an impatient gesture. "I don't know."

"Guess," Libby said.

"Several things come to mind. Maybe Darius wanted her dead because he's about to come into the find of a lifetime and he doesn't want to share it with her, or maybe there's something illegal about it and she's going to rat him out. . . ."

"Not too far a stretch, considering that was the way he supposedly did business," Libby said.

"Or maybe he found out that Septimus and his wife were planning on taking over the business and throwing him out. That would really piss me off," Bernie observed.

"Me too," Libby agreed.

"But you know what? Let's leave the reason aside for the moment. What matters is that Darius wants to get rid of his wife, right?"

Libby nodded. "Right."

"So he invites her down to the river on some pretext or other, incapacitates her—probably by hitting her on the head—and rolls her into the water. Then he makes his mistake. He leaves because he thinks she's dead. As Dad would say, never assume. But she's not. Somehow or other, she survives. She climbs out of the river. Then, when she can, she calls someone—a friend—and asks for help. Or maybe somebody out for a late run sees her and comes to her aid. No. I take that back," Bernie said, thinking about what she'd just said. "In that case, the person would have called the police."

"And the person she called brings her dry clothes," Libby said, following Bernie's train of thought.

Bernie nodded. "And she changes and leaves."

"But where does she go?"

"I don't know, but I'm guessing somewhere close by. Somewhere where she can keep an eye on her husband. A very close eye. Maybe that thing we saw on the turret as we were driving up wasn't who we thought it was. Maybe it was her."

"Let's assume you're correct. Her husband has tried to kill her. Why doesn't she call the police?"

"Because she's pissed, Libby. Very, very pissed."

Libby unwrapped a square of dark chocolate from Mexico and popped it into her mouth. "That has to be the understatement of the year," she told her sister as the chocolate coated her mouth.

"The decade, Libby. The decade," Bernie replied, enthusiastically throwing herself into the narrative. "She wants revenge. She wants to kill her husband for doing what he did to her. Sitting in jail is too good for him. And who knows? Maybe by some miracle, he'd be found not guilty and walk."

"So she climbs into Darius's window and kills him?"

"No. She didn't climb into the window. She got out that way, but that's not the way she came in. I bet she came up the stairs and knocked on his door right after you came back downstairs. By that time we were so busy, we wouldn't have noticed anyone going up. And if Penelope was in costume, Darius might not have recognized her until he let her in and she took off her mask."

Bernie thought about Darius's reaction. He would have been paralyzed with terror. It would have been easy enough to slip the rope over his neck, hook the rope to the plant hook, and throw him out. Or maybe not that. Bernie could see Penelope taking a step forward and Darius taking a step back, until he was right by the window. *Then one push and out he goes.* After all, she was bigger than he was.

"Or maybe she had a partner," Libby proposed.

"Which would make things easier."

"And Darius wrote the note to us because?" Libby asked.

"He wrote it because he knew something was wrong. Because he suspected that he hadn't killed Penelope and that she was going to come after him, and he wanted to make sure she didn't have that satisfaction. He wanted to make sure that at the very least she would rot in a jail cell for the rest of her life."

"Then who killed her?" Libby asked. "Certainly not Darius. I mean, at least we know he's dead. It may be the only thing we *do* know for sure."

"Her partner," Bernie said.

"Who is?"

"The same person who brought her the clothes she was wearing. The person who knew she was alive."

"That definitely narrows down the field," Libby said sarcastically.

"It does," Bernie protested. "Almost everyone thought she was dead. So what do you think?"

"About what you laid out?"

"No. About world peace and climate change."

"Frankly, I think it's pretty sketchy."

"Do you have a better idea?" Bernie asked.

"Not really," Libby allowed.

"Think about it," Bernie said.

Which Libby did. She spent the rest of the trip turning over in her mind what Bernie had said, and try as she might, she had to admit that Bernie's version of the events had merit. "We should probably go through the house where we found Penelope's dress in the daylight," she suggested as they pulled up to the shop. "Maybe there's something there we didn't see at night."

"Good thought," Bernie said. Then she groaned when she caught sight of Michelle pulling in behind Mathilda. Her dad's fiancée was the last person she wanted to be dealing with at the moment.

# Chapter 49

Michelle got out of her vehicle at the same time that Libby and Bernie got out of theirs.

"What a delightful surprise," Bernie said, lying through her teeth. "Isn't it, Libby?"

Libby didn't answer.

Bernie repeated her question louder this time. "Isn't it, Libby?"

"Definitely," Libby answered, though the expression on her face suggested otherwise.

"I hope you don't mind my dropping in like this," Michelle trilled, "but your dad said you were out, and he didn't know what time you'd be back." She gestured with her chin to the container she was carrying. "So I'm bringing him some dinner. My special fried tofu and kale casserole and a quinoa, carob, and stevia brownie for dessert."

Libby grinned. Her dad hated everything Michelle had mentioned. "I'm sure he'll be so pleased."

"Can't have our guy go hungry," Michelle chirped.

"No, we can't, though he's not exactly starving to death," Bernie couldn't help herself from pointing out.

"He can always go downstairs and get something to eat, you know."

"I know he can." Michelle leaned over and gave Bernie's arm a quick pat. "But I just thought this would be a nice thing to do, and it gives me a chance to see my snuggle bunny."

Libby cringed, and Bernie thought her father would die if he heard himself referred to that way. She wondered if he knew.

"We want him to remain healthy," Michelle continued.

"Are you saying our food isn't healthy?" Libby demanded, taking the bait.

"Not at all," Michelle replied in a soothing voice. "But you have to admit that superfoods and more fiber can't be bad, right?" Then she flashed Libby a brilliant smile and started up the stairs, leaving Libby commentless.

Bernie and Libby followed behind her. The sisters spent the next hour watching their dad take teeny, tiny bites of Michelle's meal while they told him what they'd found out.

"That's fascinating," Michelle said when they were through. She clapped her hands in a parody of excitement. "Going around. Talking to people. I envy you not having to stay in the shop all the time. It must be nice to feel so secure about your clientele. To not be worried that someone is going to steal them away, what with the competition and all. I know I'd be worried if I were you, but then I'm a worrier."

*No. You're something else*, Bernie thought but didn't say. Neither, through a supreme act of will, did Libby. Both sisters could see from the expression on their dad's face that he was grateful for their self-restraint.

"Can you get me a piece of pie?" Sean said to Bernie and Libby as soon as he heard the downstairs door close, signifying Michelle's departure.

"What kind of pie?" Bernie asked.

"Any kind of pie will do. Apple first, and if that's all gone, then pumpkin, preferably the one with the ginger-snap crust." He held out the dish Michelle had given him. Half of the tofu and kale casserole and all of the quinoa brownie remained. "And could you throw this out, too?"

"But, Dad," Libby said. "If you don't like this kind of food, why don't you just tell her?"

Sean looked at his daughter as if she was crazy. "First of all, I don't want to hurt her feelings. After all, she has my best interests at heart."

Libby didn't say anything, although she doubted it. "And secondly?"

Sean straightened up. "That's simple. Because then she'd ask me what she makes that I do like, and I'd have to tell her I don't like anything she makes, and I don't want to do that." Sean frowned as he thought about how wonderful his wife's cooking had been. He really didn't know how good he'd had it. Oh well. At least his daughters had inherited his wife's ability. "Oh, and by the way," Sean added, "could you add some whipped cream to the pie? And a cup of coffee wouldn't hurt, either."

"So what do you think?" Libby asked after her dad had finished eating.

"About the pie? I love your pie. You know that."

"No, about Darius killing his wife."

Cindy jumped up on Sean's lap, and he began to pet her. "I think your theory has merit," he said. "I just don't see how you're going to prove it."

"We haven't quite figured that out yet," Libby admitted.

"You should take another look around the house where you found Penelope's dress," Sean suggested. "Maybe there's something else there you didn't see."

"That's what I said," Libby replied. "Especially since no one has looked there."

"That's because no one figured Penelope for being around there," Sean observed.

"No they didn't," Bernie agreed. "They figured she'd met with some kind of accident. . . ."

"Or foul play . . . ," Libby added.

"In the city," Bernie said, finishing the thought.

Cindy butted her head against Sean's hand, and he rubbed her ear. "I'd like to come along, if you don't mind."

"Love it!" Bernie and Libby said together. They exchanged glances. This was a good sign. Ordinarily, he would have said something about having to check with Michelle first to see if they had plans. Maybe she was losing traction.

"We can always use another set of eyes," Libby continued.

Sean grinned. "That's what I was thinking, too." He motioned to the atlas resting on the coffee table that Bernie had taken from Darius's apartment. "I'd like to take a look at that if you're not."

"Libby and I were hoping you would. Maybe you'll find something in it that we haven't," said Bernie, handing the book to her dad. Although she and Libby had leafed through it, nothing had popped out at them.

"Geography used to be my favorite subject, so maybe I will," Sean replied.

Libby stood up. "For my part, I'm going to go downstairs and get the cinnamon-raisin bread and the apple-walnut muffins started."

"I guess that leaves me with the pumpkin chocolate chip cookies and the olive oil carrot cake with chocolate ganache frosting," Bernie observed.

"God, they all sound good," Sean remarked as he opened the atlas.

A moment later, he'd become totally engrossed in the maps he was looking at. He smiled as he turned the pages. The names were fanciful, and given the monsters inhabiting the oceans, the maps looked as if they had been drawn in earlier centuries. Much earlier centuries.

But as Sean looked at the maps more carefully, he realized that wasn't true. The maps were actually based on ones from the twentieth century. The cartographer had taken maps from various periods in time, combined them, and renamed them. Thus the title *The Atlas of Implausibility*. He'd done a good job, too.

But if you knew what you were looking for, you could spot the original impetus. There was no index, but it didn't take Sean long to realize the maps were grouped by continent. As he looked through the maps having to do with North America, he remembered a story his mother had told him, a story her brother had told her, and he wondered if it was true.

He rested the atlas on his lap. "Hey," he said to Bernie. "Do you think you could get me my magnifying glass and look up something for me on the computer before you go downstairs?"

"Of course," Bernie replied, standing up.

"In fact," he said, "could you bring me everything you got out of both Witherspoon apartments?"

"With pleasure," she said, and then she set about collecting the materials her dad had asked for.

Later, after she was done helping him, she had something she wanted to look up. She knew it was a long shot—that was why she wasn't telling anybody—but if it panned out, it would explain a lot.

# Chapter 50

The Hudson was choppy at ten in the morning, the water beating against the river's bank in fitful little waves. The sky was gray, the color reflected in the water. A stiff breeze was blowing off the river, making Libby glad that she'd brought along three large thermoses of hot chocolate. It helped with the chill.

Sean took the thermos and the breakfast sandwich Libby had made for him—two strips of bacon and an egg fried in coconut oil, topped with slices of avocado and wrapped in a freshly made corn tortilla—and started down toward the riverbank.

"Are you sure you don't want us to come with you?" Bernie called after him.

"I'm fine," Sean said over his shoulder.

"Are you sure?" Libby asked.

Sean stopped and turned around. "This is just a hunch," he told them. "If I find anything, I'll yell."

"Because we can—" Libby began, but Sean cut her off.

"I know," he said, the irritation in his voice coming through. "But I just want to do this by myself."

"Okay," Bernie said.

"Good hunting," Sean said. Then he turned and continued down toward the river.

Bernie watched him go. "He wants to sneak a smoke," she said to Libby when she couldn't see her dad anymore.

Libby gave Bernie her thermos and breakfast sandwich. "That's what I figured. I keep on thinking we should do something."

"Like what?" Bernie asked, unwrapping the sandwich and taking a bite.

"I don't know," Libby admitted while she started eating hers.

"Exactly. He's seventy-three. At seventy-three, I figure he's earned the right to do what he wants."

"I guess," Libby said, although she wasn't convinced.

Then she and her sister finished their sandwiches and got to work. They'd decided to look through the falling-down cottage again before they searched the surrounding area, on the theory that there might be something they missed in the dark. After half an hour they had to admit they hadn't found anything that shed more light on what happened to Penelope Witherspoon.

"This is even grosser in the daylight," Libby commented as she stepped around something that looked like a pile of dried vomit. "I'm glad I didn't step in that," she said, pointing to it.

"Ditto," Bernie replied.

The place hadn't been that bad when she and her friends had come down here. Now the floor was literally covered with trash. There were fast-food wrappers, half-eaten packs of dehydrated camping food, empty water and beer bottles, empty bottles of cheap vodka, Styrofoam coffee cups, cigarette butts, and charred pieces of wood from extinguished campfires.

"It looks as if someone was living here," she said, picking

up a moldy sleeping bag and turning it inside out. "Not just partying."

"Penelope Witherspoon?" Libby asked.

Bernie squinted at the inside of the sleeping bag. A name was written in indelible ink along the top. "George Washington," she read out loud. "Please return to owner."

"So not Penelope's."

"Definitely not." Bernie thought of the Witherspoons' apartment on Park Avenue. There was no way she could visualize Penelope staying here. She would rather have died. Well, maybe she had. With that thought, Bernie dropped the sleeping bag back on the floor and stepped outside. Libby followed.

"This is a big area to search," she noted.

"Larger than a football field," Bernie said.

"What does that mean?" Libby demanded.

"That it's a big space." Bernie took a slug of hot chocolate, then screwed the top to her thermos back on and put up the hood on her hoodie.

"It would help if we had more people," Libby observed. "A lot more people."

"And a couple of dogs," Bernie said. "But we don't, so we'll just have to make the best of what we have."

"Why do people always say, 'We have to make the best of what we have'?" Libby mused. "Why not the worst?"

"I think we've stalled long enough," Bernie said as she eyed the tangle of weeds and the low-growing brush in front of her. Hopefully, there was something else of Penelope's out there, as well, something they could bring to the police. "Let's do this thing," she said to her sister.

"Let's," Libby replied. The question was how to do it in the most efficient way possible. In the end, they decided to try to walk in a straight line, keeping about twelve feet apart from each other until they came to the end of the Berkshire Arms. Then, when they reached the end of the building, they would make another pass, shifting downward toward the river. It wasn't perfect, but it was the best way they could think of given the thickness of the underbrush.

The sisters had just started their search when Sean reappeared.

"Find anything?" he asked.

"Not yet. And you?" Libby asked.

"I wasn't really looking," he admitted.

"We know," Bernie said.

"I know you know," Sean said as he pulled his watch cap down over his ears. "Thanks. So how are we going to do this?" he asked, changing the subject.

Libby explained. Sean listened and nodded. He had nothing to say, which his daughters took as a compliment.

The three of them started walking down their allotted paths, eyes sweeping the ground to the left, then the right, then the left again. They walked slowly, concentrating on the ground. The only sounds were their feet crunching the leaves, the cries of the seagulls, and the occasional toot of a tugboat going down the river. Once in a while, one of them would stop and take a sip of hot chocolate.

Ten minutes later, Libby noticed that Bernie had stopped, put her thermos down, and was poking at something in the underbrush with a stick she'd picked up along the way.

"Find anything?" Libby asked.

"I'm not sure," Bernie said. "It's probably nothing. Just a piece of trash." But she bent down and felt around underneath the shrub just to make sure.

"I hope there's no poison ivy under there," Libby said.

"Always the positive thinker," Bernie replied as her hand closed on what the stick had hit. She pulled it out. "Interesting," she said as she brushed the dirt off a medium-size leather bag.

Sean and Libby crowded around her as she inspected it. The bag had been black once, but now the leather was a moldy gray. Bernie opened it. The inside was in better condition.

"This is a Burberry," she announced, reading the label, as she looked through the compartments. "One of the newer ones."

"Meaning?" Sean asked. His knowledge of women's handbags fell into the minus category.

"Meaning it's expensive," Bernie replied. "Meaning it's not something that you'd forget or throw away."

"You think it's Penelope's?" her dad asked.

"Well, it ain't Queen Elizabeth's," Bernie told him. "Penelope had a Burberry trench coat in the hall closet, as well as two Burberry totes that could be this one's sisters."

"Any ID?" Libby asked.

"Nope," Bernie replied. "Maybe whoever took her bag threw her wallet around here somewhere." She gestured to the ground.

"One can only hope," Libby said as the three of them started looking through the bed of fallen leaves that lay underneath the bushes.

Five minutes later, Sean put his thermos down and pulled a wallet out from under a piece of wood. It, too, had once been black. Like the bag, the wallet was covered with mold and dirt. He idly ran his fingers along the material, cleaning it off. When he saw what was underneath the debris, he grinned.

"God bless monograms," he said, showing them the remains of the letters. The gold letters had faded, but the *P* and the *W* were still visible.

"Penelope Witherspoon," Libby cried.

"Exactly," Sean said. "So she *was* here."

"Okay," Bernie said. "Which raises even more questions."

"Like where was she between the time she came out of the water and the time that she died?" Libby said. "Not to mention the matter of who killed her."

"Her partner killed her," Sean declared. "I said that already."

"We thought that, too," Bernie said.

"Has to be," Sean said as he put his collar up against the wind. "It's the only thing that makes sense if we assume that the theory about Penelope killing her husband is correct."

"I'm not so sure," Libby objected. "For openers, we don't know this person even exists."

"Logic says he does," Sean replied. "Someone brought Penelope clothes to change into, and someone gave her a place to hide out in. They had to have. Otherwise, she would have been spotted."

Libby chewed on her lip while she thought over what her dad had said. "Then how did she get in contact with this person? She didn't know she was going to get tossed into the river by her husband. If she had, she wouldn't have gone along."

"Her phone," Sean replied, taking a guess. "Somehow, her phone didn't go in the river with her."

"I suppose it could have dropped out of her pocket," Libby conceded after a moment of reflection. "Either that or it was in a waterproof case. Okay. So this person rescues her and does or doesn't help her kill her husband, after which they have a falling-out."

Sean nodded.

"But then why would this person kill her in such a public manner?" Libby asked. "Why not just kill her and get rid of her body?"

"I haven't figured that out yet," Sean admitted as he opened the wallet and thumbed through it. It was empty. "We should look around," Sean suggested. "Maybe whatever was in here fell out."

"Let's hope," Bernie said as she got down on her knees and began going through the leaves and the dirt and the twigs on the ground with her hands. Libby leaned her thermos against a tree and joined her, while Sean remained standing. He was afraid he wouldn't be able to get up again if he got down on the ground.

"Found something!" Bernie cried a few minutes later, holding up an appointment card for a haircut at the Industry Salon on Friday, November tenth, at three p.m. Penelope's name was written in cursive on the first line. "Guess she won't be needing this," Bernie observed as she handed the card to her dad and went back to looking. Five minutes after that, she found some coins and picked them up. "Interesting," she said, getting off her knees and pointing to the misshapen silver coin about the size of a quarter that sat in the palm of her hand, next to five pennies.

Libby, who had also gotten up, picked up the coin and held it up to the light. "This looks like the one the crow dropped by Darius's body," she observed.

"It does, doesn't it?" Bernie agreed.

"May I see it?" Sean asked.

Libby handed the coin to him.

He pointed to the markings on the coin. "I could be wrong, but I think this is part of what Darius was looking for," Sean replied. "I think it's danegeld."

Libby cocked her head. "Danegeld?"

"Viking money," Sean explained.

"I didn't think the Vikings came up around here," Bernie said.

"They weren't supposed to have," Sean said, thinking of the maps and the story his mother had told him. "That's why finding this would be a very big deal. Basically, it would mean rewriting history. Until now archeologists have found two settlements in Canada. Not to mention the cache's value."

"I'm guessing it would be worth a lot," Bernie said.

Sean handed the coin back to her. "Quite a bit."

"Then where's the rest of the treasure?" Bernie asked.

"With the person who killed Penelope," Libby said, hypothesizing.

Sean stifled a sneeze. "That's what I'm guessing, too."

"It has to have been buried around here," Bernie said, thinking back to the crow dropping the coin on Darius's body.

Sean nodded. He thought about *The Atlas of Implausibility* and the map of the Hudson River and the settlement on there named Langkeld, which was sited right below where Longely was now. When he'd seen the name Langkeld, Norse for "building on a spring," he'd thought it was a joke—but maybe it wasn't. Maybe that was why Darius had had the atlas in the first place. *Ironic*, Sean thought. The one time Darius had been correct, he hadn't lived to enjoy it.

Sean flipped the silver coin into the air with his thumb and caught it. "I'm going to show this to my old neighbor Frank. See what he says," he told his daughters as he slipped the coin into his jacket pocket.

Frank was an avid coin collector. If he couldn't identify it, he would know who could. Then, after Sean was positive he knew what he had—no point making a fool of himself if he didn't have to—he'd show it to Clyde, who would then show it to Lucy.

Sean opened his thermos and took a sip of hot chocolate. "You done good," he said to Bernie and Libby. "You done real good. I'd have you on my team anytime."

Bernie and Libby grinned. They already knew it, but it was still nice to hear.

# Chapter 51

Later that evening, after their dad had gone to bed, Bernie showed Libby what she'd found on her laptop.

"He's the one we're looking for," Bernie said, pointing to the article on the screen. "I'm positive."

The moment she read the article, Libby knew that her sister was correct. She wanted to kick herself. He'd been here all along, but she hadn't thought of him in connection with the two murders. For all intents and purposes, he'd been invisible.

"How'd you figure it out?" Libby asked. "What gave you the idea?"

"Being introduced to the cousin."

Libby stared at her blankly.

"The cousin at the Roadhouse." Bernie provided another clue. "He had a hyphenated last name."

Libby slapped her forehead with the palm of her hand. "Of course. And Manny was just using the first part. That's why we didn't get the connection."

"Exactly," Bernie said.

"Okay. I understand how we could miss the whole name thing, but how could Darius? How could he not have recognized his name?" Libby asked. "For that matter, how could he not have recognized *him*?"

Bernie took a last sip of her tea before answering. "He didn't recognize the name for the same reason I didn't—it just never occurred to him. And as for your second question, I'm betting he wasn't on-site when the accident happened, so he never saw him."

Libby stared at the article on the screen. It was like she was seeing vengeance made literal. "You think Manny tracked Darius here? You think he and Moran were partners?"

Bernie shook her head. "No and no. I think it was just bad luck for Darius Witherspoon. Or karma, if you believe in that sort of thing. I think our guy recognized Darius's name, and everything went from there."

"And Penelope?"

Bernie shrugged. "I think when she decided not to go to the police, she became part of the mix, so to speak."

Libby reread the article for the third time. "I think you're right. I think we should show this to Lucy."

Bernie shook her head. "Not a good idea. We'll need more than this to get Lucy to act."

"We have the coins."

"You can't tie those to the murders. We need actual proof."

"But we have no proof," Libby replied.

"Exactly," Bernie said. "But I have an idea."

"I don't want to hear it," Libby replied.

Bernie told her, anyway. "Think about it, Libby," she urged when she was done. "That's all I'm asking."

Libby frowned. Bernie's plan seemed reasonable, but then, they usually did.

"Please," Bernie said, taking Libby's hands in hers.

"Fine," Libby said, caving. "But I'm not promising any-thing."

"I'm not asking you to," Bernie told her, even though she was. "But whatever you decide, please don't tell Dad."

"That's understood," Libby said, annoyed that that thought had even crossed Bernie's mind. She spent the rest of the night tossing and turning. Bernie, on the other hand, spent the rest of her night with Brandon.

"So what do you think about what I said?" Bernie asked Libby the next morning, as she was putting the cinnamon-raisin bread in the oven.

"How do we know where he's living?" Libby demanded as she closed the oven door and set the timer.

"He's got an apartment in the basement," Bernie told her. "I saw him going down there."

"Great." Libby straightened up. Not only were they going to do something illegal, but they were going to do it in one of her least favorite places in the world.

"We'll be out of there really quickly," Bernie coaxed, di-vining her sister's thoughts. "Either it's there or it isn't."

"And if we don't find it?" Libby asked.

"Then we're gone," Bernie promised. She raised her hand. "I swear."

"How do we get in?"

Bernie went in her bag, took out the set of picks she'd "borrowed" from Brandon last night, and jingled them in Libby's face. "With these."

"Does Brandon know you have them?"

Bernie laughed. "What do you think?"

"I think he's going to be really pissed when he finds out."

"He's not going to."

Libby switched to another topic. "So you knew I was going to say yes?"

"Let's say I was hoping you would." Then Bernie showed her sister the burner phone she'd acquired last night from the Mini Mart over by Route 92 and told her what she was planning on doing.

"You should get Brandon to make the call," Libby objected.

"No," Bernie said. "If I did that, he'd be involved."

"So?"

"Would you want Marvin involved on the off chance that something goes awry?"

"I thought you said nothing would," Libby said.

Bernie crossed her arms over her chest. "And it most likely won't. Don't be such a chicken."

"You win," Libby said grudgingly. She figured she really didn't have too much of a choice. If she didn't go with Bernie, Bernie would go on her own.

# Chapter 52

Libby watched Bernie as she went outside, sat in the van and, disguising her voice, called Manny and told him she knew what he'd done, and demanded half of the Viking cache for her silence.

Bernie had half expected Manny to hang up on her, but he didn't. She could hear him breathing on the phone. After a couple of minutes, he asked her where and when, and she set up the meet for two in the afternoon at the Ez-Top Diner—which was a good fifty-minute drive from the Berkshire Arms.

At 12:45 p.m. she and her sister left A Little Taste of Heaven and drove over to the strip mall on Ash Street and tucked themselves away at the far end of the parking lot. Their position afforded them an unobstructed view of both the road coming down from the Berkshire Arms and the road Manny would have to take to get to the diner.

"What happens if he has his passport on him?" Libby asked Bernie while they waited for Manny to pass by.

"Then we go home. But he won't. Why would he?" Bernie replied. "He's not going anywhere he'd need it."

"I guess," Libby said. She was busy thinking about all

the things that could go wrong when she saw Manny's vehicle roar by them.

"And there he goes," Bernie observed, lightly punching Libby in the arm for emphasis.

Then she turned on Mathilda, exited the parking lot, and headed up to the Berkshire Arms. Bernie figured they had two hours, what with the drive and Manny waiting for them to show up. By the time Manny started back, they should . . . No, they would be back at the shop.

Twenty minutes later, the sisters were walking toward the main entrance of the Berkshire Arms. The parking lot was practically deserted, as it had been the last time they were there. Bernie parked in the same place as before, and as before the crows came flying down. Once again she scattered bread crumbs, only this time the bread crumbs were from the store and she tossed them away from her. Then she and Libby walked to the Berkshire Arms and went inside. No one was in the lobby. The place seemed as if it was already abandoned.

"Here goes nothing," Bernie said as she walked down the hallway. When they got to the end, Bernie opened the door marked BASEMENT and went down the steps. Libby followed.

She didn't like basements in general and this one in particular. It was, as most of them were, chilly and badly lit. She and Bernie walked by the furnace room, the residents' storage area, and the room where the electricity was monitored. Manny's room came next.

"I wouldn't want to live down here," Libby commented as they stopped in front of it.

"Me either," Bernie agreed as she got Brandon's lock picks out and began fiddling with the lock on the door. A couple of minutes later she had the door open, a fact that greatly pleased her, because the place was creeping her out, as well—not that she'd admit that to Libby—and she stepped inside.

The adjective that came to Bernie's mind as she looked around the studio apartment was *plain*. Except for the walls, everything was strictly utilitarian. Manny had decorated the walls with posters of Paraguay, charts of the Atlantic Ocean and the Hudson River, and a large framed print of a Viking ship, but then he seemed to have lost interest in the endeavor. His bed, a three-quarter, was made up with white sheets, two pillows, and a large navy quilt.

Had Penelope stayed here? It was certainly possible, Bernie thought. She probably hadn't been too happy, Bernie decided, since it was definitely not up to her usual standards. Outside of the bed, there was a braided rug on the floor, a nightstand with an office lamp sitting on it, a moderate-size TV mounted on the wall, and an old armchair with the stuffing coming out of the bottom by the window.

Libby went over and opened the closet door. She found five pairs of jeans, a pair of khakis, several button-down shirts, five ties, and a winter jacket hanging from the closet rod. She went through the pockets. The passport wasn't in any of them. Libby turned to the large laundry bag sitting on the floor and dumped it out.

"Look at this," she called to Bernie.

Bernie walked over. Three coins, similar to the one Bernie had found on the bank of the Hudson, lay on top of a white T-shirt. Libby picked them up and handed them to Bernie. Then she picked up the folded-up T-shirt they'd been lying on top of. The T-shirt unrolled, and the dagger that had been wrapped up in it clattered to the floor. Libby stooped down and lifted it up.

"Viking?" she asked, handing it to Bernie.

"It sure looks old enough," Bernie said, handing it back as she surveyed the clothes on the floor. They were women's.

"You were right," Libby said.

"Always am," Bernie replied as she held up a pair of jeans, checked the label, dropped the jeans, picked up a long-sleeved T-shirt and sweater, checked the labels on those, and dropped them back on the pile.

"Not always," Libby countered.

"Pretty much always," Bernie threw back while she checked more labels. The clothes all came from Old Navy and were Penelope's size. "I bet these are Penelope's," she said as she went to get her phone to photograph the clothes, the coins, and the dagger.

"He should have gotten rid of them," Libby observed as she started going through the garments' pockets. "Nothing here," she announced when she was done.

"I'm not surprised," Bernie said. She slipped her phone into her jacket pocket and went into the kitchen to look for a plastic bag to put a couple of the shirts in. If Lucy came around to their way of thinking, they'd be useful for DNA testing.

After she'd put the shirts in the plastic bag she discovered, she and Libby put everything back the way they'd found it. There was a brief discussion about keeping the coins and the dagger, but that was finally deemed unwise on the grounds that it would tip Manny off that someone had been there.

When the sisters were done with the closet, they went on to the dresser. There was one small framed picture sitting on top. It showed Manny with whom Bernie and Libby assumed was his family. The five of them were posed in a town square in what looked like a small town in Paraguay. Everyone was dressed in his or her Sunday best, and Bernie guessed that they had just come back from church. Manuel was standing in the back, with his arms around his mother and his father, while his two sisters crouched in front.

Libby pointed to Manny's father. "That's the man whose picture we saw in the paper."

"It certainly is," Bernie replied, getting out her cell and taking a couple of snaps. Then she checked the time. They had to get going soon.

She started going through Manny's dresser drawers, while Libby searched under and around the mattress. When that didn't yield results, Libby started on the chair. Fifteen minutes later, Libby found what she and Bernie had been looking for. Manny's passport had been hidden inside the chair, between two springs. It was a good hiding place, Libby reflected as she leafed through the pages, and if there hadn't been a piece of stuffing visible, she would never have thought to look there.

Libby pointed to a stamp on the fourth page. "Manny was in Paraguay a week after his dad was killed," she noted. "Judging from the number of stamps, he's been back and forth to Paraguay a lot. At least he's been telling the truth about that."

"Nice to know," Bernie said as she took the passport from her sister, put it on the bed, and photographed all the pages, taking special care to make sure she got close-ups of Manny's full name, Manuel Rico-Perez, as well as the relevant dates stamped on the pages. When Bernie was done, Libby put the passport back where she'd found it. Then she and Bernie looked around the studio apartment, checking to make sure that everything looked the way they'd found it, after which they left, carefully closing the door behind them.

"You think Lucy will listen to us now?" Libby asked as they hurried to the van. She could hear the crows in the distance. They seemed louder than usual, more restless, too, as small flocks of them took off, wheeled about, then landed back where they'd taken off from.

"I don't think he's going to have much choice," Bernie said, walking faster. She was anxious to get out of there.

"We did good," Libby told her sister when they reached the van. They were just about to get in when Manny emerged from the bushes. He pointed a Glock 9mm at them.

"But not good enough," Bernie observed.

# Chapter 53

Manny smiled. Bernie decided he seemed perfectly relaxed. She wasn't sure if that was a good or a bad thing.

"You should have left things alone," he said. "Everything would have been fine if you had."

"I don't know what you're talking about," Bernie replied. She had to raise her voice to be heard over the cawing of the crows. She watched as two alighted on Mathilda's hood. A moment later, three more flew down.

Manny waved his Glock at them. "Don't bother pretending. I saw you and your sister."

"Doing what?" Bernie asked, keeping up her act.

"Looking through my things. Nanny cams," Manny explained, even though neither Bernie nor Libby had asked. "I have an app on my phone, and speaking of phones"— he held out his hand—"I'll take yours now, if you don't mind."

"Or you'll do what? Shoot me?" Bernie asked.

"I wouldn't push it if I were you," Manny said, and the tone in his voice and the expression on his face left no doubt of his intentions. "Shooting you now or later makes no difference to me."

"It does to us," Libby said. "Give him the phone, Bernie."

"I was going to," Bernie told her sister as she handed her cell over to Manny. *I just have to keep him talking*, she thought. *The more he talks, the more time elapses, the better chance that something will distract him, and either Libby or I will be able to get the gun.* "I'm curious," Bernie continued. "How did Penelope get in touch with you?"

"Luck," Manny said. "Pure luck. I was fishing, and I saw her coming out of the river. Naturally, I ran over to help."

"Naturally," Libby said.

"When she told me what happened, it seemed like fate."

"So you knew who Darius Witherspoon was?" Bernie asked.

Manny nodded.

Bernie stalled for time. "But he didn't know who you were?"

"No."

"And you were thinking of killing him before then?" Libby asked.

Manny nodded again. "The idea had crossed my mind, but I couldn't figure out how to do it and not get caught, and then Penelope came along and solved my problem for me."

"She did it all by herself?" Libby clarified.

"No. I let her into Darius Witherspoon's apartment before he came in. She was waiting for him underneath his bed."

"I'm surprised he didn't have a heart attack when he saw her," Libby commented.

"From what Penelope said, I think he was in the middle of one when she put the noose around his neck and threw him out the window," Manny told them. "Then she climbed out of the window and went into the basement through the window I left open for her. No one saw anything. I guess you don't see what you're not expecting to."

"But why hang him?" Bernie asked.

Manny licked his lower lip. "Because that's how my father died," Manny said.

"I thought his death was an accident," Bernie told him. She watched two more crows land on Mathilda's roof.

Manny shook his head. "That's what Witherspoon told the *policía*, but it wasn't true. Witherspoon was teaching my papa a lesson. He accused him of stealing a gold nugget, and this was his way of making sure no one else on the crew did it."

"And did he steal the nugget?" Libby asked.

Manny shook his head. "His partner . . ."

"Ezra Poland?" Libby asked.

Manny nodded. "He had taken it to show someone. Poland took Papa down right away, but it was too late. My father was already dead."

"And Penelope? Why did you hang her?" Libby asked.

"Because she tried to cheat me. We were going to split the danegeld fifty-fifty. And, anyway, Witherspoon said he was doing it for her. At least, that's what my cousin said he said."

"Maybe your cousin lied," Libby pointed out.

"He would not do such a thing," Manny said as he motioned for Libby and Bernie to start walking toward the river. "Mr. Darius Witherspoon was a bad man, and he deserved to die."

"So what are you going to do with the danegeld?" Bernie asked. She had to yell to be heard over the crows. There were more and more of them. They were perched on the telephone line, and they covered the van.

"I am taking it home," Manny said. "Now move."

Bernie and Libby exchanged glances. Bernie was just about to trip and "accidentally" fall into Manny when a crow swooped down and landed on Manny's head. Manny shook his head, and the crow flew off, to be replaced by another one.

Manny cursed. "Damn birds. I should have shot them all."

A third bird landed on Manny's shoulder. A fourth landed on his other shoulder and nipped at his earlobe. Manny grabbed at the bird, and Libby turned and grabbed for the gun. The gun went off, and a crow fell to the ground. It had been shot. Suddenly the crows on the van and the telephone line rose in the air and descended on Manny in a black, swirling cloud. He dropped the Glock and started running toward the river.

"I told him he shouldn't try to poison the crows," a voice behind them said.

Bernie and Libby whirled around. It was Mrs. Randall. They hadn't heard her come up.

"I told him they wouldn't forgive him," she said as she listened to Manny's screams.

Bernie and Libby got the impression that the screams didn't bother her. In fact, she seemed to be enjoying them.

She turned to them and smiled. "The behavior you're watching is called mobbing. Corvids do it to protect their young, and occasionally for other purposes, as well." Mrs. Randall shook her head and pulled up the collar of her pale blue peacoat. "He wasn't a very nice man, and he shouldn't have done what he did."

"Try to kill the crows?" Libby asked.

"No, silly. Kill the people."

# Chapter 54

Four weeks later Mrs. Randall, Libby, Bernie, and Sean were sitting in the Simmonses' flat, drinking hot spiced apple cider and tea, eating maple-glazed doughnuts and apple kuchen, and discussing what Mrs. Randall had christened the Costume Party Affair while they watched the rain drizzle down on the pavement. It had been a wet fall, and it seemed as if winter was going to be more of the same.

"So they never got another super for the Berkshire Arms?" Sean asked Mrs. Randall.

Mrs. Randall shook her head and readjusted the neck of her black turtleneck sweater. "The bank is foreclosing on it, anyway, so there really wasn't much point. I got the eviction notice two weeks ago. When I ran into Moran's son—"

"Gus?" Libby asked.

Mrs. Randall nodded. "He said the two murders were the final straw. There was no way they could sell the rest of the condos now, especially with the Witherspoons' pictures being pasted all over the Internet, not to mention CNN, and the dailies."

"That's what Gus's dad said, too," Bernie noted.

"I can understand why the story is all over the media,"

Libby noted. "It has all the elements. Buried treasure. Two murders. Vengeance. I wouldn't be surprised if it became a made-for-TV movie." She added a lump of sugar to her tea and took a sip. "So what's going to happen to the property?"

Cindy hopped up on Sean's lap, circled around three times, and lay down. He gave her a pat. "Talk is that they're going to demo the building and turn the place into a park. After all, it does have nice views of the river."

"Excellent idea," Libby said. "As far as I'm concerned, the sooner that building is gone, the better."

Bernie turned to Mrs. Randall. "So where are you going to go?" she asked.

Mrs. Randall smiled. "My sister has a camp out in Saint Vincent, so I'm planning to divide my time between there and Berkeley. My son got a faculty position teaching mythology there. I guess it does pay to read to your child. He always loved folktales." She broke off a piece of her doughnut and ate it. "Delicious," she said.

"I didn't see any crows when I was up there," Libby said. She'd gone up with Lucy the day after her and Bernie's run-in with Manny to reenact the scenario for their chief of police.

Mrs. Randall spread her hands out. "That's because they took off and went somewhere else."

"Why would they do that?" Sean asked.

Mrs. Randall smiled at him. "The fanciful among us would say that their job guarding the treasure was done, while the less fanciful among us would say that they were tired of being disturbed and decided to roost in a quieter spot. They do change their nesting area from time to time," Mrs. Randall said. "Of course, if we're being entirely accurate here, if any birds were guarding the treasure, it would be Huginn and Muninn, who are ravens, not crows. But, really, all the corvids are basically the same." She paused. "So what's happening to the treasure?" she asked, switching gears. The police had found it in a suitcase in the trunk of Manny's car.

"I read that the Museum of Natural History has it, although I read something about it going to Norway in three years as a special traveling exhibition," Bernie replied.

"Well, the find has certainly upended a great many assumptions about the Norsemen," Mrs. Randall said, sitting back in her armchair. "I know that there have been stories about the Norsemen coming this far up the Hudson and setting up a colony, but up until now there's been no evidence to substantiate that."

Sean took a sip of his cider and put his glass mug down. "My mother used to tell me a story about men in long boats sailing up the river and making a home here on the riverbanks. Her brother used to find the occasional coin on the banks of the Hudson, right beneath the Berkshire Arms."

"Which makes sense," Bernie said, "considering that Darius found it buried in a well right by the building's foundation. One of the archeologists working on the site says he thinks there's more stuff down there. A lot more stuff. And there could be another settlement upstream. Evidently, Darius thought so, too, because the archeologist found some notes to that effect."

"It wouldn't surprise me if there is," Sean said. "I remember Uncle Henry finding a knife once. It looked really, really old."

"What happened to it?" Bernie asked.

Sean shook his head. "It disappeared. My guess is that it went in the trash when he died."

Bernie leaned over and cut a piece of apple kuchen for herself. It was the perfect fall snack food. Light and not overly sweet. The softness of the baked apple slices melded with the chewiness of the cake. Sòmetimes simple was best.

"May I have a slice of that?" Mrs. Randall said, indicating the apple kuchen.

"By all means," Bernie replied, then cut her a piece.

"Excellent," Mrs. Randall pronounced after she'd taken a few bites. "It's too bad I won't be around for Manuel Rico-Perez's trial."

"I have a feeling there won't be a trial," Sean told her. "He'll probably take the deal the prosecution is going to offer him."

"How do you know they're going to offer him a deal?" Mrs. Randall asked.

"Because that's the way these things usually go these days," Sean replied. "Jury trials are expensive."

Bernie ate another piece of cake and thought about the last time she'd seen Manny as he ran toward the river. He'd been covered in crows pecking at him. They'd left him only when he dove into the river. Even then they'd circled overhead, cawing at him, until a fisherman who'd been coming in to shore pulled Manny out of the river. He'd been covered in blood. The expression *pecked to death by ducks* had entered Bernie's mind.

"He's lucky he didn't die from hypothermia," Bernie observed.

"Or the crows didn't peck his eyes out," Mrs. Randall said.

Libby suppressed a shiver. "They wouldn't do that, would they?"

"They might," Mrs. Randall replied. "Corvids can be vengeful, and when you add in the fact that they never forget a face . . ." She took another sip of cider. "I told him and I told him and I told him that crows and ravens aren't to be taken lightly, but he didn't listen. After all, I'm just an old woman. What do I know?"

"Well," Bernie said, "I don't think he's ever going to make that mistake again—not that he's going to have a chance to, given where he's going."

# RECIPES

I have three recipes for you today. The first one, salmon chowder, comes from my cousin Joan Bernstein, who is an excellent cook. The second recipe is called a Swedish pancake by some and a German pancake by others, but whatever you choose to call it, it makes a wonderful breakfast treat. And my third recipe is for Swedish glogg—a hot spiced wine.

There's a loose theme here, very loose—Scandinavia. The other thing these recipes have in common is that they are quick, easy to make, tasty to eat, and will, I promise, be in your repertoire for a long time to come.

## JOAN BERNSTEIN'S SALMON CHOWDER

This is the kind of recipe for a busy weekday night. Add some bread and a salad and you're ready to go.

6 small new potatoes, cut into quarters
28 ounces vegetable broth
1 medium ear of corn, kernels removed, or ½ cup frozen corn
One 2-inch sprig thyme or ½ teaspoon dried thyme
12 ounces skinless salmon, cut into 1-inch chunks
1 cup baby spinach
¼ cup sliced scallions
Salt, to taste
Freshly ground black pepper, to taste

Combine the potatoes and the broth in a medium pot, bring to a boil over medium-high heat, and then reduce the heat and simmer until the potatoes are tender but not cooked through, about 5 minutes. Add the corn and the thyme, and bring the broth back to a boil, reduce the heat, and simmer, covered, until the corn is tender, about 4 minutes. Add the salmon and simmer, uncovered, for 3–5 minutes. Stir in the spinach and scallions, season to taste, and serve.

*4 servings*

## *GERMAN (OR SWEDISH) PANCAKE*

This recipe goes by different names and you can find variations of it in many cookbooks. The one thing they all have in common is that the pancake finishes cooking in the oven. My kids love it and I have been making it forever.

Combine and stir till smooth:

4 beaten egg yolks
2 tablespoons cornstarch
¼ cup lukewarm water
¼ cup lukewarm milk
¾ teaspoon salt
1 tablespoon sugar
Grated rind of one lemon or orange

Beat 4 to 5 egg whites until very smooth and fold into the yolk mixture.

Melt 2 tablespoons of butter in a heavy 10-inch skillet. When the skillet is hot, pour in the batter and cook over low to medium heat, partly covered, for about 5 minutes, until the batter is set. Then place the skillet in a 400-degree preheated oven until the pancake is puffed out. Total cooking time is about 7 minutes. Serve immediately with powdered sugar, sugar, and cinnamon, or jam. Homemade apple compote is also a nice accompaniment to the pancake.

*2 servings*

## SWEDISH GLOGG

This is a very nice party punch, as well as something to sip on a cold winter's night. There are literally hundreds of versions of this drink; some are made with wine, others with hard liquor, and some with both. This version is based on Martha Stewart's, but feel free to make it your own. I have. Part of the fun of making this is adding a little more or a little less of things and seeing the results.

1 bottle dry red wine, such as Pinot Noir or Zinfandel
1 bottle port
2 cups water
1½ cups cognac, brandy, rum, port, or vodka or aquavit
Rind of 1 orange and 1 lemon, cut into strips, plus their juice
5 cardamom pods
2 sticks cinnamon
10 whole cloves or ½ teaspoon allspice
5 slices peeled fresh ginger
2 tablespoon granulated sugar
10 teaspoons blanched almonds

In a nonreactive saucepan mix together the wine, port, water, cognac, and spices. Bring to a boil over medium-high heat, and then reduce heat to low and simmer for 5 minutes. Remove from heat and let cool. Cover and refrigerate for at least 12 hours and up to 24 hours.

Strain wine mixture and discard solids. Reheat wine over low heat (do not boil) and stir in sugar to taste. Add 1 teaspoon almonds to each of 10 mugs. Fill with wine mixture and serve.

*10 servings*